Something Bigger

Sheila Killian

CARITAS PRESS, USA

Something Bigger

Sheila Killian
Copyright © 2021 Sheila Killian

First Edition
10 9 8 7 6 5 4 3 2 1
ISBN 978-1-940209-43-2
For reorders, visit CaritasPress.org

Something Bigger is a work of fiction. Events, conversations and characters are works of the author's imagination, though based on historical occurrences and climates. The author takes sweeping artistic liberties in her portrayals of all characters, real and imaginary. Situations and dialogues, even those concerning historical figures, are fictional. For resources that give a factual account of the events of 1921, see www.sheilakillian.com/history.

CARITAS PRESS
CaritasPress.org

To Aoife, Cian, Finn and John, with love

"I will call them 'my people'
who are not my people;
and I will call her 'my loved one'
who is not my loved one."

Romans 9:25

Part I

Chapter One

1962

These are the things that remind her of him: hot tea, piping hot, with almost no milk. Black shoes with laces, double-tied. A man writing, not looking up, lost in his own words. Paleness in eyes. A quick striding step. The creak of a swing, even in a playground, even though it's not a porch swing. Trains. She doesn't know why that should be. They hardly ever travelled by train together, but there's that wail, that fading cry of a train that reminds her of him.

Zundel's diner on Lafayette, a place he never even saw. That conveyor belt they have for taking away the trays of empty plates and dirty cups. He'd have loved that. Marcella can see him stopping to look at it, a hand on his hip. 'Well would you look at that, Siss', he'd say. That's just the kind of modern that he loved.

What else? Things she has read that she wants to read to him. Songs on the radio that were written after he died. Birthdays. She's older than him now, and that's impossible, so she wants to talk to him about that. Flowers when they're just past their prime, curling and drying. Old men remind her of him, he who was never old. Young men in a hurry. Boys who think they will run the world one day. Crows flying home in the late evening, silent and straight in her imagination, that determination about them, the way they follow some path they can see in the sky. Something no one else can see.

Funerals, obviously.

She is seventy-two years old. She has lived longer without him than with him.

She comes to the cathedral early when it's empty and echoing and sits in the half dark watching the sacristan opening doors. If it's bright outside, sometimes a single shaft of sun catches him like a spotlight as he strides up the centre aisle, and she almost expects him to dance.

She walks out in the middle of the day – in the heat or rain or sometimes snow. In the afternoons she watches people. Hardly anyone comes in to pray now. They just come tired, overwhelmed by Fifth Avenue, setting down their bags for a while in the shadow of St. Patrick's, inhaling the candlewax smell, wafting out on softened air. They don't see Marcella, and if they did, what would they see? Just a little old lady, thin and quick, harmless as a bird.

If they are tearful and young, she might offer them a kerchief. They remind her of all that's happened. Young women wrapped up in whatever new thing has them crying in front of a plaster St. Jude. When she talks, they only hear her Alabama voice. She doesn't tell them she is Irish, though she watches for Irish ones. She has a soft spot for them; they make her feel especially invisible. And the flint-faced Southern ones,

Chapter One: 1962

they don't know the secret she carries. Some day it will be Bessie Stubbs. She'll walk right in here. She never could stay away from a place like this.

Marcella doesn't ask questions. She lets them talk if they're talkers, or tells them a story. She talks about Fran sometimes, or Bessie when she was small, or Johanna when she used to sing, until they're distracted from their own trouble, smiling. She doesn't tell them the bad parts. She never mentions hate. She doesn't talk about Jimmy either, though later she tells Jimmy about them. After they've gone, she lights a candle for them, for their days. She lights one for Fran too. For Tommy and Johanna. And Bess. Wherever she is. Sometimes she lights one for Jimmy and he laughs, but quietly. 'What do I need candles for, Siss?' he'll say.

That's true of course. He doesn't need candles, but she lights one anyway. There were candles there, that day, and she lit them all. They flickered as though the church door had opened. Did the church door open? And would it have mattered? Surely it began long before that. Maybe when little Bessie wandered into their front yard instead of someone else's carrying her homemade toy and her trust. Or when Jimmy read about what happened in Dublin and couldn't get there. Or when his name went up in Alabama. Or when he asked Marcella to come, or when the war ended. Maybe she can just blame the war. Still, she plays the story up and down, and tries to find a single moment, as if she could change something. As if she could change him, and the way he treated everyone the same regardless. Nobody knows the story now but Jimmy and her. And only Jimmy knows how it ends.

Chapter Two

1904

Marcella stared out the dirty window, ignoring the drone of her teacher reading at the front of the class, his back to the turf fire. Rain streamed down the glass, thickening it, bending the weak, spring light into a small rainbow on her page. She watched it strengthen and then fade across the algebra she was supposed to be doing while the teacher read to the smaller ones. As usual, she had finished ahead of her peers. In a one-teacher school, she found, there was a lot of time to dream. This teacher seemed happy enough to let her drift through the day, as long as she didn't disturb anyone else. People called him the young teacher, ever since he took over from her father seven years ago, but he didn't seem young to her.

Her father had never been young. Nor really old. She shook herself quickly away from that thought and looked across the schoolroom to find Tommy Banahan staring at her. He winked and smiled, pleased he'd

Chapter Two: 1904

caught her eye. She smiled back — a small one, looking away again. She liked Tommy.

Turfsmoke hung in the air at the front of the room, drifting slowly in a shaft of light from the window. Like that dream she'd had again last night. It was a memory, really. She was sure it was, but in the dream, she saw herself from above, maybe six years old, a skinny girl with serious eyes and her hair cropped too short. She was here in this schoolhouse, watching her father standing at the blackboard, chalk dust swirling around him in the sunlight. He was writing numbers, and then something else that wasn't distinct that she was craning to look at. Then in the dream, he began to turn towards the class, and just as she was about to see his face, and what he was writing, the whole scene faded. That dream came often, every few months, and she'd wake from it feeling like she was on the edge of something. It was always vivid but never reached a conclusion. It had to be a real thing that had happened. It was one of the few memories she had of her father, before he died. She had so few memories of him, so few of him noticing her. She wanted this one to be real.

Remembering the dream now in the middle of the school day unsettled her. The schoolroom seemed so small, so much the same every day, like an enclosure she was outgrowing. Staring out the window again, she found herself wondering what else there was, beyond the treeline and the parish road. And what would it be like to just walk away, and never come back?

She became aware of a scuffle around her, and realised the teacher had stopped reading, and they stood for prayer to mark the end of the day. The teacher was checking his pocket watch, closing his books. Across the room, Tommy Banahan lingered, waiting for her.

Something Bigger

She slowed down too, so that the classroom emptied, and they could walk out together towards their homes. She had business to do, collecting eggs from his mother, but really, she just liked Tommy. He understood something unsaid about her. His house was fatherless too, the same deadening quiet in the evenings, the same absence hanging over everything like smoke.

Today, though, was different. Her house was bustling, her mother cleaning and Fran baking, everyone distracted by Jimmy coming home. Aren't you looking forward to seeing him, Siss, Fran would say, and Marcella would smile and say yes, she was, but really, she could hardly remember Jimmy. He was twelve whole years older than her, and he'd been gone for years now. That made it hard to remember a brother.

Everyone else remembered, though. The whole parish seemed to be looking forward to his return — Jimmy Coyle, a priest home from America, no less, who might say a special Mass in a neighbour's house, or bring news of one of their sons and daughters who went out there years ago, and from whom nothing had been heard. Coming home from America was a rare thing. Coming and going more than once as Jimmy had done was unheard of. All week, women had been offering her mother apple tarts or fruit cakes. Good china was carefully washed for the visitors who would surely call. Blankets were aired and the boys' old room was emptied and cleaned with his bed made up under the window, like it used to be, small and flat: a bed for a boy, not a grown man. It was as though he were not just family now, but something more than that.

All she could really remember about Jimmy was his tallness, the quick way he moved, that way he had of smiling to himself, a private, pleased smile. His off-key singing in church. Mostly, all her life, he had been gone, or going, but still at centre of things for all that. She remembered visiting his seminary in Limerick when she was small. It must have been winter because the hulking grey building with its dark windows chilled her. A stone eagle clung to a round stone at the top of the front steps. One of its chipped talons was bigger than her hand. It stared past her with empty, plaster eyes. She couldn't imagine living there, sleeping so far from family. And there was his ordination day, the longest Mass in the world and the grey dress with daisies that Fran made for her, the one that was then her Sunday best for a year. She had scuffed her new black shoes that morning, before she even left the house, and Fran had saved her, rubbing in some boot polish before Mother saw. Then he was in Rome for a year and then America, one place as far away as the next. Since then he'd lived mostly through the letters Mother kept behind the kitchen mirror. She'd take them down often, and smooth one out to read to herself by the fire. Marcella would watch her face, jealous of the rare softness that came over her as she read. Sometimes she'd try to distract her, to tell her something about her school day, anything to break whatever tie seemed to come through the flimsy airmail paper. When she read the letters herself, they seemed ordinary, describing good news always, things going well in towns with strange names. Like a book, not like real life. She couldn't see what it was that her Mother was getting from them. And it was hard to compete with a printed page. Sometimes he sent parcels too, with clothes for her that were too small or too bright, and postcards of his city, looking beautiful and imaginary, with a skyline of tall buildings and a washed-out sky.

Something Bigger

Black, white, shades of grey. Hard to imagine him walking there.

Fran knew him differently because she was so much older. They had been young together once and must have played together like real brothers and sisters before Marcella was born. She could hardly imagine Fran young. Since Father had died, it was just the three of them in their stone cottage, the sisters sharing a bedroom while the boys' room was kept empty like a shrine. There had been five brothers. Dermot and Denis and Peadar and John had left for Australia, or England or Canada, all gone years before, as boys did if there was no land to hold them. One by one, like swallows off a roof they flew, but not like swallows at all, it turned out, because they never came back. Only Jimmy did that. Jimmy came back often enough to just about be real.

Girls didn't have to leave. Fran worked at home as a seamstress taking in work from their neighbours, stitching britches and frocks and bright cottage curtains, making bonnets for Marcella, dressing her up like a doll. Fran had style and Marcella did not. This was accepted. Marcella was the smart one, no good with her hands. It was thought she might be a teacher. That way, she could marry, but would not have to marry for land. She could marry anyone if she was a teacher. Anyone at all. She herself wasn't sure about marrying, but there was plenty of time for that.

Banahan's house was a half mile outside the village, a smaller cottage than Marcella's, with only two people living in it. Mrs. Banahan was a wisp of a woman who always wore brown. She came late to Mass and sat on the outside of any pew at all, not like respectable women who came on time and knew their places. She

Chapter Two: 1904

sang every hymn, high and loud, her falsetto voice carrying over the whole chapel. People called her a widow, but everyone knew her husband wasn't dead at all, only gone to England and not coming back. She wrote letters, so the postmistress said, every few months to a different address, but she never got an answer. They seemed to get by for money. She sold eggs, and Tommy did a bit of work on the farms. So far, he was managing to stay in school.

Tommy was the best thing about Banahan's. Marcella had always liked him. People said he was slow, but he seemed quick enough to her. At school, he got low marks at anything that involved reading, but he made her laugh, often witty and always kind. She liked the tiny birds he sketched in the margins of his copies, and the fantastic animals he sometimes drew in and around the words in the books he used that were not his own. The books belonged to the school, only on loan to him, but he showed her the drawings even though he knew the teacher would cane him if he saw. It was a small, warm secret they shared. It was only pencil anyway. They could rub it out at the end of the year, and nobody would be the wiser. He told her once they had no books at home and she laughed and didn't believe him, but Fran told her it was probably true. "Unfortunate" is the word she used. "That poor unfortunate, with only his Mam in that little cottage and his father either dead or as good as." Marcella had never felt sorry for him, but the word made her notice things: the untidy patches on his clothes; the fact that he never had new ones; the filth of his fingernails, grained in. Still, she liked him best of all the boys in Rockfield, and all the boys in school.

"So you're walking me home now, Marcella Coyle, is it?" His smile was mocking but warm.

"Just for duck-eggs, Tommy. That's all that brings me to your house."

Outside the schoolhouse, the grass was high and wet, and the evening seemed full of expectation. Beads of dew glinted when the light caught them. Later, maybe, the sun would burn it off, but this early in the summer, it could stay damp for days. The high sound of bees poured off the hawthorn hedge but there were no butterflies. Not yet. Tommy's house was cold and darker than hers. He gathered the eggs into a box for her, picking a spider from the straw and placing it carefully in the window before continuing.

"Is Jimmy staying long this time?"

She helped him wrapping the eggs.

"Just a week. Then on to Rome for a few days and back to America. To hear Mother talk, you'd think he was going over to advise the Pope."

Tommy laughed. He was an easy laugher. That was one of the things she liked about him.

"So, will we see you at all, now, with your brother home? I suppose you'll be entertaining all the neighbours, and going calling with him?"

Marcella knew it was true, and before she thought about it, replied.

"Sure we might call here as well as anywhere. Maybe we'll come around for tea?"

"Hardly now, Cella. This isn't the sort of place a returned yank wants to call to."

Marcella looked around at the grimy floor, the chipped crockery. It wasn't that the place was small — her own home was small. It was something else, the underthings hanging in front of the fireplace, the grubby windows, the half-empty bottle of tonic wine on the high shelf. Then she became conscious of Tommy following her gaze and snapped on a smile.

16

Chapter Two: 1904

"Ah who knows where he'll go, Tommy? And people are visiting him in our house too. Call down if it suits you."

"I might," he said, and she knew straight away that he wouldn't.

* * * * *

Jimmy hauled his bag from the overhead shelf and walked to the door between carriages long before the train reached Athlone. He slid down the window, and rested his elbows on the sill, looking out at the boggy midlands wheeling past, smoking his last slim cigar. These fields, so dark and damp that were once so familiar. He thought of old schoolfriends he might meet during the coming week, the few who stayed, only the firstborn and lads with land behind them or who had married into it. That was never going to be his path, working land until the land owned him. Like his father, he was more drawn to ideas, to books, and then to God, the biggest idea he ever found, and the one that brought him out of the small fields of Rockfield and off to the Jesuits. There was no coming back from that. At first, he'd only wanted to be the local priest. He'd pictured himself giving benediction, wearing the bright vestments, bringing communion to the sick in the small cottages. But time passed and his world grew, and by the time he was ordained he needed something bigger. And what was bigger than Rome? The centre of it all. It took only a year, scholarly and intense, to see that he was too young, too much of an outsider to make his mark there. Instead, he chose the colonies, using the term lightly, half joking. That turned out to mean Birmingham, Alabama, a city founded on coal and steel, on ambition and ruthless hope. He'd been assigned a parish very young, following the sudden death of an older priest, and he didn't know yet where it would take him.

The train slowed, approaching the town. As he tossed the end of his cigar onto the shingles, he caught sight of a small boy half hiding beside the track. He remembered how he and Fran would play on the railway tracks when they were young, a secret they never told. It had seemed a great playground, a road with no people, going who knows where. They would wait at the side of the track, holding on tight to a post or a tree as a train passed so as not to be pulled in under the clacking wheels. They would walk along the track, one balancing on each rail, to see who would slip first. It was never Fran.

Fran was most of what he missed about home. Only two years younger, she knew him differently to anyone else, more than his parents, or his friends, or the brothers who left before him. She knew him as he was. Not like his Mother who, right from the first Christmas he came home from the Jesuits started seeing him in a different way. She saw the priest in training, the Roman collar he would one day wear, not the boy he was. She saw him at the local church, where he had first seen himself. She saw him hearing the neighbours' confessions, marrying them and burying them and all the time she saw herself reflected. He tried, God knows he had tried, but he wasn't sure he had ever really forgiven her for not just seeing him.

Fran, though. She never changed. It was going to be good to see her again. The train slid into Athlone, crossing the Shannon on the big metal railway bridge. The only thing he disliked about taking the train was this: that crossing the bridge meant he didn't get to see

Chapter Two: 1904

it in all its fullness. He loved the structural steel, arching over the river, landing on the western side beside the army barracks and the rows of terraced houses running down to the marshy bank where the non-commissioned married men lived. He missed that view. Sometimes it seemed everywhere he lived made him homesick for another place. Birmingham, with its politics reminded him of Rome. But there was no ecclesiastical power there. Mobile was place for that, a far more refined city, and the head of the diocese. For now, he was grinding down the debt he had inherited on the big city church, but after that perhaps, he might make a move to Mobile, to work with the bishop. Perhaps to be bishop himself. Five years or ten, then he'd wind his way to where he should have been going to begin with. Meanwhile, he could bring his sister out to join him. He could do that much for the family, for his mother. Birmingham wasn't a paradise, but it offered a better life than here.

The train wheezed to a halt, and he hailed a jarvey to take him home. The small town of Athlone seemed more or less the same. The army barracks was busier, perhaps. He found himself frowning. He wasn't a rebel, but these British soldiers stationed here never seemed to stay long enough to belong. There were still no streetlights, he noticed, and he mentally braced himself for Rockfield, for a small cottage in a small place. He had brought a camera this time and planned to photograph everything he could. Not for them, though they would think it was for them. No, he wanted pictures when he went back to Birmingham, so he could hold their faces clearly. Right now, for instance, he could hardly remember Marcella's face. He tried to focus on the colour of her eyes – blue, of course, like all the family, but which blue? Pale like him, or darker and flecked with green like Fran? She'd been a skinny little girl when he saw her last, not long after Father died. And Mother — how was she? It was so hard to read from her letters how things really were at home, or what she might think of his plan. And Fran? How would it really seem to Fran, when it was talked about properly, not just hinted in a letter?

He put away his wondering and wrapped his scarf around to keep the wind out. Rockfield was not far, now. It was getting dark, and the warmth was gone from the day.

* * * * *

Marcella watched Jimmy all the time, from the evening he walked in the door, casting a long shadow on the kitchen floor with his importance, his holy orders, his tall hat. His dark foreign suit was made of some thin material, so he started to catch a cold as soon as he arrived. All week, he was never still. From early morning he strode around the place as though he had never left, up early to say Mass in the convent, in and out of the presbytery to talk to Fr. Davis, stealing time to take Tanner the dog out running on Gorry Bog. That dog loved to run, and though he shouldn't even know Jimmy — how could he remember him? — he seemed completely and immediately loyal to him. Jimmy seemed to do that, to people as well as to dogs. He'd breeze into a room, and everyone's attention would turn on him like a compass needle. She watched as he joined the Sunday morning queue in the shop after Mass. People stepped out of line to talk to him. Far older men asked his views on things he had no way of knowing the first thing about: a son in England, the weather for turf, the price of cattle. The

Chapter Two: 1904

small crowd shaped itself around him. Marcella tried to see how he did it.

Men came to life in his presence, calling in to smoke with him in the kitchen, and to hear the stories he brought home with him, the new politics of America, of French Catholics, and Ulster Scots, of unknown races, what they all wanted and how they all lived. They would argue with him late into the night by the dying fire about things closer to home. About revolution, and whether one would ever come in Ireland. Mother was alive in a way she hadn't been in months. There was something about Jimmy's life that she could bask in. Jimmy was a favourite of the bishop in Mobile, she said. Jimmy was running a big city parish now. Jimmy knew what was best, she would say, and Fran would just agree, and get on with things.

Everyone said Jimmy was like their father, but Marcella had no way of knowing. Father's face in the few photographs they had was inscrutable, his grey hair stiff and impeccable, shiny round glasses that obscured his eyes. Jimmy's eyes were clear, framed by thick black curls, and his face was mobile, showing every thought he had. He was always half looking over the shoulder of whoever he was talking to, giving a wink to someone who came in their cottage, even in the middle of another conversation. He was quick, and he got what he wanted. She had no idea if Father had been like that. Mother though, that was a possibility. She never talked politics. She sat quietly by the fire, but at the end of the night, whenever she was ready, she would chime in with a word that would just close the conversation down. It wasn't so much what she said. It was usually something inane. "Well now, that's that." Something meaningless, and all the visiting neighbours would stop their arguing. The men would stand, and gather their pipes and coats, and in five minutes they'd be out the door. That way she had of turning a room on a word. That seemed to Marcella to be completely like Jimmy.

People said Mother was delicate, but Marcella didn't think so. She was quiet but hard to ignore. They said she had changed since Father had died, but Marcella couldn't ever remember her being happy. Sad days were always sadder for Mother; happy days were an effort. Her smile never exactly fit her face, her laugh was low and strained. Fran was the life of the house, caring for Marcella, sewing for money, cooking and cleaning. Fran always knew what to do. Marcella helped, but often she set out on long summer evenings to Banahan's or up the fields alone. She had her own secret places – flat stones under low bushes where she could read; that one spot on the hill by the pond that was comfortable to lie down when the grass was long, a warm place in the turfshed, out of sight on rainy days. She often lingered on her way back in the evenings, standing alone in the shadow of the henhouse, watching the windows of the cottage light up yellow as the sun leached from the evening sky. She was comfortable out there, holding her own space for a little longer, seeing the small house as its own world without her. Now with Jimmy home, the house seemed different, a more public place, less her own. The kitchen was always filling up with visitors and she found she could disappear easily and not be missed. So that's where she was, up on the Liss hill on the third evening when Jimmy came walking up the slope towards her, and sat, looking across the bog towards Athlone in the distance. She was surprised but pleased to finally have his undivided attention.

"You'd hardly see the town there, would you Siss?

Chapter Two: 1904

The buildings are so low."

She had never thought of the buildings of Athlone as low. Some of the townhouses along Queen St. were three stories high. But now that he pointed it out from this distance, she could see it was true. It was a low river town, clinging to the foggy fields.

"I suppose. Compared to your city anyway. Tell me about Birmingham, Jimmy."

He leaned back on the damp grass, looking open and relaxed and talked for a while, painting word pictures of long streets with bright stores and fancy houses, streetcars and gas lights, tall smooth city trees and jabbering jaybirds; hot nights with steam coming off the roads after rain; red dirt roads twisting through high, hot forests outside town. He hadn't opened up like this before, not to her, and when she listened, even when she couldn't understand the context, she felt important. Then he stopped in the middle of a story, and looked right at her for a long moment, like he was weighing her up.

"But why don't you come over, Siss? See it all for yourself?"

She laughed until she saw that Jimmy was not laughing at all.

"I mean it, Siss. You could finish your schooling there; get yourself a proper qualification; make a life for yourself. What do you say?"

It was suddenly very quiet. Thin streams of smoke were ribboning up from the cottages below the hill. The first of the evening crows shawled silently overhead. Jimmy waited.

"But all my family is here, Jimmy."

"And me? Amn't I family, Siss?"

Her throat thickened and her eyes grew hot and dry.

Something Bigger

"It's like this, Siss. What are you going to do here? When you're done school?"

"I don't know. What does anyone do?"

"Not much around here. And what would you really want if you could do anything?"

She thought about this.

"I'd be free, I suppose, Jimmy. I'd like some job, something that's just my own. And I'd like to be able to travel, and see things, see the world like you. But I haven't even finished school yet."

"Now, Siss. You're smarter than that. What good will this school of yours do you here? If you stay here three more years, you'll marry some small farmer, or worse, some labourer with no land. That's what Mother tells me. And where will you be then? No. Come to Alabama with me and get a good education. You're well able for it."

"And what would I do with this education?"

"Anything you want, Siss."

"Really?"

"Really. You'll teach, I think."

"I might not want to teach."

"Fair enough. But come, and you can choose."

He made it sound easy, talking fast now, about making arrangements for her to come over in what, just two months? About schools and opportunities. She would always remember how it felt, exciting, and paralysing at the same time. She never could remember saying yes.

That evening, Fran was away, unusually, so she couldn't talk to her about it, and Mother acted as though she didn't know anything. But at night, after she'd gone to bed, looking over at Fran's empty bed she heard scraps of low argument drifting up from the kitchen.

Chapter Two: 1904

"... Marcella has what, only one more year of school to go? ... she's running out of time ... Fran, fair enough, she has a trade, but you know she'd have a better life in America. Are you going to deny Marcella too?"

"James!" Mother's raised voice was clear. "Do you know her at all? She's only fourteen?"

"I was younger when I went to Limerick, and I never lived here again."

"She's a girl, James. And young for her age." Mother's words sounded thin, as if all the power had passed to Jimmy. There was quiet, and then his voice again, low, and insistent.

"You didn't like my first idea, Mother. Let me at least do this. What else is waiting for her here? Who else? That boy you talked about? What's he going to do for her, or for you?"

"Well, sure enough. There is that."

She kept her eyes closed, waiting for Fran to come to bed so they could talk together, but she didn't come. Marcella was afraid she knew why. Jimmy's first idea wasn't to ask her. She was a second choice.

In the morning, the house was quiet for once. She stepped out of the bedroom into the kitchen where her mother was taking out ashes from the open fire, and hardly looked up as Marcella came in.

"Mother, Jimmy asked me ..."

"Sure I know, pet. Isn't it a great thing? A young one like you to get such a chance."

Her mother's voice was determined, but her eyes were glistening.

"And we'll see you all the time, Marcella. You'll be home with Jimmy every couple of years. And won't you write? It will be great to be getting more letters from America. Jimmy doesn't write half enough."

"I will. If I go, I mean, I ..."

"Yerra of course you'll go. How would you say no, girl?"

"I don't know. I need to think."

"What thinking is there in it? You go tell your friends about this, and they'll tell you. Quick enough. Then we can start making plans."

* * * * *

"Don't be soft, Marcella."

Mary Catherine chewed the last of her lunch with an air of absolute authority.

"Why would you even think about turning down a chance to go to America? You know I'm getting out of here too as soon as I can. So don't wait around here on my account. Still, I can't believe you're leaving me here. I was sure I'd be the first to go."

Marcella looked away into the middle distance. Mary Catherine had been her best friend since they started school at four or five years old. Even then she'd seemed older and sharper, always looking ahead to the next thing.

"Look at it this way — what will you do if you don't go? Are you going to marry that Banahan lad and move in with his drunken mother? Come on. You can do better than that."

Marcella flinched, and Mary Catherine caught the expression on her face and interrupted her own flow.

"Wait. You're not seriously thinking you could do that? Marry Tommy Banahan? And you the Master's daughter?"

"There's a new Master now, Mary Catherine. And even so, what of it? If I wanted to, and I'm not saying I do, but if I did, why wouldn't we marry?"

Chapter Two: 1904

"Because money, Marcella. Because he doesn't even have the makings of it. You'd be scrambling always to bring in a few shillings and I don't see you sewing like your sister. What would you do? Sell eggs with his mother? God. I can't believe we're talking like this. I always thought it would be me going somewhere exciting, and you staying home. Are you really thinking of saying no? It's not like it's forever. You can always come back."

"Nobody comes back."

Mary Catherine looked at her, coolly.

"Alright, Cella, you know that's not exactly true. There's Roisin's older sister, what's her name?"

"Rita, I think. That's true. She's working in Dublin now, isn't she? She's a nurse or something."

"And the Carroll's who used to live near us – their father went to England and came back with money and bought a farm up in Leitrim. And one of the Cliffords is supposed to be coming back from Philadelphia one of these years."

"Not to Rockfield, Mary Catherine. Nobody comes back here, do they?"

"Except your brother now and then. No, you have to come back. I'm not having you leaving me here unless you're going to come back."

She paused.

"OK, let's think about it, Marcella. What stops people coming back, when they go?"

"I don't know. Maybe other places really are better."

"Or maybe they're not, and they can't afford the passage home." Mary Catherine looked thoughtful.

"How did the ones who came home do it? Tim Carroll made money to buy land. Rita Fleming came back a nurse or a teacher or whatever she is, so ... well look. That's it."

Mary Catherine sat back, looking suddenly smug.

"What's it?" Marcella was getting irritated now.

"They got something out of going, Cella. They got money or became something there. That's what you have to do – save your money, get trained at something, and you'll be swanning in here just as fine as your brother in a few years. This is the twentieth century — anything's possible now. And your brother is practically running the place if your mother is to be believed. That has to make it easier for you. I wish I had someone like that. Even London would do, if I can't get to America. But you're sure to do well with Jimmy there helping you."

Marcella started smiling in spite of herself.

"Maybe."

"No maybe about it. Isn't this what you wanted? Look, I'll miss you, but if I had this chance, I'd be gone. But be sure to get work and save your passage home. It can't be that hard if one of the Carrolls could do it. Imagine you, a returned yank, all style on a Sunday? Nobody would care then who you were married to."

"I never said I wanted to marry Tommy Banahan."

"Of course you didn't. Perish the thought. But the main thing is you could. And you could bring me back an American man. There's nothing taking my fancy around here, let me tell you."

"How will I manage without you, Mary Catherine?"

"I don't know, Cella. Much the same as I'll manage without you, I suppose. Badly, but it will be worth it. Sure it will only be a few years. Go."

* * * * *

28

Chapter Two: 1904

The day before Jimmy left for Rome, he took out his camera. It was a bright wet day, and between the showers he hurried them outside and posed them. First Mother and Fran standing awkwardly in the front doorway, their faces oddly blank. Then the postman, who happened to call, theatrically handing a letter to Mother. Finally, Jimmy gave the camera to Mother to take a picture of him with his sisters, the only picture from that day that would survive. They stood behind the five-bar gate, eyes straight on her as she fussed with the camera. Their faces came out serious because the exposure was slow, and they had to be very still. Jimmy stood in the middle, the important one, leaning slightly forward over the gate, his two arms stretched down to grip Tanner's collar. The dog was on his hind legs, jumped up and held still for the picture. Jimmy was tall in priestly black, white collar, pioneer pin in his coat lapel and the brim of a top hat curving above his pale face. His brass-topped walking stick was thrown to one side for the picture, leaning on the broken pillar. His pale eyes faded into the whites, producing an eerie effect when the picture was printed in black and white, and he looked watchful, his head a little to one side as if commanding the camera to work.

Fran stood to his left in a long black skirt that covered her boots and a wide bonnet with an ostrich feather pinned on her thick, curly hair. Her blouse was lace with broad black ribbons woven in and around collars and cuffs, and a cameo brooch at her throat. Of course, later, the sisters could not remember if the ribbons were black. They might have been purple or blue velvet, but dark, in any case, and immaculate. Fran held a sprig of flowers and leaves with her long fingers loose around the stems. Her jaw was squared a little, and her eyes, as anyone at all could see later, were incredibly sad.

Marcella was on the other side of her brother with her head barely reaching his shoulder. Her skirt was shorter, just below her knee, and her blouse was plainer than Fran's, with the sleeves pushed up unevenly. Even so, she wore a small hat with flowers, looking as elegant as she could. It wasn't every day they were photographed. She held a spray of leaves and flowers to match her sister's, but in a tight grip, and in the picture, it was plain that her fingernails were short and broken. Hands for footing turf and climbing trees. Marcella's lips parted a little as she watched the camera, somewhere between defiant and curious. Later she would see that she was beautiful then, her face a perfect oval and her features even and clear. Behind them, a hedge of whitethorn was all tight buds, ready to burst into full bloom once there was some warmth in the days, and it was caught in a sudden dazzle as the sun found a gap in the rain clouds. Marcella stared straight through the lens, waiting for the shutter to snap. She was fourteen years old, and everything was about to change.

Chapter Three

1904

In the following weeks, she found everything already changed by the fact of her leaving. Later she would try to remember intangible things that were lost in the blur of preparation: last times of closeness with Fran; any signs of regret from her mother; Tommy's face and the way it moved. Most of what she would recall would be a blur of excitement that spilled over to irritation; growing impatience with things that would no longer concern her now; the odd ache, when someone talked about the end of the school year, or summer, and most of all, the speed with which the days went by. Jimmy booked her passage for a month's time, and there was a disconnect between the excitement and fear of undertaking that journey alone, and the everyday of school, homework, housework and Tanner, her trusting, unknowing dog, to bring on long walks up the fields. And there were her friends, fussing over her plans. She was the first of them to go, the youngest to go so far, the only one to go alone. This made her a celebrity for a while, and then as the day of departure neared, an outsider to their shared plans for the time after she left. Most of the girls were going to stay in school for two more years and then train for office work. Noreen Barry, the only daughter of a strong farmer, was expected to marry young. Sinead Cahalan and Muire Browne were going to England as soon as they could, to work as nurses or teachers or who knew what. They didn't plan to come home. But Marcella did. She would be almost the first to do that, too.

And then there was Tommy, distant at first, almost angry, ignoring her for weeks, and finally waiting to speak to her one evening as she stepped outside the schoolhouse.

"So, Miss America. How are you going to manage in New York City when you're in a school your father didn't start?"

She flushed. It wasn't the words – he was always teasing – but there was something hard there now.

"I'm not going to New York, Tommy. It's Birmingham, Alabama. And what difference does it make to me if my father started this school? Isn't he gone now, as much as yours? I mean ..."

The words were out before she could stop them, before she remembered his father was dead, or as good as.

"You mean what, Miss America? It's alright. My father probably couldn't have run a school anyway. He was good with his hands, Mam always said, and you know what that means, don't you? Not good with his head is what it means."

Chapter Three: 1904

They fell into step together walking up the hill, away from the village. His stiff smile softened a bit.

"Tell me about Alabama? What sort of a place is that?"

"I don't know. Jimmy sends postcards. It looks like a city."

"And will you be gone for good, Cella?"

His voice was serious now, and kinder.

"No, Tommy. I'm going 'til I finish school, and then I'm coming home here to be a teacher. Or else I'll train over there. But either way, I'm coming back. And Mother says I'll get to visit, like Jimmy does, every couple of years."

"So, two or three years then?"

"More. To learn to be a teacher. Maybe a few more then, to save to come home."

"That could be ten years then. We'll be older. Alright, Miss America. That'll do."

He was holding back a smile, but he couldn't stop it reaching his eyes. She was doing the same. Their hands brushed against each other. His was warm. She hoped it was true, what she had just said.

* * * * *

Her last day in Rockfield school came a week before the end of term, the day before her leaving home. The school day had dragged, and at the end, it was finally time to say goodbye to her friends.

"You're to write now, won't you? If those American men are all gorgeous, find one for me. And if they're not, well, do your best, alright?"

"You never needed my help, Mary Catherine, finding a boy. I don't see why you'll need it now."

Something Bigger

They hugged, glassy-eyed, and Mary Catherine stepped out of the classroom. The ache in her gut was instant and painful. It was exciting and lonely, this stepping away into the black and white world of Jimmy's postcards. She shook herself and went on with the task of clearing out her school bench. On an impulse, she tipped up the wooden seat to chalk her initials underneath, to leave some sign that she had been here. It was difficult, holding up the heavy bench with her right hand, inscribing "M. M. C." in solid cursive with her left. She was so absorbed in it, bent over on the floor, that she didn't hear footsteps until she saw Tommy Banahan's shoes on the floorboards in front of her.

"Well Marcella Coyle. Damaging school property, no less."

"Tommy. Well, I know you won't tell."

He picked up a copy from her desk and started to read it.

"Can I keep this?"

"My copy? Are you that hard up for copies?"

"No, just this one. Can I keep your English copy?"

"Why? Are you getting soft on me? Don't you know I'm leaving?"

She saw his face grow still for an instant.

"Ah not at all, Cella. I know you're leaving. I'm slow but I'm not stupid. I just thought this could be a handy thing to have. You always do well in your essays, don't you? And here's a whole copy full of them. I'd say these would see me right through school if I spread them out enough. Here, I'll swap you."

His face was almost back to normal, his smile a bit clenched, his eyes a bit too bright. He pulled a small stone from his pocket, one of the pretty white ones from the riverbank, worn into a soft pattern like a small cliff face. She held it, smooth in her open hand.

"Go on then. Take the copy, and maybe you'll get good enough at writing to write me a letter sometime, would you? Mother can give you the address."

"Indeed your mother wouldn't give me your address, Cella Coyle, and well you know it. What would she want with me writing to her precious daughter? No, you'll have to write first and give me the address."

"I will"

"Promise?"

"I promise, Tommy."

It was an easy promise. It cost her nothing.

"Grand. Well, I will write then. And I'll see you, Cella, in five years or ten, isn't that what we said? We'll be proper old people in our twenties then, but," and here his voice became gruff, "I'll wait."

They hugged quickly and awkwardly, and then he was gone too.

At home, her father's old suitcase – her suitcase now – was laid on her bed, almost full. What would he have thought of her heading away like this? She slipped the white river stone into the toe of new black boots tucked at the bottom of the case. Her half of the wardrobe was almost empty. What was she leaving behind? She looked out the low window. She'd slept in this room all her life, and that window had always seemed big. She remembered standing on this spot when the bed was so high, she had to climb on to it, looking out the window at the sky, the top of the chestnut tree, the wheeling crows. Now she was taller, and the window seemed low, so she just looked down on yard, the path to the gate, the start of the road stretching away to the brow of the hill.

"What are you moping at?"

Something Bigger

Fran's voice was softer than her words.

"Nothing. Just thinking, you know."

"Well they looked like serious thoughts. Tell me, Siss?"

"I just realised I don't see the sky anymore out this window. I used to always see the sky from here. I don't remember when it got so low down."

"You're grown out of it, Siss. Grown too big to be standing in here, looking up at the sky. Sure you'll see plenty of sky where you're going, don't worry. Here, look what I have for you."

The coat was brand new, shop-bought, not home-made or a hand-me-down, a beautiful pale blue. She slipped it on, soft and light. It came to just to below her knee.

"Oh, I love it, Fran. It's so light. Is it too light?"

"Jimmy said light is what you'll need. Hard enough to find something light around here, but this looks fine on you. Remember that when you're buying clothes – don't get something that doesn't look good on you, just because it's what you think you should buy."

"But Fran, I won't be buying clothes for myself, surely?"

"You don't think Jimmy will buy you clothes, do you? What would he know about it?"

Fran stopped, seeing the expression on Marcella's face.

"Look, it will be alright. The money over there is easy – just dollars and cents, no shillings, or farthings. Jimmy will give you money, I expect, and you just need to buy the best you can afford. No skimping. Oh, I should have talked to you about this earlier. I should have taught you to sew a bit. Can you sew at all, Siss? Can you mend a hem?"

Chapter Three: 1904

Marcella nodded, though in fact her hemming was dreadful. She'd never had to think about it, with Fran in the house. She'd never spent her own money on anything more than sweets. Fran leaned back against the closed door, her arms folded. She had stopped smiling.

"Listen here, Siss. I have something to say to you. It's important, and I'm not going to be sentimental about it. Are you listening?"

Silence was answer enough.

"You're going to be living in new places. Big cities, and fancy schools that we can't imagine now. You're too young, but you'll be fine. Here's the thing, Siss. You have to be sure to see all you can, all the new people and the new food, and write it all down in letters to me. D'you hear?"

"Of course I'll write. You know that."

"Not just any old letters. Write to me about real things, Siss. You can write anything at all to Mother, but you have to tell me what's really going on, what the place is really like, because I'm never leaving this place."

"It should have been you, Fran."

"It couldn't be me. How would you mind Mother? What money could you bring in? No. This is the only way. But you're to make the best of it. Jimmy's letters are no good. You can't tell what's going on with him. You have to show me this new life you're going to have. Will you do that, Siss?"

"I will, Fran. I'll try."

"Good girl. That's a promise?"

Marcella nodded. That evening, she tried on her new coat in the kitchen to show her mother, twirling on her toes to catch sight of herself in the high mirror over the fireplace. She caught her mother watching her with an expression she had never seen before.

"Cella, you're to be good, and mind yourself now, over there in America. Keep your hands in your pockets when you wear that coat."

* * * * *

The stern deck of The Lucania emptied as it slipped out of port and passengers moved in out of the drizzle. Marcella stood in the shadow of the funnels, looking back at the grey wake of the ship. Looking back only because of the wind, she told herself, because looking forward made her eyes water. The ship was the most new thing she had ever seen, a gigantic machine that outside smelled of oil and smoke, and in the cabins of wet wool and sweat and fried onions. It teemed with a thousand third class passengers, and hundreds more on the higher decks, but still she felt completely alone.

It was one of the fastest liners in the world, Fran had said. Marcella could be in America in a week. Wasn't this the adventure she'd longed for? For now, it only felt cold, gliding, almost silently out of port. Queenstown passed by to her right with its tall pastel houses stacked up on top of each other like shoeboxes. She imagined people inside all the little lit up windows, looking out into the gathering dark, not seeing her leave. Then the engines kicked in. There were only two men left on the deck with her; smokers in the shadow of the cabin wall, the twin red glows of their cigarettes brightening and dimming as they inhaled, like tiny lighthouses. She turned away from them, remembering her mother's strange advice and putting her hands in her pockets. She wasn't hungry, though she'd hardly eaten all day. She had no plan for this

Chapter Three: 1904

journey. She seemed to have spent all her time over the last weeks packing, saying goodbye, planning to leave and finally leaving. Now she was here at the end of her departure, being carried out into the dark with nothing to do. Nothing to think, even. Nothing to say, if she ever managed to get words out.

In fact, she hadn't spoken since she went on board. In the cabin, she left her locked trunk on her narrow bed, smiled mutely, and heard the older women behind her back whispering 'shy', and thought yes, maybe she was shy now. That was a change. Mary Catherine would laugh at the idea. She wished she were with her now. She didn't feel brave enough to talk to a stranger. What if she went all the way across the ocean and didn't open her mouth to another soul? What if her voice dried up from lack of use? There was a book she read once about a girl who lived at the side of a lake in Switzerland. She came home one day from school not talking, and nobody knew why. That was the mystery of the whole book, the thing she had seen that she was afraid to talk about it. But then she got out of the habit of talking, and found it easier to pretend she couldn't. And then, sure enough, she really couldn't. Remembering that, Marcella grew afraid that her voice might just be lost if she didn't use it. The engines roared behind her. The smokers stamped out their cigarettes and turned to go inside. Finally alone out under the big funnels, the noisiest, emptiest part of the ship, she walked to the rail, careful on the slick, glistening deck. She coughed, the sound in her throat like a hoarse kitten. Leaning forward against the rail, and shouted "Goodbye," letting the wind whip her words out of her mouth. "Goodbye, Rockfield. Goodbye school. Goodbye Tommy. Goodbye Tanner." She stopped then, thinking of the dog. What if she never saw him again? He wasn't young. How old was he going to be in, say, five years? What if it was ten years? How long could he live? Why had she not thought about this sooner? She straightened her shoulders and called again: "Goodbye, Tanner. Stay alive." And then "Goodbye Fran. Goodbye Mother. Goodbye Mary Catherine. And Tommy, stay in school." She remembered the daffodil bulbs she planted only three weeks ago, way too late in the year. She knew for sure she wouldn't see them bloom. But she wasn't going to cry for flowers. Her throat was beginning to hurt now but she felt stronger. Black smoke began to drift back over the deck, and Queenstown was now just flickering lights, growing smaller.

Maybe all that was wrong was loneliness. In the cabin, she lay shivering under a thin blanket waiting to feel better. The light was harsh until it was turned off, and then darkness was absolute. She listened to the shuddering drone of the ship, and to the other women breathing. One was seasick all night long, and every few hours her companion would call out from another bed: 'Are you alright, Kathleen? Are you going to get sick again? Do you need a drink, Kathleen?' Marcella turned to the wall, and eventually slept.

The days on the boat ran together. It was neither fun enough to be exciting, nor ordinary enough to be comforting. The other passengers were friendly enough once she started talking to them. The Dublin women in her cabin dispensed second-hand advice about arrival, the port, what not to say to the immigration officials, warning her about the strange dark-skinned people she would meet. They told her to stay clear of Italians, especially Italian men. The Italians warned her that Greeks were all pickpockets and told her to never lend money to anyone Polish. The country ones told her lurid stories about Dublin gangsters, and nodded significantly at the sisters who shared her cabin. The city ones warned her off men in general, laughing when she didn't understand their slang. Most of them were first-timers, emigrants, like her. A family in the next cabin spoke only Irish, and the mother lay in her bed and cried day and night. After two days, Marcella stopped hearing it.

She felt loneliest in the mornings when she woke. It took a minute to remember where she was, feeling the loss of home fresh each time. She read her book slowly, making it last. Reading stopped her from thinking about home, but at night before sleeping she could think of nothing else, especially of her mother who had kept a stern face all the way up the railway platform, but when she looked back as the train moved off, she saw her standing there, weeping openly. In all her life, she had never seen her cry like that. Fran kept up her crooked smile, her arm around her mother. And now there was just this massive absence, strangers everywhere. So many people and nobody she knew. The sea behind the ship was churning and wide and when she looked back, scanning the horizon behind, it looked completely empty.

The morning they drew near to port, the mood changed like the light going on at the end of a play. Flirting girls put out their cigarettes and gathered their things. Lads who had been fighting forgot their differences. Everyone seemed to find the energy to pack up stray belongings, fish out forms and papers from secret pockets. Her traveling companions, even the weeping mother next door, became loud and fast-moving, excited or apprehensive. None of them seemed lost like her. She went to her cabin and waited for someone to tell her what to do, but nobody came. She made herself imagine Fran was there, and how she might tell her to pack and take her place out in the crowd on deck, and then she did that.

This port was pure chaos, a world away from Queenstown. A bigger ship eased past only yards away, like a slow-moving, metal wall. Small tugs milled around below like hens under a feeder. The water churned mud-green, smelling rank after days of clean sea air. The ship's thrumming engines fell silent, and that absence filled with whistles and sirens, shouts in strange languages from the dock. There were men there with black skin, just as she'd been told, and buildings that were higher than anything she remembered from Jimmy's photographs. She was scared and uplifted. She tried to soak it all in for Fran.

The Lucania clinked to a halt like a steel door closing. She shuffled on the crowded gangway, carried along through a blur of queues and questions, waiting and fretting. And then she was released from immigration. This was it — America, and she the first of her friends to see it. She stepped onto the dock where a young, preoccupied priest met her, not talking much on the cab ride through the city to Penn Station. She was glad he didn't speak, staring out at the incredible, fast-moving city, so many people, so many unfamiliar smells and sounds. Penn Station bristled with menace and purpose, and she followed as quickly as she could behind the priest. He walked her onto a hissing train and manhandled her trunk down the narrow corridor between sleeping cars.

"Here — number 5. This one's yours, Miss Coyle. You're a lucky young woman - you have the car to yourself all the way to Birmingham. Give my regards to your brother."

"I will. But aren't you coming, Father?"

He laughed. "My work is done now. You just sit in here, and the guard will look after you. He'll call you up when it's time to eat. Don't be leaving the train when it stops, until you get to Birmingham. The guard will tell you. I'll have a word."

Then she was alone in a tiny cabin of a room. She bolted the door and sat up by the window, hugging her knees. A window all to herself. The train sped out of the tunnel and as it left the city behind, she stared out at tall, redbrick factory chimneys, wheeling fields of barley bigger than any field she'd ever seen before. The first time the train wailed, low and emotional, not at all like the whistles of Irish trains, she felt comforted. At each stop men stepped out and smoked beneath her window, and some ladies too, the guard placing a step beside the door for them, with their long skirts. She watched from only inches away behind the glass, feeling as though she were hiding in a safe nest. It was good to be properly alone.

They were passing through a small town — barely a railway crossing, really — when a knock on the door startled her. She'd forgotten about the guard. His accent was so strong, she could barely make out the words, but his face was kind. He seemed used to travellers who didn't know their way around. She tried not to stare at him as he talked, the first Black man she'd ever seen up close. He gave her a ticket for the dining car where she tried to sit properly, crossing her legs at the ankles as Fran had taught her. The other passengers wore clothes that all looked different to hers. Her very best skirt now seemed heavy and rough. She tried to capture it in words, for a letter to Fran, what was different about the way they were dressed, but it evaded her. It wasn't just the fabrics. Maybe it was the shoes, so clean and impractical, even the men's. She thought of her father's leather boots still behind the kitchen door in Rockfield, eight years since he had worn them. She thought of Fran's hand-knit socks and couldn't imagine even her, the most stylish woman she knew, in this company.

After dinner, she found her bed made up, and curled up with her head against the window as the train twisted through dark green forests, lush and dripping. The weather had turned while she was away, and now lightning flashed from a muddy yellow sky. In little darkening towns the streets were empty, and after rain, the muddy roads steamed just as Jimmy had said. She thought of Fran at home, hanging out clothes in the damp air, and of the work involved in drying wool, the constant cycle of taking out ashes and bringing in turf, how hard it was to keep things warm and dry. And here, after a downpour, the earth seemed to dry itself. She felt exhilarated, completely alone. She was far from home but making her own way.

Sleep when it came was fitful and she dreamed she was back on the ship, but bearing too far South, missing the coast of America completely and heading out into dark, uncharted waters, with her looking back at the wide wake, trying to pick out, on the horizon, the fading lights of home. And though the dream was troubling, she woke peaceful, early, lulled by the rocking of the train. She had made it to America. She was traveling well, and she didn't want the journey to end.

Chapter Four

1904

Marcella arrived in Birmingham at quarter to three, black hands flat across the station clock, thunder looming in a steel sky. She dragged her luggage off the train into a wall of heat. It was a busy stop, but the crowd of passengers thinned quickly as the train pulled away, leaving her alone on a suddenly quiet platform, dust hanging in the air. She felt conspicuous, even ridiculous in her white dress and gloves. The still air smelled of sulphur. There was no sign of Jimmy. Gradually, she became aware of being watched, and turned to meet the eyes of a man watching from the shade of the station room veranda.

"Hey there, little Miss. You need a little help with those trunks?"

She stiffened and turned away, but he walked slowly around in front of her, taking his time. He was taller than he had looked in the shadow. More burly.

"Don't worry, Miss, I ain't fixing to hurt you. You new to Coaltown? Need a little help?"

Something Bigger

He looked foreign, she thought, with his sallow skin and dark brown eyes. Then she remembered she was the foreign one here. His suit was worn to a shine at the knees, and the cuffs of his shirt were grey and frayed. There was a smell that might have been whiskey. He smiled, not entirely a creepy smile, and she was smiling back by reflex, about to answer when Jimmy came striding up the platform followed by a breathless porter. He was frowning as he swept her into a rough embrace.

"Well now Siss. Here you are in all your finest. Come on. Leave the trunk to Henry here. We're going to walk."

He turned on his heel, expecting her to follow. She looked back, but the man had retreated under the awning. She hurried after her brother.

"Who was that, Siss?"

"Who was who?"

"You know very well, Marcella. Who was that man you were talking to?"

"I don't know. Just some man."

"Just a man?" His voice took on a dangerous edge. "Nobody is just a man, Marcella. Nobody here. Why were you talking to him? No, better question, why do you think he was talking to you?"

"He asked if I needed help. He was just being friendly."

He stopped and turned, his hands on her shoulders.

"Look, Siss. I'm sorry I was late, and you weren't to know, but this is important. Maybe this one was just a friendly man. Maybe. But this isn't Rockfield. It's not a safe place to talk to strangers. Not ever. Do you understand?"

She nodded. Jimmy's voice softened.

Chapter Four: 1904

"This is a big city, Siss, and we live right in the middle of it. There are all sorts of people here, good ones and bad. They all came here for something, and we don't know what that is. So well, just be careful, won't you?"

Jimmy's accent, which had always seemed American to her at home, reminded her now of Rockfield, and of how she hadn't heard another voice like it in, was it really only ten days? It seemed so much longer. Her head ached suddenly, and a wave of exhaustion came over her. This was the start of her new life. It was supposed to be exciting, wasn't it? So why did she feel tears coming? She didn't want to cry like a child. He hugged her again, her face to his shoulder.

"Ah, never mind, Siss. We'll be grand. You'll see."

But she did mind. His warnings changed the way she looked at people as they walked up the hill from the station. Jimmy walked fast, and she was thirsty. After days of being carried by boat and train, she struggled to keep up. The sidewalk was hectic. A small bevy of nuns almost collided around a corner with an eagle-faced man who glared at them as they walked away. Black women pushed baby carriages with pale, bonneted babies, avoiding sharp-dressed businessmen and delivery boys with teetering loads. The street was loud with hammering from high over her head, where it seemed half the buildings were still stretching up to outdo each other. She was far too hot, and she knew she was slowing Jimmy down. And then he stopped and pointed ahead.

"Look Siss. Look up."

Over the low roof of a grain store, two dark gothic spires towered up from the next block.

"Is that your church?"

"It is indeed, Siss. Come on"

Something Bigger

He slowed now, seeing she couldn't keep up. He looked a little flushed, almost shy, his anger evaporated. They rounded the corner to 3rd St., and there was a church that looked like a cathedral. Pale marble pillars flanked steps that led straight from the sidewalk up to a dark oak door. How strange not to have a yard, or a space for carriages. Did people not stand and talk outside church in America? Jimmy took the steps two at a time and pushed, but the door with its heavy black hinges did not give way. Marcella waited. Down the street her eyes caught a flash of sunlight off metal, a barber standing in the shade of his doorway, watching them without expression, sharpening his blade.

"Locked, Siss. I'll show you later."

Marcella, feeling lightheaded now, only wanted to sit on the shady steps and wait, but Jimmy was already pushing open a low iron gate beside the church and she followed. Dwarfed between the church and a high courthouse building on the other side, the low wooden rectory was not much bigger than their cottage in Rockfield. Different, though, with faded, white-painted boards and a long wraparound porch shading a swing seat under the front window. There was a sparse and weedy garden, one small tree, two stone pots overflowing with bright marigolds. She leaned on the gate for a moment. Jimmy was almost at the front door. She went to follow, but stumbled, falling on the paved path. Struggling up, embarrassed, she tightened her face as though she wasn't hurt, and then saw blood seeping through the knee of her best ivory stockings. She shouldn't have worn them and now they were ruined. She could hear her mother's voice in her head telling her so – "Marcella, you shouldn't wear all your best clothes all at once. What are you going to wear tomorrow?"

Chapter Four: 1904

The nagging inner voice was cut off abruptly by a stick-thin Black woman who swept out the door holding a washcloth full of ice. Before she could say anything, Marcella was bundled up the path and into a swing seat on the rectory porch with the cold compress pressed against her knee. The feel of the damp cloth against her skin, the sheltered seat and shade disarmed her. There was such concern in the woman's brown eyes, such a pure kindness.

"There now, honey. There now. Don't cry, baby. Don't you cry."

There was something familiar about her. It was in the way she moved without hesitation, the way she looked her in the eye as though she already knew her. She felt cared for. The woman caught Marcella's left hand and showed her where to hold the ice in place. She was so obviously and completely in charge. She didn't look at all like Fran, but Marcella realised that's who she reminded her of.

"I see you've met Johanna." Jimmy stood in the hall, twirling a set of keys. "I'll give you a while to settle."

Johanna showed her to a narrow white room, with a large bed, too big for the space. There was a little dresser with a mirror on top in three parts – one flat against the wall and two more hinged to it on either side, swinging like doors. She found she could twist them to reflect almost any part of the room. She closed the door and sat on the end of the bed, and pressed her face forward between the mirrors, turning them to face each other. She looked left and right, watching herself endlessly reflected, smaller and smaller into the distance like the pattern on the front of a tin of Royal Baking Powder. Shrinking Marcellas all overlapping in both directions into infinity. It was all hers, this room. She exhaled.

Something Bigger

Here she was, after all, at the beginning. It was going to be alright. She pushed the mirrors closed as the door opened and Jimmy was there, bright and excited.

"Come on, Siss. Let's show you the church."

In the sacristy, her eyes adjusted to the dark. The only window ran along high under the ceiling, its yellowed glass casting a soft light over the cool tiled floor. A bank of locked cupboards took up the opposite wall, and the long wooden table in the centre of the room was laid out with account books, notebooks, and a dark pile of missals. Another priest was working on the books, and nodded his greetings, distractedly. There were no flowers. Nothing soft or tactile. Jimmy fumbled with the keys and opened the door to the altar and the cavernous space of the church itself, turning back to talk to the other priest.

Her footsteps were too loud for the enormous silence held there under the vaulted roof. While the sacristy had been cool, the church was chilly, with a trace of incense hanging in the air. It felt wholly familiar: the way light fell from stained glass windows; the rows of empty pews; the soft feel of air purified by candles burning in the side altars, dripping their wax on the gleaming terracotta floor-tiles. It was grander than any church she had seen, more polished, but a church was a place she knew very well. She wandered, finding back steps leading to a balcony, and climbed them quietly, assuming this was not allowed. It was comfortable to be up there, quiet and invisible, looking over the wooden rail at the altar below, the rows of silent seats. Two pillars came right through the balcony floor so she could touch the ring of plaster flowers on the top. The ceiling was close as a cave and sloped down on either side, lit by soft and pretty stained-glass light,

Chapter Four: 1904

pink and purple in the top frames, with green and blue saints below. The nearest one, Saint Patrick, had the same gothic green panels as in the big church in Athlone. A small organ was set near the balcony rail. Its lid opened easily. She sat and her hands hovered over the keys. Pushing the foot pedals produced a breathy empty sound. She hesitated, then pressed a key. The note was sweet, and though it seemed really loud in the silence, nobody came to stop her. She settled herself and began to pick out a tune.

"Good to hear you play, Siss."

She hadn't heard him come up the stairs.

"Is it OK, Jimmy?"

"Yes, this place needs a bit of music. I like it. Come and play here anytime."

She smiled, said nothing.

"Siss, it might be hard for you sometimes here. It's alright to miss home, and it's alright to talk about it. I miss it too, Mother and Fran, all the old things. But we're here now, the pair of us only, and ... well, go on now, play something else."

She started to pick out an old song by ear, one she had learned in school, and he hummed along a little off key. Neither of them could remember the words.

"Remember Father used to sing that one in the morning when he was shaving?"

"Did he? I don't remember."

She really didn't. In fact, she could hardly remember his voice at all. Or how his face moved, apart from that incomplete dream in which he almost turned around to look at the class, in the schoolhouse in Rockfield. She wondered what colour his eyes had been, really? She realised Jimmy was still talking.

"Ah you do. You know the way he used to always

hum to himself when he was getting the water outside, and then he'd be full on singing by the time he was shaving. He was a terrible singer. Only nobody could ever tell him."

She smiled properly now, because Jimmy himself was unable to hold a tune and everyone knew it but him, especially in Rockfield where he sang sometimes in church, his high benedictions all flat. She played on, trying to place her father's voice along the melody, but she couldn't make it happen. She could see him standing in the front of the school room, his back to the class, chalk in hand. She could almost see him turn to face her. His voice? Try as she might it was gone. She realised she wasn't playing anymore. Her hands just seemed to stop of their own accord. But Jimmy was already on his way back downstairs and hadn't noticed, so it was alright.

As she passed back through the sacristy, Jimmy introduced her to the other priest, Fr. Tony Brennan, and then they were absorbed again in the record books. She crossed the rectory yard, and Johanna smiled at her through the kitchen window. A warm smile. She straightened her shoulders as she went to her room to unpack. It was going to be fine. It was only for a few years after all.

* * * * *

She unpacked and set Tommy's river stone on the white dresser. The thunder that had been building all afternoon broke suddenly, crashing so loud she thought the walls had fallen. Rain hissed straight down outside her window, pooling on the thin brown grass. She ran to the front porch and watched from under the overhanging roof: rain steaming off the hot gravel, plopping on dead leaves, shining every surface. At first it smelled sharp, a chemical smell like damp soot, and then the air seemed cleaned, not just cooler, but sweeter, and a breeze rose to pull at her hair, soft and damp like home.

"It's a relief, isn't it, Siss? The rain?"

Jimmy was so quiet in the swing seat behind her, she hadn't seen him.

"Yes. I never thought I'd miss rain."

"It's surprising what you'd miss."

"It's so different though. Is it always like this? Does it get worse in winter? Are there seasons here, even? Those trees, do they lose their leaves? What will they be like in Autumn? Will they ..."

"Fall."

"What?"

"Fall." Jimmy tried to hide a smile and failed. "It's called Fall here. Not Autumn."

"Fall. Alright. Fall. What I meant was, I don't know if those leaves will go brown or red or just stay on the trees. I don't know if there will be frost here, even. Or when. It's like being a child, not knowing anything."

"Like a child?" He was teasing her. Just a little bit. Not being mean.

"Yes, like a child. A little one. I mean even the way it gets dark here – I don't even know if that will change at all? Are there longer days coming or is this it? This pitch dark at seven o'clock in the day?"

"This is it, Siss," He was grinning openly now.

"What?"

"What?"

"What's so funny? Don't tell me you didn't wonder all this stuff when you came first?"

"I hadn't time, I think. And who could I ask? I

could hardly ask Johanna when it was going to get dark. Who had I to ask about those things?"

She threw him a sharp look and was quiet for a while. He was looking off down the street, his face turned away a bit. Rain drummed on the porch roof.

"OK," she said. "Well, you have me now, Jimmy."

He smiled at her, a quick, tight smile that was all in his eyes. Marcella found herself smiling too. They stood close together, looking out at the rain without speaking for a long time.

Chapter Five

<svg>⌒∞⌒</svg>

1904

Birmingham Age Herald, June 1904

ROLLER COASTER STARTS TODAY

After many disappointments and un-
avoidable delays, the roller coaster will
commence operations today at East Lake
park. The tracks have all been laid and
tested, the big structure and slide well
lighted with electric lights, and everything is in first class order to make this,
one of the most enjoyable entertainments
ever presented to the people of Birmingham and vicinity. All the attractions
at the park are now in operation, and
Calman's orchestra gives free concerts
every afternoon and evening. On Sunday
Memoli's band of sixteen pieces will render free concerts to the public.

Something Bigger

St. Paul's Rectory
221 Third Avenue
Birmingham,
Alabama.
June 1904

Dear Tommy,

I told you I'd write. I don't think you believed me, but here it is. That's my address up there, so I want letters from you now. No excuses. This place I'm living they call a rectory — it's like the parochial house. There's me and Jimmy, another priest from Ireland called Tony Brennan, and there's a woman called Johanna who is here all day but goes home to her own place at night. I like it now, I've got used to it. I have my own room. The house is made of wood, but so are lots of the houses around here. It's as solid as stone. I like it now, I think.

I haven't started school yet. It's going to take another week, Jimmy says. I don't know how I feel about school. I mean, I know I have to go. That's the point of being here, but I don't know what it will be like. Everything else is really different here, so I guess school will be too. People are dressed up all the time, like it's Sunday every day. We live in the middle of the city, so I suppose who I'm seeing are the townies, but they're stylish right down to their shoes. What if they're like that at school? I might say the wrong thing any time. Even the simplest things are new and unfamiliar. The food is all different. There are bugs that would frighten a dog! The weather is hot all the time, even at night. Even when it's raining. Mostly it's the crowds that are different. All day people are walking and riding carriages and drays just outside the fence in front of the rectory, only a few yards away from the house. People from all over the world, it looks like. Rich and poor. I've never seen anything like it. And at the same time, the heat! I don't know how they walk down there without collapsing. I'm worn out from it, and I don't go anywhere.

I'm not explaining it properly. I'll try harder next time. And I'll send you cuttings from the paper every time so you can see more than I can explain. Will you be ok with all that reading, Tommy Banahan? Ah, you know I'm only teasing.

Write to me, and tell me all about Rockfield, if everything is the same, what the news is at school. I miss it all, miss talking to you. You all, I mean.

Write!

Your friend,

Cella

Marcella's first Birmingham days were all dull, debilitating heat that slowed her walk and slowed her thinking, made her impatient but lethargic. Nights were long and lonely. She'd wake thirsty in the bright window light, disoriented, afraid to leave her bedroom to get a drink.

She spent her days with Johanna in the kitchen or hiding away from the city's coal dust and chaos on the church balcony or in the swing seat in the deep shade of the front porch, watching people walking outside the low fence — so many strangers walking by so close, not even seeing here there. She came to recognise the young bellhop of Tutwiler hotel, always hurrying, always late; the flat-faced woman who walked slowly and unevenly, dragging her soft shoes in the dust; the parade of Black men and women, Johanna among them, walking in from the other end of town every morning to cook and clean and garden, walking home again in the dark evenings; the flint-faced barber across the street who smoked and stared from the shade of his shop door; nuns in groups of three or five, priests in ones and twos; careering carriages, even some motorcars and slow horse drays. She soaked up the street like a drink of water, all the untold stories she could imagine, and she wrote about them to Tommy and Fran. She told Fran about the rectory, being funny about the people she saw, describing their clothes and the way they moved. She wrote to her mother about Jimmy, the size of his church, the length of his sermons, the way he held the congregation in the hollow of his hand as he spoke from the pulpit. She wrote to Tommy about everything: how she felt, what she saw, the three-legged stray kitten she'd started feeding, how she named him Captain, how she stored away kitchen scraps for him, trying to make him hers. She told him how lonely she was, how busy Jimmy was, how little time he had for her. How after Jimmy finally said it was time she went to school, it was a relief.

School was a light, airy convent within walking distance, smelling of lavender floor polish and pencil shavings, overlaid by the faint scent of talcum powder from the nuns in their pale blue habits and wide wimples. Her first day was horrible. The other girls had some clean confidence she lacked. They mocked her shoes, the way she parted her hair, her ignorance of French, of American history, American literature. At the first recess they circled her in the schoolyard, laughing, asking her to say this word or that, mocking her accent,

Chapter Five: 1904

and after that they ignored her. It took her a week to find a friend. Lucille was another late-coming outsider, tall and pale with something fragile in her eyes that her quick smile couldn't quite cover. She came from Atlanta, living with an aunt in Birmingham to attend the convent school. They stuck together because the alternative was being alone. In time, they grew close. Lucille showed Marcella how to apply rouge, how to fix her hair. She lent her lipstick. She walked with her out the school gate in the evenings which was when Marcella had felt most alone. She taught her how to be in an American school, how to speak up just enough in class to pass the endless tests, all she needed to know about the subjects that were new. It was Lucille who first befriended Mimi, a rule-breaker who liked to make people laugh, making them a circle of three. Marcella was so grateful to be pulled into any kind of a group, it felt like friendship. Not like the friendship she'd had with Mary Catherine, but something new. She told Fran about the things she and Lucille and Mimi did together, about occasional evenings in the Lyric Movie theatre, treats in the ice cream parlour. She told her the good bits, writing a life that was better than her own, but a fine life, and almost real. She just never told Fran how she didn't fit in. Not yet.

Her letters to Tommy were different. She wrote short letters often, without thinking too much about what she said. She tried to make him laugh, tucking postcards and dried leaves into the envelope at the last minute and without explanation. Sometimes she sent cuttings from the newspaper, unimportant stories, small ads, black and white photos of broad-faced men, boosting the city, drinking whiskey. She wrote honestly about how lonely she was, about embarrassment or boredom or small things she feared or loved. She knew he was reading them, but it seemed to her that she was writing to herself. It occurred to her the letters were like a diary, or a scrapbook, though she had no time for diaries. Sometimes she wondered if he kept them, if they were building up in that dirty cottage he lived in. She wondered if she might sit with him, in years to come, and they would read them over again, together, when she got home.

She wrote to Mary Catherine every week, but after one or two letters, Mary Catherine stopped writing back. That was a hurtful surprise. Tommy, however, wrote often, and this was also surprising. He made her laugh with stories from Rockfield school, though after a while she struggled to put a face to the names he mentioned. In passing, he said Mary Catherine had left Rockfield and gone to England. Marcella supposed she'd left in a hurry, with no time to write. That would be like Mary Catherine. Tommy wrote about Fran, and what she was wearing at Mass, and who from the men's side of the church was watching her style as she came down from communion. He wrote about how he missed her at school, only he didn't put it like that. You're missed, Cella, he'd say. Not "I miss you." He wrote about Tanner who still ran out to greet him as he went by to school in the morning "the only one in your house who'll acknowledge me, Cella. Your mother would have a fit if she knew I was writing to you, her precious daughter talking to a Banahan." Marcella didn't argue the point. She knew it was true. All his letters had birds on them, robins perching on the ends of paragraphs, rooks spreading away in the margins. She loved them. She'd have framed them to hang around her bedroom if she could. Writing to Tommy seemed easy, so much easier than it had ever been to talk in person. She could say anything, and never have to explain.

Try as she might to learn all the unwritten ways of the city, she was often ambushed by things she didn't understand. She was at ease with Johanna, and often worked with her in the kitchen, drying dishes while Johanna washed, with an easy unspoken rhythm between them. She was relaxed enough there to ask questions without worrying if they were foolish. Johanna's life unfolded for her slowly. She'd been fifteen years in Birmingham, she said. That was Marcella's whole lifetime.

"Fifteen years in Birmingham, child. Ten years in this house. I came to this city for work when I was little older than you. Married like a fool. For love, I thought, but he left me with a child on the way, and no work. Then I came and found service here. Steady work. This is a good house, child."

Marcella didn't ask what "a good house" meant. If this was a good house, what was a bad one? How would you know? Instead, she asked about Johanna's child. Jackson, it turned out, was a boy a year older than her. A good boy, his mother said. A quiet boy, not likely to get himself in trouble. Still in school. Marcella thought about him coming home from school to an empty house, while she came to a kitchen full of Johanna and sweet cooking smells.

"Where does he go to school, Johanna?"

"Up in Longfield, where we live. Your brother helped build that school. He's a good man."

Marcella had heard of Longfield, and imagined Johanna's life there as similar to her own. That is until one evening she walked into the kitchen just after dark. Johanna had her coat and scarf on, ready to go home, and was fishing something out of the trashcan. A small paper bag, folded tight and slipped quickly into her pocket as though she were trying to hide it.

"What's that, Johanna?"

Afterwards Marcella was ashamed of the sharpness in her tone – as if she owned everything, as if she could demand an answer from this woman who had been nothing but kind to her. As if she thought Johanna was stealing, although actually, she had to admit, that's exactly what she thought.

"Nothing child. Just that chicken neck — see?"

Johanna held open the soggy bag in her hand. Marcella could see the twisted gizzard of the chicken they had for dinner. The bag was wet with blood and the sweatiness of the meat. Her face crinkled in disgust.

"You don't like that? You don't like that kind of meat. Only white chicken meat for you. Or good dark meat. No bones, no neck, no liver. This is just trash for you, child. Nobody here wants it. You see?"

But she didn't see. Not yet.

"But why are you ... is it for a dog, Johanna? I had a pet dog, at home. Is your dog a big one? The big ones are more gentle, Fran says."

Babbling. She always babbled when she was nervous.

Johanna waited, with her head a little to one side, letting Marcella talk. Once she was quiet, she explained.

"This ain't food for a dog, honey. This is meat, not trash."

Johanna's face was stiff, but her eyes were full of pity. Marcella struggled to find words.

"But, we were throwing it away. We just threw it away. Why ..."

Chapter Five: 1904

"Hush, child, don't you mind. It's just things you don't understand yet. Ask your brother. He'll explain."

Jimmy was out on the front porch. Marcella knew this, but she didn't ask him. She wasn't sure if she wanted to hear what he might say. Instead, she wrote to Tommy again, telling him about what had happened. There was a short French poem she had to learn for school the next day, so she copied that out too, onto the end of the letter. She guessed he wouldn't understand that either.

In time, things got better. She learned to dress well, to flirt a little. She dated sometimes, chaste double dates with Lucille. She studied hard at school — wasn't that what she was there for, after all? — and caught up with her new subjects. She'd always been good at math, as they called it here. They had learned far more of that in Rockfield than these nuns taught. Sometimes she dreamed a bit as St. Levinus was explaining algebra, and that half picture of her father hovered on the edge of memory. Always turned away from her at the front of the classroom, a shaft of sunlight from the grimy window catching the individual motes of chalk dust as he wrote numbers on the slate. She found the memory comforting, as though he were here with her, in this light, American place.

* * * * *

Summer turned to winter, and to spring again. Marcella sat out on the front porch in Jimmy's deep swing seat, with a glass of water, a wide-brimmed hat, and a half-written letter home. The seat was tucked away to one side of the porch, near the looming shadow of the church, almost out of sight in the deep shade of the afternoon, and she could sit sideways, curling her feet under her, wrapping an arm across her stomach, half watching the street without being seen. She was sitting like that when she saw the child.

She was not much more than a toddling baby in a washed-out floral dress, stood just inside the open gate, gripping the railing with her left hand, and dangling something — a sock? a rag? — from her right. There was dirt on her bare feet — old dirt, ingrained, not just today's dust. She didn't move or speak or cry. She just stared with an unnerving intensity. Her blue eyes seemed too big for her face, and Marcella got the quick impression that they were the only bright, clean part of her.

"Hello, baby. What's your name?"

The child didn't turn away, as Marcella half expected. Instead, she took three steps forward into the rectory yard, as though she belonged there, as though Marcella was someone she knew and could trust. The pout on her lips made her look serious. She walked on her toes, like a tiny, grimy ballet dancer, light as a bird, and, like a bird, she looked as though she might fly. Marcella crept down the porch steps and along the path towards her, went down on one knee, coaxing.

"Are you lost? Are you thirsty? Would you like some water?"

The child reached for the proffered glass, and that's where she was, drinking from Marcella's hand, spilling water down the front of her dress when the sharp voice came from the street.

"What are you doing? What do you think you are doing with my girl? What's in that drink? Bessie Stubbs, get back here at once!"

The woman was in the gate before Marcella looked up, snatching up the child like a stolen handbag. Her hair, tied back too tight, was thinning about

Chapter Five: 1904

the parting. Her forehead was low. She wore a high lace collar which wasn't as white as it might have been, and a brooch pinned at her throat. Her mouth was limp, and her lower lip trembled. Her eyes in a broad, pale face, though a little mismatched, were furious. Marcella flinched under their intensity.

"How dare you! How dare you take my child."

"I didn't. I ..."

"If I see you with my girl again, I'll ..."

"But she just came in. She was there on the street and she just walked in the gate. I was just ..."

"I know what you were doing very well. You can't fool me, young lady. I know your tricks and ways. But you won't get away with it. Not with my Bessie."

"What tricks? Now look here ... you don't know me at all, Ma'am. You can't say ..."

"Is there something the matter here, Miss Cella?"

Johanna's voice was calm, and she strolled down the path as though she had all the time in the world. She was talking to Marcella but never took her eyes off the woman, who in turn ignored her and continued to berate Marcella.

"If I see you talking to my Bessie again ..."

"Can I help you at all, Mrs. Stubbs, Ma'am?"

"You won't get away with this. I know what you're doing. Bessie's just an innocent child."

"Would you like me to fetch the Father, Ma'am? He's just inside."

Johanna was louder now, standing up real close to Mrs Stubbs. Too close to be polite. She had stepped between her and Marcella, and slight as she was, she filled the space with her calm, challenging presence.

"No. No. I don't want to talk to ... No. Come on, Bess."

"It's no trouble, Mrs. Stubbs, Ma'am. I can go fetch him right now."

The woman hurried to the gate, pulling the girl by the hand. Johanna walked slowly behind her, as Fran might if a horse had wandered into the cottage garden; that easy way she'd herd it back out to the road without saying a word. Bessie was trying to look back, but the woman held her wrist too high, so the little girl had to dance along with her, out the gate and out of sight. Marcella sat back, and realised she was shaking.

"What was that, Johanna? Who is that crazy woman? And what ... why was she so angry?"

"Oh never you mind, child. She's old man Stubbs' wife. You know Stubbs? Tall, hard man, works down the barbers shop where the Father goes now and then. That's his missus, just fit to explode, I reckon, seeing her little girl in here."

"But she just walked in, right off the street. She ..."

"I know that, Miss Cella. But Mrs. S? Well she's scared and angry with herself for letting her baby wander off like that. Why she must have walked two blocks and crossed that street, all on her own. No wonder her Momma was in a state. And you know, she'd be anxious, a child of hers in this place of all places. The Father can explain."

"Is he here? I thought Jimmy was gone to Mobile today?"

"He's gone since early. Back tomorrow."

"But you said you'd fetch him for her. How...?"

"I did. Didn't I?"

Johanna's quick grin made Marcella feel protected, but the incident had unsettled her. There was more to it than a wandering child. The woman had seemed to really believe Marcella might harm the little girl. She walked down to close the gate and saw the rag

Chapter Five: 1904

the child had been holding had fallen half out of sight under a bush near where her mother had pulled her away. Picking it up, she saw it was a rough-stitched toy rabbit of sorts, small enough to fit in her palm, stitched together from an old sock with skewed button eyes. The felt ears might once have been red. The left one was ragged and frayed at the top. It looked chewed.

"She's going to miss this" Marcella thought. She carried it to her room and pinned the raggy sock-bunny to the side of her shelf.

"You stay here, little rabbit, " she said. "Serves that woman right to lose you. You wait 'til your girl comes back to find you."

* * * * *

Up the street, as darkness fell, Abner Stubbs stood outside his barber shop and smoked, ignoring the sound of crying from the upstairs window of his home. That was just Bessie, fussing 'cause she'd lost her little Brer Rabbit, and Ethel fussing 'cause she couldn't quieten her. That was woman's business. He inhaled, thinking maybe Ethel was scared, in case he'd get mad from the fuss. He thought maybe he should make like he was mad, like the man of the house ought to, but the truth was, he didn't feel angry at all. Bessie was sweet when she was upset. He loved to see her pretty little face all puckered up, like she didn't know whether to cry or scream. He reckoned she was prettier than anything then.

A regular customer passed by on the evening street, and they nodded greetings at each other. His business was slow these days. Building, but building, slowly. From the upstairs window came the sound of a slap, and then only muffled sobs from the child. He could picture her — his fiery little one, that sweet little face all angry. Ethel didn't get like that anymore. She used to be so easy to rise, when they came here first, when they were walking out together and first came to Birmingham. It seemed to him, looking back, like her whole mood used to hang off his then. He recalled the day he'd opened the barbers, the lease all signed, his name painted over the door as big as any other name on the street. She'd been so proud of him. It made him feel ten feet tall, she so happy to be his woman, and he the whole world to her. And then she started losing babies, one after another, two in a year sometimes. It was like something died in her, until Bessie came, and Bessie lived, and that thing that was dead came back, but not fully. Not for him. From the first week of Bessie's life, Ethel was all wrapped up in that bitty little baby just like she used to be in him. He could hardly reach her now.

He missed coming upstairs in the evening, and having her there, waiting for him. Even if she didn't make dinner. Even if she didn't have the place so clean, she used to want to know everything about his day. She used to care if he was happy. She used to fear him, just enough, if he was not happy. He wasn't the kind of man to make a fuss about food or cleaning, not back then, but he wanted her waiting. He wanted her attention.

But those years, those babies she lost, they moved her away from him. And now he could see Ethel really did care more for Bess more than she cared for him. It made him think maybe she never cared for him at all. These days, he paid attention to what she had and hadn't done all day, to the food and the cleaning, and everything that made her take notice of his needs. But it was no good. He could shout and hit, but it was like he couldn't even hurt her, and God knows, there were

Chapter Five: 1904

times he tried. Nothing he could do made her look at him like she used to. Now she walked in and out of his barber's shop like it was something shameful, like it was not good enough for her and her daughter. Like he should be a bigger man in this big city. Like he wasn't big enough or good enough for her.

His cigarette was almost done, and he cupped the stub in his palm, inhaling the last. Still, he was here, wasn't he? His own shop, his own business, here on this street. And Bess was his daughter too. Little Bessie still had it, pretty little thing. She still loved her Daddy and she took heed of him too. Like it should be. She was the best thing in his whole sorry life. He'd do anything to keep her like that, pure and simple and belonging to him.

* * * * *

In later years, Marcella would look back and see her school years like a silent movie, moving too fast, out of focus, with some cheery soundtrack added later by her own memory. School was a haven, a small world of fiercely loyal friendships, schoolwork, summer dances and gradually, her growing up, no longer an awkward child, but becoming someone the boys smiled at, the mining men looked after as she passed by with Mimi or Lucille, their books clutched to their chests, walking to or from school. Meanwhile, Jimmy worked; that's mostly what he did, as far as she could tell. She did not get involved in those years, or try to understand. The rectory was full of talk — men's talk, mostly, priests and newspaper men and Catholic business owners being hit up for donations for who knew what it was that absorbed Jimmy so. Marcella often sat with him in the evenings on the front porch, she with her homework and he writing, or reading, or sometimes dozing off in the wide swing seat. She liked that. They were family, together, and they didn't have to talk. These were the peaceful years that she would remember always, but vaguely, blurred, like a drift of smoke on a summer day.

Then graduation came charging towards her like a runaway train. Suddenly the nuns wanted to know what she and her friends would do with their lives, bringing it up directly or indirectly every day. The girls cooked up plausible lies with which to respond, since they had no real idea of how to make their own way in the world. Lucille said the nuns were only hoping one of them would have a vocation. The thought of staying any longer in that convent was anathema to all of them. Their real plans were simpler. Mimi was headed for New York, to stay with a cousin and train to be a teacher.

"Don't be silly, Mimi. You can't be a teacher. You know you can't follow the rules. How do you think you can make other girls keep them?"

Mimi was undeterred. New York City was a city far away, made from good times and excitement as far as she could see. Lucille wanted only to marry.

"It's really all I want, Cella. A good enough man with a big enough house, so I can fill it with babies." Marcella could see her doing that, like a golden mother in a fairy tale. Lucille's own family was small — just a brother, an aging father, a sickly mother. She would go home to Georgia after school and find work, but she didn't plan to stay there long. Marcella saw all the little ways Lucille was different when they were in the company of young men. She lifted her chin a little higher, talked a little louder, laughed more often, and differently. Her boy voice was intimate. Her boy laugh was thin and high like breaking glass. Marcella saw men

Chapter Five: 1904

drawn to her, and could imagine that if she chose to marry, it would not take her long. She could imagine her in a beautiful house, looking pretty as a china doll, entertaining well.

"What about you, Cella? What will you do?"

"I'm going home too, eventually, but first I need to earn my fare. I may work in a store, or anywhere, really, so I can save."

"Home to Ireland, you mean? To that boy you keep talking about?"

"I do not."

"Oh, you do, Cella. He must be a fine one."

She didn't care to talk more about Tommy with Lucille. His letters, which she loved, were always on the edge of asking her if she was coming home, and her replies, always on the edge of saying maybe, or soon. Yes, but not yet. Not now. As the years had passed, it was harder for her to imagine life in Rockfield, the dark cottage with no electricity, her mother, waiting. And anyway, she didn't have the fare yet for a passage home. Even Jimmy wasn't traveling now, the parish and the expanding church taking his money as well as his time.

Jimmy was clear about her future.

"It's simple, Siss. You'll teach. Like your father, and his father. You've the head for it."

"And what if I don't want to?"

"Why wouldn't you? Isn't it a fine job for a woman? And didn't you plan for this? What else would you do?"

"I don't know. But I don't want to spend another day in that convent, Jimmy. Aren't we ever going home?"

"We could, Siss. You could. But what would you do there? Even if you were a teacher, would you teach

71

in that one-room school that was Father's? Teach all those barefoot children reading and writing when you could be a scholar here, teaching French, or short-hand, or history?"

"I don't want to, Jimmy."

"Why wouldn't you? If you don't like St. Eliza-beth's, there's plenty of other places. The parish could use you in any number of schools – maybe not pay you, but what do you need money for anyway? Can't you stay here 'til you meet someone?"

"Meet someone?"

"You know, Siss. A young man. In the meantime, teaching's a fine job for a woman. It's secure, and re-spectable, and our schools are new, but we can make them good. You can live here for a few years, and then find your own home, not too far away."

"I could work with you here, in the parish. But how would that earn me a passage home?"

"Home? Do you mean Rockfield? Is this not home now, with me?"

His face was serious now.

"Yes. It is, but what about real home? I thought we'd be travelling over and back every few years. I didn't think I'd be here so long without seeing Fran and Mother."

He looked hurt for a minute, then it passed.

"There isn't the money yet, but there will be. In a few years, I promise."

"Maybe I don't have to wait that long. If I get my own job, any job, with regular money, I can buy my own ticket."

She stopped, trying to interpret the way his face seemed to have suddenly closed down, with something more than disappointment. She couldn't explain why she didn't want to teach. It wasn't that she had other plans. She just wanted something else, something new; some story that was all hers, not just a part of the parish. They didn't talk about it again. She finished up in school and did well in her exams. Her graduation dance was on an unseasonably cold May evening. The girls all wore thick wraps over their organdie dresses, and she looked, she knew, as beautiful as she had ever been. They had planned the night for ages, but it felt unreal, in a way. She danced and laughed, and it was golden. When she got back to the rectory, Jimmy was waiting. He took out a small box, wrapped in gold paper with a lacy pattern, and handed it to her without a word. She rattled it and held it to her ear.

"What's this, Jimmy? This doesn't sound like a kitten. Didn't you promise me a kitten?"

But he didn't laugh at all.

"Go on. Open it, Siss. See what you think."

A brown velvet box with a golden clasp, and inside, a delicate gold ring with a twisted pattern and a single pale blue stone.

"Jimmy! Is that a real opal?"

"No, it's a kitten. Of course it's real."

"But it must have cost a fortune, Jimmy. I mean it's beautiful. I love it, but it must have cost so much."

"Ah but Siss, it's not that much. It's a big day for you. And I suppose I wanted to say, it is for me too. I'm proud of you, Siss, and I wanted to mark it. You're educated now, and you're of age. And, well, you can make your own decisions. I know how proud father would be if he were here, to see you graduated, the first of us to graduate from an American school. He'd love that, you know. He'd be really proud of you today, whether you teach or don't teach. Ah, shush, don't be crying now. What's that about, Siss?"

Something Bigger

His arm was around her, and she tried not to cry. She was missing home in a wave that almost drowned her. She would have given anything to be back there, just for an hour in the dark kitchen with Fran and Mother — and Father alive again so she could see him looking proud of her — and ask Fran about what she might do next. Instead she was here, with this shiny ring. She slipped it on her right hand, and it fit as well as if she'd picked it out herself. A ring from her brother. Jimmy's shoulder was warm, and she leaned in to it, hiding her face from his, so he would think she was happy.

She graduated from the convent. She had done well. She was eighteen years old, with a high school diploma and a small sheaf of congratulation cards, mostly signed by priests and nuns. Everyone told her that the world was as wide as an open field, and that her possibilities were endless.

She found herself an apprenticeship in Loveman's Department Store only four blocks away. On her first payday, she opened a savings account and started building up money for the ticket home. Meanwhile, the work was easy and pleasant. She started on the haberdashery counter, selling pretty small things to rich ladies who liked to talk and be seen with their baubles, and small expensive gifts to men who came in flirtatiously or furtively, buying for their wives, or others. Sometimes they gave tips, and this all helped. Lucille and Mimi both moved away, to Atlanta and to New York. She and her new friends went out sometimes, met boys, went to the Lyric Theatre together. After a few months she realised she liked her life. There was more to her work than the slowly mounting bank balance. She liked living in the rectory, earning her own

Chapter Five: 1904

money, sitting with Jimmy in the evenings, still with that aura about her in the church circles – the priest's sister, in the rectory, someone to be acknowledged. She thought perhaps this might be freedom.

Not as free as Mimi, of course, who had abandoned plans to teach, and instead found work in a garment factory in New York. Her letters showed that this meant boarding houses, shared rooms, making her way up the back stairs at the end of a long day, going out to dances with all her dazzle on. And there was Lucille in Atlanta, living at home with her aging parents, working in a department store not unlike Loveman's, waiting to meet that rich man who would give her a big house to fill with children. Were those lives better? Marcella could not imagine the loneliness of boarding houses, or Lucille's fear of not meeting a man. Weren't they only young yet? What was the rush?

She wrote to Tommy to tell him about her savings. It would take six or seven years, she said, to get her fare together. He wrote back almost immediately. He would make the place ready. He would fix up the house. He would find real work and be waiting. It was only a few years. They'd be still young then, with their lives before them. I'll see you, he wrote, in 1914.

Chapter Six

∽

1914

Rockfield,
Athlone,
Ireland
June 1914

Dear Marcella,

Thanks for your letters, and for the pattern. It's such a fancy cape – I don't know that I could begin to think about wearing it around here, mind. Well, I'll make it anyway – it will be the talk of the parish. You sound happy, Siss. And older. You sound so much older than when you left. It's not just the talk of your job, and all that. It's something else. I wish I was there to see you with my own eyes.

But about that lad Jeff that you mentioned, you're right, don't write to him. It's his job to write if he's the one who went away. And don't be in a rush to write back either. Here, while we're talking about young men, do you remember Martin Coleman? He lives down towards Crancam, in that white house over the hill from Noone's. You might remember him from Mass — halfway up the church on the right. He sits with his brothers, but he's the tall one. You know him — moustache and glasses? Good dark hair? Anyway, we've been walking out. I like him. Mother likes him, which is a wonder in itself. I think sometimes she'd like to keep us like little children forever. But she likes Martin.

I met Nora Caulfield the other day on King St. She was in your class, wasn't she? She's finished up with school now and working in the army barracks in town. In the kitchen, I think. She looked older too, like a grown-up woman almost. I suppose all you babies are growing up. That young Tommy Banahan called by the other day too, asking Mother how you were, bold as brass. You asked after Tanner – well he's fine. Slowing down. He doesn't jump up like he used to. Mother is talking of getting a pup to keep him company, but I think he likes having the place to himself. And since we have hens again, it's best not to disturb them with some new dog. So we'll stay on our own, Tanner and Mother and me. For now, at least.

Take care, Siss. And remember, don't fall in love with the first boy who asks you to dance. Or don't stay in love with him for too long! I don't know whether to wish I was there to see you, Siss, or that you were here instead. Even for a visit. Tell me, how is Jimmy, really? His letters tell me nothing. He only writes about his work. Is he happy? Will he be coming home again? Maybe I'll get married, and then you'll both have to come home.

Your loving sister,
Fran

Something Bigger

St. Paul's Rectory
221 Third Avenue
Birmingham, Ala.

Dear Fran

Martin Coleman? I can't place him. I hope he's a good man — he should be, for you. Where do you go on dates? Do you get in to Athlone? Is he handsome? Do you have a photograph? You're right about Jeff. It's not like we were serious or anything, but I miss going out to the movies with him. It was something to do. Lucille wrote too – I told you about my friend Lucille? She's coming back to Birmingham, so that will be lovely, to have her nearby. But the reason she's coming back is she's getting married. Isn't that young? She's only my age, but Georgie Vaughan, the man she will marry, is a lot older. The wedding is next month. Jimmy doesn't approve. He says he doesn't like his politics. You know Jimmy – he sees the best in everyone, but this man is a bigot, he says, and that's the one thing he won't stand for. Our other old schoolfriend Mimi is coming back from New York for the wedding, and we're both to be maids of honour. There will be a reception in the Tutwiler Hotel, which honestly, Fran, is the fanciest place in the city, so no matter what Jimmy says, it is going to be fun. This Georgie man is rich.

Jimmy is doing well. I do think he's happy. He sings around the house often, if that means anything. He works hard, but he loves that. Sometimes he falls asleep reading his Office out on the front porch in the evenings. He writes a lot these days. He's started writing poetry as well as letters and sermons. He doesn't publish the poems, but I've read some, and I'm starting to put them in order so he could publish a collection some time. He writes them very fast and doesn't go

Chapter Six: 1914

back over them at all. I think they'd be better if he took a little more time about them, but they're not bad. Most of them are about God, or America, but he wrote a lovely one about Father. I'll see if I can find it again and write it out for you.

How is Mother? Her letters are getting shorter and she says the same things in all of them. Am I minding myself? Am I going to Mass? As if I could avoid Mass, living in this house full of priests right next door to the church. Is she alright? You haven't told her I'm coming home, have you? By next year I will have enough saved, but there's no point in getting her too excited about it until I have the ticket bought. I can hardly wait. Jimmy said I must buy a return ticket, and they're almost the same price from here. So I will. But you know, Fran, I might not use it. I might stay. I've been here a long time now.

Anyway, you take care of yourself, Fran. And don't be springing a wedding on us without giving us a chance to plan for it, you hear? Give my love to Mother as always.

Your loving sister,
Marcella

Drumdoo
Rockfield
Athlone
June 1914

Dear Marcella,
How are you? It was good to get your letter, and even better to know you'll be home soon. At least a year feels soon now, after all the time we've waited. It

will be good to see your face again and hear your voice. I bet you haven't changed. I think I have, but sure we were only children when you left, and now we're all grown. It will be good to have you home.

I suppose you've heard Fran's news? She's getting serious with one of the Colemans, and they're like to marry, everyone says. She could do worse, in fairness. And so could he. If she does marry him, you're not to worry about your mother being on her own. My Mam often calls in there with a few eggs, and I think they're getting fond of each other. So that's company for both of them, I'd say.

Do you know who I met last week? Do you remember Mary Catherine Egan that was in school with us? You were great friends with her, weren't you? Years back, not long after Mary Catherine took off, in the middle of school, she disappeared off to England and never wrote to a soul. Not even when her father died, she didn't come to the funeral. I thought she must be gone altogether, but she's back now, married to a man from the far side of town. She met him in London, she said, and now he's got work in the bank or somewhere like that in Athlone, so she's living inside in town. I was up in the graveyard when I ran into her. I got a bit of work off the priest, cutting the grass and that. Well she was something to see, in her long camel coat and a hat with a feather and all. She didn't know me, of course, hardly looked at me there with my scythe, but I said hello to her anyway, and then she was friendly enough when we got talking. She was on her own.

She was walking through the new section, looking at all the names on the graves. I remembered all of a sudden that she might not have seen her own father's gravestone. So I took her to it, careful like, so as not to

Chapter Six: 1914

upset her, but she wasn't one bit upset. She just looked at his name there, and there wasn't a stir out of her. I'd cleaned the grave up only that morning, and the flowers her mother planted were all out and lovely, but she never commented. She was more worried about getting her boots wet in the long grass. Calfskin she said they were. Leather, she meant. Just leather. She was like a stranger in her fine city clothes. Last time I saw her there, she was gathering nuts at the gate like a boy, and now there she was, lifting her skirt and stepping high, like she'd never seen grass before. The notions of her.

And then a funny thing happened. She was on her way out, and she stopped dead in her tracks at one of the new graves like she'd seen a ghost. Pale, like she should have been, if I'm to be honest, at her own father's stone. It was Harry Wilde's grave. Do you remember him? Ach you mightn't have known him. He was from up in Loughkinn, and only came to Mass in Rockfield the odd time. He was our age, nearly. He fell off his boat in the river, not long after you left. Well, you should have seen Mary Catherine when she saw his headstone. All the tears she should have had for her Da came pouring out of her. And she was crying out questions. "Did Harry die? How come nobody told me?" That kind of thing. Well I told her straight what happened, and still she kept asking how come nobody had told her. I felt like telling her to cop herself on. People die all the time, and we've more to be doing than trying to tell everyone who is gone about it. But I stopped. She was like a ghost – white and stuck to the ground. I don't know what came over her. But then she straightened herself up in a bit and picked her way down the path like it was made of cow dung or something. The state of her, Cella. Like she forgot who she is. You won't be like that now, will you, when you come home?

That's all the stories I have for you. I know you're saving your money, but I want you to know I'm saving now too. The bit of work from the priest is good and there will be hay to raise on all the farms around here soon. It will be a good summer for it. We'll get a nice little nest egg together between us.

Keep the letters coming, Cella. I might not write back as often, but I like them. I like them a lot.

Yours,
Tommy

Marcella read Tommy's letter three times, trying to work out how it made her feel. Normally she loved to hear from him, but there was something in this letter that unsettled her. She also had a prized pair of calf-skin boots, new from Loveman's last season range, and she wondered what it would really be like to go back to a place where this was considered to be strange. She tried to picture herself wearing them there, and it made her remember open fires that threw ash all over the floor, the endless warming of draughty cottages, tick mattresses, scratchy wool blankets that were hard to wash and dry, the effort of ordinary things. She was suddenly glad she had a year left in this bright city. The thought came unbidden into her mind of the money she had saved, and she questioned for the first time, if going to Ireland was the best way to spend it.

* * * * *

Jimmy stepped down from the cab, glad to be in Mobile for a couple of days. He liked the peace of it,

Chapter Six: 1914

the cleaner sea air, the French and Creole accents on the streets. He would have a good fish supper later. He was fasting until sundown, so it would be better still. He'd liked being near the Bishop too, or at least close to where decisions were made. Sometimes Birmingham felt as far away as Ireland. Life in Mobile seemed easy and sophisticated, but also a little unreal. It felt like a vacation, whereas the work in Birmingham was important. He was making a difference there. He ran up the shallow steps to the Bishop's front door, and with a quick smile to his secretary, strode into the study. The Bishop took a while to look up from his writing: long enough for Jimmy's smile to fade, but not long enough for his toe to start tapping.

"James."

"Your Grace."

"I'm glad to see you, James. I'm glad you came. It's been a while, hasn't it? I was worried we'd lost you to that lawless town."

Bishop Dineen's thin voice dripped with concern. Jimmy was immediately alert. He was familiar with that tone.

"Yes, I'm sorry, your grace. It was difficult to get away. We've had ..."

"Oh call me Michael, James, please. We're old friends now, surely? How long have we known each other now, hmm? And indeed, I'm sure it's not been easy. A lawless place, Birmingham. A difficult place."

He pronounced the three syllables of difficult separately, lingering over the word. James said nothing.

"But you've done well, James. Indeed you have. To grow the parish income like that so quickly ... to bring the debt down to such a manageable level. You've done well. You'll leave a strong legacy there, no doubt, even for a relatively short stay."

The words settled in the still air. The silence stretched. Jimmy forced himself not to speak.

"You have no questions, James?"

"I'm not sure what questions I might have, your ... Michael. I am content in my post, if that's what you mean. We have plans, you know, to ..."

"Plans. Yes, James, the thing is, you've done well, as I said. You've brought the debt down. It's manageable now. Manageable by a less capable man than you are. And I have many such men, you must know that?"

Something small exploded in Jimmy's head.

"Well, yes, manageable, if that's all you want, Michael? But there's more to be done there. Sure, it's lawless, but ..." Jimmy stopped, conscious that his voice had risen.

"But?" The bishop's prompt was soft as a cat.

"Your grace ... Michael ... the place is full. Full of people and less than half of them Catholic. And more coming in every day, pouring off the trains and down the mines or into the mills. And yes, sometimes they're out of work and causing trouble, but the point is, Michael, we can build something with all those people there. Something better than we've seen in the whole of the South. "

"Fine ideas, James. Fine ideas. But are they practical? Is it wise, in these days, to be building like that?"

"Is this about the coal strike, your Grace?"

"Michael. Please. I won't ask again. No, James. I'm not talking about your outspokenness. I heard a little of your getting involved, and it's true it was not wise, not your customary judgement, not the judgement that could be expected of a leader of the Church. Why would you take the side of the ragamuffins, and speak

Chapter Six: 1914

against the ones who could fund your ambitions? There are people there who could change the city for all of its people, and they're not the ones working down in the mines."

"I only said what I thought was right, Michael. The way men were treated in the coal mines, well it wasn't Christian."

The bishop laughed a little, softly.

"Well that's as it may be. But no, this isn't about what fool thing you might have written to the papers about the coalminers. The truth is, I have roles here that need a man like you. A vacancy has arisen here in Mobile. We have received a bequest for a new school for the most promising young men, to learn Latin and theology, and prepare for the seminary. And Italian, if you liked, I know you have a soft spot for that language. You could set it up from the start. You're a teacher at heart, James, you know that. This would be a scholarly life. A safe life, for you and your sister – we'd find something for her here. A good, scholarly life."

Jimmy said nothing.

"Think about it, James. I won't force your hand, though I could, of course. I want you here, close to me. I could rely on your counsel, and it would be a good use of that brain of yours. What are you doing with it out there, among those barbarians?"

"Isn't that the point, your grace?" Jimmy's voice was quiet again.

"I'm sorry?"

"Wasn't it to the barbarians we were called? Isn't it barbarians who need us? I'm telling you, out there, we can build something that can grow."

"Do you seriously think you can grow the church there, James?"

Something Bigger

"I know I can, Michael. Don't make me choose. Give me five years and I'll give you five new churches. I'll give you half the city."

It was the bishop's turn to be quiet.

"Can you stay out of trouble while you're doing it, James?"

"I can, Michael. More or less."

"And your sister, James? What of her? Wouldn't she have an easier life here?"

"Marcella is fine, Michael. She has work. Five years, that's all I need."

"Indeed it's not, James, and you know it. If you want five years you may as well take ten. If you make your mark in Birmingham, you're turning back from here, from the diocesan work. And you know where that work leads, James. You know where your potential could take you."

"I don't know, your grace, I ..."

"Oh come now, James. Let's have no false modesty here. You're young, but I won't be here forever, and with your skills? You could fill this chair one day, James. A new bishop will be prepared and in time, appointed. But he won't come from Birmingham. Do you hear me?"

"I do, Michael. And I appreciate your faith in me. But if you knew Birmingham, there's potential there too."

"Think about it, James. I won't force you. I want you here either willing or not at all. But I want a decision sooner than you want to give it to me. I can fill this school post, but I won't wait five years for you. Two or three years, and this offer is gone. Take your time going home, James. Take some time in the city to look around. Think about the life you'd have. And let me know when you're ready, if I have you or not."

Chapter Six: 1914

The bishop picked up his pen again and began to write. Jimmy knew he was dismissed. He let himself out, walking more slowly than when he came in. When he looked back at the house from the gate, he thought he saw a face looking out from the bishop's study, but there was bright sunlight on the window, and he couldn't be sure.

* * * * *

St. Paul's Rectory
221 Third Avenue
Birmingham, Ala.

Dear Tommy,
Do you see what they're writing in the newspapers here? War in Europe. Not in Ireland, surely? Write to me now. Tell me what it's like there.
Your friend,
Cella

Marcella sat on the front porch in the evening heat that showed no sign of abating, with a jug of cold, sweet tea and a basket of distractions. She was taken aback by this news of war, hoping it would not come near Ireland, though she could hardly see why it would. She had some needlework, a piece of tapestry she needed to unpick for the second time because it had not turned out as she had hoped, and a brand-new notebook. This was a gift from Jimmy who said she wrote so many letters, she might as well keep a journal. She liked it. The lines were spaced prettily, pale and wide. It seemed almost a shame to put ink on those pages. She looked out towards the street, thinking about how to begin, and that's when she saw the girl on the sidewalk, staring in at her through the open gate.

"Bessie?" She sat forward, calling in a soft singsong voice, as though trying to coax a wild animal. "Bessie Stubbs?"

The girl had grown a lot. She couldn't be more than ten or eleven, could she? With her hair piled up like that though, she could almost pass for a teenager. Her eyes were broad and steady, her lips full and a little sulky. No smile. She didn't answer Marcella but walked right up to the shade of the porch with a limp that was barely noticeable. Marcella remembered how she used to dance on her toes when she was very small, and wondered what had happened to the leg that now seemed to drag a little. She gestured towards the seat beside her, unexpectedly lost for words.

"Are you alright, Bessie?"

"Yes, Ma'am. I'm fine. I was just looking. Nothing wrong with that, is there? Free country, ain't it?"

"Yes, of course." The silence felt oddly awkward, as though it was the child who was at home, and Marcella the intruder. "I'm Marcella."

She extended her hand, conscious as she did so that it was too formal a gesture for a child. Nonetheless the girl reached to take her hand with barely any hesitation. She had a surprisingly strong grip.

"I know who you are. And I'm Bess. Nobody calls me Bessie no more."

"Pleased to meet you, Bess. Though of course we've met before."

"No," said Bess, flatly. "We ain't met, Ma'am. I've seen you. You've seen me. We never spoke before. We ain't met."

Marcella's cheeks burned at the tone of the girl's voice, and the implication that she was mistaken, or a liar. What was it about Bess that made her feel so

Chapter Six: 1914

wrongfooted? She picked up her diary again, more for something to do with her hands than anything else.

"Well, no, Bess. We met years ago when you were not much more than a baby. You walked right up this pathway to meet me then."

"You're lying, Ma'am."

This flat hostility was shocking. Bess's face looked completely relaxed. Marcella breathed slowly. It was ridiculous to be angry with a child.

"What you writing?"

"This is my diary. It's good to write things down. That way you remember."

"What kinds of things?"

"Anything you like. Do you keep a diary, Bess? Do you write down things about your day?"

Marcella was gathering herself, feeling more in control now.

"No Ma'am. I don't write nothing. I don't need to. I ain't old like you. I just remember."

"Well perhaps you should. Then you'd remember things like when we met before. You really don't recall?"

Bess shook her head, not breaking eye contact. Marcella smiled.

"Wait here then. I've got something to show you."

Marcella stepped inside, and was back in no more than a few minutes, triumphant, holding in her hand the handmade woollen rabbit that Bess had dropped so many years earlier in the rectory yard. But the girl was nowhere to be seen. Marcella looked up and down the street but there was no sign of her among the evening crowds. Annoyed, she jabbed the bunny on to the lowest spike of the garden gate, and took her place again on the porch, unpicking the mistakes she'd cross-stitched into yesterday's tapestry. Irritation made her too rough with the scissors, straining the white base fabric, at risk of ruining the whole picture. She wasn't sure she liked it anyway — a sentimental scene of a guardian angel following a child who was about to run over a cliff. The angel had no expression on his face, and his arms, reaching out to the girl, were long and out of proportion. The little girl was looking up at a butterfly as she ran, rather than watching her feet. The angel was quite far behind, perhaps too far away to save the girl, though surely saving her was the whole point of the picture? She'd been making it for months now, on and off, and still, it was not nearly finished. The piece of fabric, which had been neat and rectangular when she started, was stretched out of shape from stitching and unpicking. For perhaps the tenth time in as many weeks she wondered if it was worth continuing. She was holding it up to the light, frowning at it, when she heard the front gate creak. Expecting Bess, she was surprised instead to see Jackson walking in. She moved to the side porch, so as to meet him as he came to the back door, but instead, he walked right up the pathway to the front. It was years since they had met. He had grown tall and broad at the shoulder. She found herself smiling and saw that he was too. Proper warmth in his smile, like his mother.

"Jackson. It's been a long time. Johanna tells me you're married now?"

"Sure am, Miss Cella. I'm a family man now. With a baby coming too."

They talked easily for a while, though later she wouldn't remember what they talked about.

"You here to see Jimmy? I think he's in back. I'll get him for you. Sit down, have a drink. That sweet tea is still good."

Chapter Six: 1914

When Jimmy and Jackson moved into the study to talk, Marcella, who had no real interest in the project at Longfield, came out to resume her needlework. She noticed that the tattered rabbit was gone from the garden gate. How quick that child was to pick it up again.

Later, she saw that the notebook Jimmy had given her was also missing from the basket of threads and needles. Her first suspicion fell on Jackson. Why would he take it? But also, why wouldn't he? He had been sitting right there, on the porch, on his own for a while. Then she remembered that Bess had also been alone there, if only for the few minutes she'd gone inside to get that darned woollen rabbit. Could she have snatched it so fast? And why? When her irritation subsided, she thought she didn't really need to keep a diary anyway. She wrote letters, and she was sure Tommy was keeping them all for her. Time enough for diaries when they were back together, with no need to write to each other.

* * * * *

Lucille's wedding took place at the Episcopal Church on nearby 20th St., smaller, simpler and prettier than the gothic grandeur of St. Paul's. Jimmy had showed no interest in the event after Marcella first told him the news, calling George Vaughn "the blackest-hearted True American in the city." Certainly he was not as Marcella had expected. The bridegroom was old and square-faced with pale hair swept back from his low browns and green, hooded eyes. She whispered to Mimi, beside her in the front pew of the small chapel.

"He must be fifty, is he, Mimi?"

"Sixty more like, Cella. Look at that chin? What was she thinking? Really. An old man is one thing. But one so ugly? Lucille never did know what do to with that beauty of hers."

Marcella didn't like that way of talking about Lucille, but had to agree. George was not only old and plain, but his eyes were cold even when he smiled. His mouth was set down at the corners, and as Mimi said, there was that chin, flabby and blotched. Lucille by contrast was radiant, looking perfect in white tulle. Her father had not made the journey. Her mother was nervous and pale, relying on Marcella for support as they crossed the street to a reception at the Tutwiler Hotel. Her brother Will was there too, tall like Lucille, and sharing her good looks, but more bookish, a junior attorney in New York now. In the hotel, the party was larger, with many more people than had come to the service. Marcella had brought a date, Carlo Moretti, a boy she'd met through her job in Loveman's. Mimi had come alone, so Carlo danced with her as often as with Marcella. There were no other friends from school, and few from Atlanta, but it seemed like half the businessmen of Birmingham were lined up at the bar.

Lucille flitted from one group to another, with not much time to talk to her friends. When she did, she seemed older, as though marrying had lent her some new status.

"It's a wonderful wedding, Lucille. So many people here. What a party."

"Well, Georgie knows a lot of Birmingham. And it's an exciting time, you know, with that new war in Europe."

"Exciting? But it's war, Lucille."

"I know that, Cella. But it's not going to last. Georgie says it will all be over by Christmas, and there's no

Chapter Six: 1914

chance of America getting involved. No, it's exciting for these men, because they're going to get rich for sure, with all the steel and coal the war will take."

Marcella looked down to hide an unexpected hot resentment. Since when did Lucille know anything about such things? Mimi laughed.

"Good — next best thing to a rich man is one who's about to be rich. Lucille, you introduce us to some of these boys."

"You don't need me to do that, Mimi. You must have half of New York City chasing you."

"Well, maybe, but there's nothing like a Southern man, you know? Now you've both got men at your sides, maybe I'll go get to know that brother of yours."

"Will? You're welcome to, but you know he only cares about the law. He's never been a ladies' man."

"Not yet, you mean."

Mimi laughed that new, big city laugh of hers. She spoke lightly of beaus in New York, cocktail bars, and fancy meals. Marcella felt a pang of jealousy. Here were her friends, married or living a glamorous, free life. And what was she doing? Looking around, she met the eyes of George Vaughan, on the edge of a group of men huddled at the bar. He stared right at her before raising his hand to his lips and blowing her a kiss, right across the room, with a chilly smile. His hand looked mottled and old, and his signet ring, an elaborate dragon's head design, was too tight, embedded in the flesh of his fingers. She didn't want to smile back, but he didn't look away so eventually she had to, just to break eye contact.

Later, he walked right up to her, shorter than you'd think when he was up close, but also broader, his face flushed from what was probably whiskey.

Something Bigger

"So, little lady. Time for your dance."

He swung her out on the floor with an unexpected energy, eyes flat and shining. His dancing was jerky and out of time, and he pulled her too close for the last tune, so she felt his breath on her neck, the clunky pressure of that dragon's head ring moving down her back. Afterwards he bowed to her and moved away without a word. She realised that this was how he danced with everyone, even Lucille. He grew louder and more tactile as the night went on, hugging the men, arms around the women. His eyes glittered, and when he caught her eye again across the room, she turned away, repulsed.

Later, when Jimmy asked about the wedding, she amused him with imitations of George's ponderous speech, and his cold smile. She didn't mention how he danced, held her too tight and stared at her afterwards with his flat, dead eyes. She didn't mention the feel of his dragon-head ring on the small of her back, even though that seemed the hardest for her to forget. Jimmy laughed in such a familiar way, it made her feel good again. She found herself relaxing, letting go of some tension that had been building up through the evening. So what if her friends had their lives, their husbands and their beaus. She and Jimmy were family, weren't they? That had to count for something.

* * * * *

July 30, 1914

Dear Diary

You are my very first diary. I found you today. Well, I stole you. I'm gonna write in you every day, or as near as I can get to that. I'm gonna tell you all about

Chapter Six: 1914

my life, so I don't forget things, like that lady said. To-day was way too hot. Hot as pepper on the street when I came walking home. I was on my own, like I always am, like I like to be. I can stop when I want or dawdle if it pleases me with nobody to tell me what's what. I stood in the shadow under Huckston's canopy, just across from St. Paul's, the big Catholic church, watching like I do. I wanted to rest in there instead of out on the street. The door was open, and it looked so dark inside, and like it would be cool in there, but Momma would kill me if I went in.

All the time, there was people coming in and out. There's no service. It's Thursday. But every minute there were old ladies and young women with their babies, not even all white women, stopping in there, staying just a while, coming out again. They used the same door, the coloured women. Not the one on the side but the front door. In and out just by the white ladies. In and out. I wanted to go in so bad, see what was in there.

I don't know why it was all ladies. Ain't there no Catholic men? Maybe they all turn into priests. Maybe the men come at a different time. I got to watch out more and see. I can't think why anyone would go to church if nobody was preaching. First chance I get, I'm going to fix a way I can get in there, and find out. As long as Daddy don't see. I'm might pick a lady to fol-low, and walk right up the steps after them. It's going to be audacious. That's my word, today. Aunt Kay gave me a dictionary, and told me to learn a new word every day. She says I gotta better myself and learn when I'm young. I'm not so young, though. I'm eleven years old and folks say I look older.

Anyway, what I did next really was audacious. I

moved up real close to the priest's house, to see if I could see who all was in there. I was right up at the railing, staring, and then suddenly I saw that lady on the porch. I seen her before. She sits there sometimes. This time she saw me before I could get away. Well I walked up like I didn't care none, and we got talking like she was a regular person. She said she knew me since I was a baby, and I didn't believe her. But she did have that little bunny rabbit of mine. That's when I got you, diary, when she went inside. I was quick and I was gone before she got back. But she left my little Brer Rabbit on the fence and I came back for it real quiet. Yeah, I guess it was mine. It looked like one of Momma's little doodads that she made when I was little. So maybe I really was in there when I was a baby. Maybe that's where Momma and Daddy got me from. I guess I could be one of those church babies. Maybe that's why Daddy hates them so, the Catholics, and Momma is afraid of them. Maybe they're scared they'll steal me back, now I'm grown and pretty.

Nobody's gonna steal me.

Next Friday when Daddy is away, I'm gonna slip right into the church, and see it for myself. Momma won't know. I can't tell her, 'cause she'll just go and tell Daddy, and then there'll be trouble. I don't need no trouble. This is just my adventure. Audacious.

I'll tell you all about it then, Diary

Your new friend

Bess

Chapter Seven

1915

Springtime, Marcella thought as she walked home from work, gave a measure of beauty even to smoky, noisy Birmingham. Lately, as the balance in her bank account crept towards her target for travel to Ireland, she had begun to notice and appreciate the life she had here, her friends, her independence, the warmth of the rectory, Johanna and Jimmy. Her work was becoming more important to her too. She'd started at the counter in Loveman's, aiming only to earn money to go home, but now she was studying at night to become a bookkeeper, almost qualified, with the promise of a move to the office, promotion, a career of her own. Tommy continued to write, happy and waiting. She was going to miss her American life when she went home, so she was determined to enjoy it while she could. Dropping her pocketbook in the hallway, she picked up the mail. A letter from Ireland — was that Mary Catherine's writing? And a second

Something Bigger

from Fran. She smiled to herself and sank down on the porch seat to read. Late evening sun still warmed the wooden boards. She had been on her feet all day at Loveman's, and she was glad to slip off her shop shoes and read.

Mary Catherine had been writing again since she reappeared in Athlone. Her letters were sharp and funny, her voice familiar. She was married now, living in rooms above the insurance company where her husband, Sylvester, was assistant manager. This gave her an unparalleled view of Northgate St. and all its denizens, and she wrote about them like characters in a play. Delia O'Connor was walking out with a soldier from the barracks across the river, hiding this from her brother who had, in Mary Catherine's words, "turned republican" and was all against anything to do with the British forces. Fran featured sometimes in the stories, looking stylish and slim in her own designed coats and dresses, catching the eye of passing men, but oblivious, Mary Catherine said, now she and Martin Coleman were walking out together. Mary Catherine sounded so happy, so free of that shadow Tommy had implied when he wrote about meeting her in the graveyard. Her letters brought Athlone to life in a way she had never seen it when she lived in Ireland, too young to go to town alone. Perhaps she and Tommy could live in the town instead of out near home, and there she could have a life that was not possible in Rockfield?

The second letter was from Fran, with all the usual news of her relatives and neighbours, and then, thrown in almost casually near the end, the news that Martin had asked her to marry him, and she had said yes, with a date set for the start of July.

Chapter Seven: 1915

"So you'll have to come back now, Siss, to be my maid of honour. And Jimmy must come too. I hope he can marry us. God knows, Mother won't countenance anything else! I'll write to him tomorrow, but you talk to him first. It's so long since he's been over, and it's well past time."

She began to make plans for both Jimmy and her to travel back for the wedding. And then in May, news broke all over the American papers of the sinking of the Lusitania. It's not that the Germans hadn't been sinking ships before, but this one seemed different. This ship had Americans on it, and it was sunk right there off the coast of Ireland. Eleven hundred people on board, or over a hundred American lives, as the papers said. As though all lives weren't worth something, Jimmy said, derisively. This was the biggest ship in the world, they said, though of course they'd said that about the Titanic too. That one sinking ship seemed to change everyone's views on the war. It was like it brought it closer to them. President Wilson said he wasn't for war, and the radio said that Germany wasn't trying to start a war with America, but people talked. Everyone talked back then about the Lusitania as if they'd all just lost a brother. Jimmy said it meant the boats weren't safe anymore, crossing the Atlantic. It was too much of a risk, he said. They argued about it for weeks, but he would not be moved. Eventually Marcella was resigned to waiting until the seas were safe again. Disappointed at missing the wedding, she wrote to Tommy explaining they would have to wait until after the war before she could come home, that traveling was too dangerous now. She felt a kind of guilty relief as she posted the letter.

Something Bigger

St. Paul's Rectory
221 Third Avenue
Birmingham, Alabama
May 31, 1915

Dear Fran

How are you, my good sister? And how is that man you are marrying? You've no idea how much I'd love to go see you both, to see you wed, Fran, and spend time with you. We could go walking up the back boreen and pretend we were young again. Remember how we used to go together when we were small? Gathering blackberries and arguing over who had the most, and telling each other yarns under the hazel trees. Remember when I decided I should go be a priest, and I told you before I told Mother? I knew with you I could talk about it, where with Mother, once I'd said it, it would be written in gold letters on the sky. I miss that, Fran. I miss you for talking to and walking with. I'd go home in the morning to see you, U-boats, or no U-boats, only that Mother would be too heartbroken to let me come back here again.

You're right, I think, in what you wrote last time. I believe I am her favourite. But only because I'm a priest. It's not really me she loves. Not me as a man. Sure, she hardly knows me. Nor even the boy I used to be. She was a hard woman in a lot of ways, wasn't she? Strong of course, and it can't have been easy for her seeing all our brothers leaving the land and never coming back, but it made her hard at the end of it in a way it never made Father hard. Once I became a priest — even when I was training in Limerick — I was more than her son. I was like a prize she won, or a pension; something she would always have. Maybe it would have been different if Father had lived, but she's closed in on herself now.

So I can't go back, Fran, because I know it would break her to see me leave again, and Father isn't there now, to talk sense to her. Oh I miss him. I miss him every day. I wonder what he'd think of what I'm doing, and if I'm living up to all he might have expected of me. There's that war now in Europe, and if I were home, I might have been in it. Instead I'm here, living a sheltered life of pens and pulpits. I hope I'm doing something that would make him proud.

Do you understand? Does that make sense to you? Ach, maybe I'm wrong about Mother. Maybe I'm the one being hard, and maybe it's me that can't face her, and can't leave her again. Maybe I'm afraid to leave this place in case all I've built here falls apart while I'm gone. I suppose I'm the one wrapped up in my own importance.

But I can't do it, Fran, is what it comes down to. I can't go home again, and I never will. That's the truth of it.

Can you forgive me?

Your loving brother

Jimmy

* * * * *

In July, Fran sent a photo of the wedding, her dressed smartly in a suit of coffee and cream standing beside a tall man with a spectacular moustache, a little uncomfortable in his dark suit. They both looked happy. Marcella thought yes, perhaps she remembered this Martin from Mass, back in Rockfield.

Fran's letter was short. Curt, even. She addressed

herself to Marcella, not to Jimmy. She didn't even ask after him. But it was the last paragraph that really caught her.

"Mother was upset, of course, not to have Jimmy here. Well, we all were. I was sure he'd be the one to marry us. It would have meant a lot. I know you can't come now, Cella, with the war. Nobody can. But I hoped to see Jimmy here soon. Mother is talking about the war like it's all about her, keeping her from her son. You know how she is, it's always Jimmy. But there isn't a loss on her. It's far from her the war is. Not like poor Mrs. Banahan now, with her Tommy gone to France and not a word from him. I met her yesterday, and she said it came out of the blue. He had no plans to go fighting until the week before he left, and now he's signed up and gone. She's a good woman, Mrs. Banahan, for all her misfortune. She started calling in to Mother every day now, checking she's alright for everything, and all Mother does is give out. Still, maybe her young lad will get home again. Stranger things have happened."

Tommy at war? That was impossible. He couldn't hurt a fly. Sure enough, though, a few days later his letter arrived with an unfamiliar postmark, confirming that yes, he had joined the British army, and yes, he would be going overseas.

"I had to go, Cella. This is better than sitting at home waiting, and maybe this way I can help end it faster, get you back here sooner. I mean, I was never one for fighting, but I might as well do that as pull weeds for the priest. And then when it's all over, I'll have money, and we can make a new start for ourselves. That's what we'll do. There's no point you writing to me now for a while. But don't worry, I'll be safe as houses. The lads here are mostly English, but they're alright. They think it's funny my name is Tommy. I didn't know why first. Turns out that's what they call themselves. So better I'm called Tommy than anything else if I'm to fit in here. Sometimes they call me Irish. That's alright too. They're decent lads, and they don't look down on me like some we could name. I'll see you in Rockfield, Cella, after the war. We'll both have adventures to talk about then."

* * * * *

Marcella visited Lucille every Monday, and they sat and talked together. Lucille didn't go out now, but stayed in her townhouse, a respectable wife. Marcella rarely met George Vaughan when she visited, and soon realised this was no accident, that Lucille suggested times when he might be out, and that suited Marcella well. They would sit together in the drawing room, having coffee. Sometimes one of them would have a fresh letter from Mimi and they'd work together to decipher her great looping scrawl, making out hilarious stories of accidents and coincidences that seemed too wild to be true.

"Except, you know, that could have happened to Mimi," Lucille mused. "That girl attracts chaos like a magnet."

"Does she still see Will?"

"Sometimes. He and Mimi have gone out to a few shows, but they're not steady, as far as I know. I don't know that she's in his social class."

The judgement in her tone was new. And sure, it was surprising that Mimi was actually walking out with

Something Bigger

Lucille's brother, but wasn't it a bit much to think he was too good for her? Since getting married, Lucille had changed, subtly. She seemed smaller in some ways, as though she needed less space to live. She crossed her legs at the ankle as she sat, in exactly the way the nuns could never persuade her to do in school. When she laughed, it was not raucous. Her lipstick was a shade less red. She read serious books, or at least had such books on display on low tables as a reader might. She sewed. Her conversation was topical, informed, impersonal. Marcella looked for the warm ambitious friend she once had, and hardly recognised this still, beautiful shell of a woman. Was it marriage to an old man that had done this to her? Or was it her choice, this walled-in life like a doll in a doll box? Lucille could have done anything.

Marcella liked her own life better. She enjoyed her work and was making good progress there. She was still seeing Carlo, and they often went on dates. The Lyric Theatre was her favourite. When they talked, they sometimes struggled to find things in common. He always had some new plan to make a lot of money fast, but he grew impatient when she questioned him. Soon enough, she stopped asking, and lost interest, realising the plans kept changing, and perhaps none of it was real. But in the Lyric, she could sit with him in the dark, near the piano player, watching some Cecil B. DeMille melodrama play out on the big screen. Her mind could wander, and she'd think of Tommy, and wonder if there was a movie theatre by now in Athlone that they could go to together, when she went home. If she went home. If Tommy came back. If he stayed safe, in the war she didn't want to read about. She had an anxiety about it that never left her, even as she was

Chapter Seven: 1915

laughing with Johanna, or sharing gossip with her work friends. The absence of Tommy's letters, the absence of news about him stayed with her, like a small, hard stone in her stomach. It made her scan Fran's letters for any casual mention of his return, but nothing reassuring came.

Crancam,
Rockfield
Athlone
May, 1916

Dear Jimmy and Marcella,

How are you both? I'm writing to tell you that Mother has been unwell but is making a good recovery now. This war is wearing her down, she says, though I can't see why. It's not like she's in it, or any belonging to her. She talks about you both a lot but says she won't write. Or has she written? She wants to see you both, and you, Jimmy, she misses the most. She keeps saying she wants you to come say a Mass in the house. I explain to her about the U-boats, and how they're keeping you from her, but I don't think she wants to understand.

We are well in our little family. Martin does more around the house since the baby came. He's a fine little boy, Jamesie. Martin takes him out now sometimes on the cart, strapped in beside him when he's going to visit his mother. They make a fine pair. I can't say who he's like. Sometimes I think Father, but he has Martin's smile. I wish you were home, Jimmy, to take a photograph.

Something Bigger

We're blessed that we all have our health, but I'm tired with the baby. I can't wait to get off my feet when I can. Of course, Mother doesn't understand – you'd think she never had children herself. She still thinks I can walk up there twice a day to see her, but I can't now. She's grand, though. Mrs Banahan is still calling in, pretending it's only for eggs. There isn't a loss on her really.

Poor Mrs Banahan. Her Tommy is in France and she gets no news from him at all, and of course no money though he promised. There is three or four of the lads from around here gone off to fight with England. You'd think it was to the moon they were gone. And now with this trouble in Dublin, people are saying they shouldn't have gone at all, but stayed and looked after our own business. Have you heard about that? I suppose you have. Martin is very excited about it. They took over all the big buildings in Dublin and proclaimed us a Republic. They say we're free now altogether from England, and we're our own people at last. Little sign of it around here that I can see; it's the same work and the same lack of money and the same hens to be fed. Martin says they'll try to execute the leaders, though some of the young lads around here say if they do, they'll have more to reckon with than they expected. They're fired up rightly about it all, though there wasn't a word out of them even only a few weeks back. Martin's the same – he says it's only right for Ireland to strike now when England is at war. He says we'll show them what war is. He can talk and talk about it. It's not worth arguing with him.

How is the job, Siss? Are you still in that Department Store or whatever you call it? Is it grand to be out and earning your own money? I hardly get time for sewing at all anymore, so I've lost all my good cus-

Chapter Seven: 1915

tomers. I do a bit of fixing for Tessie O'Neill is all, now and then. She still buys too small for her, but at least she's learned to look for big seams. But that's it. Sure there's no time, with the hens and the house and the baby and all.

Write when you can, Jimmy, and you too, Siss. Tell us all your news, but don't mind the bonnet patterns. It's far from all that I am now.

Your loving sister,
Fran

Marcella finished reading the letter.

"We have to get home, Jimmy. We have to see this baby. And we still haven't even met Martin."

"We can't, Siss. Not yet, and not for a long time, I'd say. First the Lusitania, and just now the Sussex. Sure those U-boat boys don't care what ship you travel on."

"We should have gone when we could."

"You'll be home before that little lad is walking, never fear."

Jimmy seemed not to care at all about traveling. Fran was not just married, but a mother now, and yet he seemed more interested in the "trouble in Dublin." He couldn't get enough of it, even buying the New York papers to read more details. They were calling it the Easter Rebellion, and then the Easter Rising. He loved the symbolism of that. He kept saying what a shame it was their father hadn't lived to see Ireland free, to see freedom won. Marcella couldn't understand his obsession. It was only a fight, far away from Birmingham, and if Fran's letters were anything to go by, it seemed remote from Rockfield too, and Ireland was no more free than it had ever been, as far as she could see. But still, Fran's Martin was all excited about it, and there was Jimmy reading and writing about it every spare minute. She began to wonder if all men loved war.

He wrote poems, less about America now, and more about this new theme, the birth of a nation. When the leaders of the Irish rebellion were executed, he wrote about them as martyrs, their names to be carved in history. He started sending his poems to the newspapers, and soon all over the city, his name became associated with the Irish cause and the Easter Rebellion. One newspaper even referred to him as "The rebel priest," and he chuckled over that.

All this made him popular among his own people, but less so among a group of men who were also following news of the war and preparing for America to join. These men, the owners of mines and mills, met in other rooms, making their own plans to make new fortunes selling coal and steel to the allied powers in the war. They owned newspapers too, and soon articles began to appear commenting on Jimmy's stance, often in anonymous editorials, taking issue with what they called "his cause." Britain was an ally, they argued; an enemy of Britain was surely an enemy of America. They were not alone in this. No less a person than Woodrow Wilson, the President of the United States attacked what he called "hyphenated Americans," of which Jimmy now, as a self-proclaimed proud Irish-American was one.

"Why do you keep going on about it, Jimmy? It's over, the rebellion. It didn't succeed."

"Did it not, Siss? And why do you say that?"

"Well, they're all dead who led it, aren't they? All shot?"

"So?"

Chapter Seven: 1915

"So they failed. It was a waste."

"Is that all you see, Siss? A waste? Not a free Ireland?"

"Where, Jimmy? There's no free Ireland, just a few new graves in Dublin. Fran's still doing what she always did, and now she says they've been rounding up young lads even down in Athlone, who had nothing to do with the trouble, and sending them off to be locked up. It's only made things worse."

"Worse now, Siss, but mark my words, something will come of this. Something worth dying for."

"Nothing like that is worth dying for, Jimmy. It's only a place."

"Everybody dies, Siss. At least those men made it count."

She knew she was the only one who would argue with him, but she also knew when an argument was pointless. After a while, she sat back and let him write his poems. It kept him happy, and poetry was harmless enough, surely.

Mother's letters grew more and more petulant. Finally, she asked Marcella, why wasn't Jimmy writing. If he couldn't come home as he should, the least he could do was write.

"Jimmy — are you not writing to Mother? She says here she hasn't heard from you."

And he confessed that no, he hadn't written in months. He hadn't time, he said, but she could tell it was more than that, that his heart wasn't in it. She understood, in a way. Writing to Mother was harder now that so much of their lives couldn't be explained to her. Her own letters had become shorter, more dutiful. Jimmy looked haunted, confessing this to her. She saw a chance to help.

Something Bigger

"Look, Jimmy. Why don't I write for the pair of us? You give me some bits of news to put in, and I'll sign our letters to her from us both, and she'll be happier then."

So that was how it began. Jimmy would supply her with a story, something cheerful or absurd: a tennis game at which he was badly sunburned, or a trip out of town to visit another Irish priest. And if he didn't, Marcella just made something up. She'd imagine things they did together, describing a drive to Tuscaloosa, a day spent painting the back fence, the adoption of another cat named Captain. Simple, foolish things. It made writing to Mother more fun, and as her letters grew longer, signed with both of their names, Mother's replies grew more content. Like Jimmy's poetry, it kept her happy, and seemed harmless enough.

Chapter Eight

1917

Birmingham Age Herald, April 1917
HOUSE PASSES WAR MEASURE

After hours of wearying debate, vote stood 373 to 50. Cheers Greet Announcement Of Vote.

With Signature Of President And Vice President, The Actual Conflict Will Begin.

Greatest Resources In History Of The World Are Being Mobilized

Washington — America, the richest and mightiest nation that ever existed, is preparing to make war to its utmost strength in men and money. Actual and potential resources which, all told, probably have never been equalled by any other nation in the history of the world are brought into the war under the American flag.

Something Bigger

**In the balance against Germany
are thrown a navy in strength and ef-
ficiency among the foremost afloat; an
army comparatively small, but high-
ly efficient, backed by a citizenry of
20,000,000 capable of military duty;
industrial resources incomparably the
greatest in the world already mobilized
for public service, and the moral force
of more than 100,000,000 Americans.**

Carlo was excited by America entering the war,
like most of the young men Marcella knew. Lucille's
brother Will, had already joined up, straight in at offi-
cer class. Carlo was considering it too. It was like a big
adventure to him, something to band them together as
Americans, the greatest nation on earth, stronger than
the English, and ready now to help them.

Marcella thought it was ridiculous, but she kept
that to herself. She was glad when he called, glad to go
out with him, to dress up and get away from the rectory
for a while. At the Lyric, the movie was new so there
were queues down 19th Street for the box office. It was
a hot evening and all the young couples were dressed
to kill. Marcella knew they looked well together. He
bought her root beer and they sat in the dark, near
the back. She loved the film — Chaplin's funny, dis-
reputable little character, the bright, made-up eyes of
the men, the arch looks of the women. Around them,
the air was thick and close. Young men draped their
arms over their dates' shoulders, getting as close as
they could. After the show, the street corner flooded
with couples who didn't want the evening to end. Yellow light poured out the Lyric doorway, turning the
broad sidewalk into something like a stage. When they
stepped outside, Carlo's arm was light on hers. From
behind her came a familiar voice.

Chapter Eight: 1917

"Evenin' Miss Cella"

Out of context, it took her a moment to recognise Jackson, enough time for Carlo to slip his arm around her waist possessively.

"Who's this, Cella? Who's your, uh, your friend?"

"Jackson! Gosh, it's been ages." Without thinking Marcella stepped away from Carlo and hugged him, resting her hand on his shoulder.

"You look well, Jackson."

"You too, Miss Cella."

His smile was wide but controlled. Out of nowhere, she remembered her notebook that had gone missing on the front porch years ago. She'd wondered at the time if he had stolen it. Did he steal it? She stepped back a little.

"You hardly come around the rectory anymore, Jackson. How's your family? How is your wife — May, isn't it?"

She realised the crowd had grown quiet and Jackson stiffened in the sudden attention. Young men were gathering around them in a loose circle. Carlo reached for Marcella's waist again. There was a tension building around Jackson's eyes.

"April. She's fine, Ma'am. She ..." Two of Jackson's friends appeared by his side, muttering urgently, trying to draw him back. Marcella could see a group of young women behind them. She wondered which one was April. Jackson managed another smile.

"I'd best be going, Miss Cella."

His friends drew him back on the 17th St. side and the circle that had opened around them filled again. She heard snippets of conversation from the strangers around her, thin and sharp.

"It's not right, them coming in here. Ain't they got their own theatre?"

"They got their own entrance. They should stick to it. What's he doing, coming round here, talking to that white girl?"

"What's she doing, you mean. Who is she, any-way?"

"She's a sister of that crazy priest, that Father Coyle."

"Well, what would you expect from one of them? Those Irish Catholics should have their own entrance too."

Carlo pulled her away and walked her home, not speaking. She was glad of his silence. She didn't really want to hear his opinion on what had happened. A quick, dry kiss on the cheek and he turned away, al-most running down the street. She wasn't sorry he was gone.

Next morning Johanna was clattering pans and plates in the kitchen, working fast and roughly. Marcel-la hadn't seen her in such a mood, and hesitated before going in. She forced brightness into her voice to deflect whatever was bothering the older woman.

"Morning, Johanna."

"Mornin', Miss Cella. And you? You enjoyed your movie last night?" Johanna's voice was controlled, as though she were holding something tight behind her teeth.

"Jackson told me he met you down at the Lyric. He said you spoke. He said you spoke to him right there in front of all those young men. Is that true, Miss Cella?" Her face was impossible to read.

"Yes, I saw him after the movie. He looks well."

"Well better if you hadn't, Miss Cella. Listen here. Don't you go talking to my Jackson again, dragging him into the middle of a crowd like that. It ain't good and it ain't safe. Don't know what fool thing you thought you were doing, Miss Cella, but I'm telling you right now, he doesn't need that. He's a good son, and we don't need trouble."

"We were just talking, Johanna. Where's the harm in it?"

"If you can't see the harm in it, Miss Cella, you're blinder than I thought. Didn't you see how people looked?"

Marcella felt slapped and needed to defend herself.

"It was just a few mean people. They talked about me too, about Catholics."

"That ain't the same, Miss Cella." Her voice was slower now, quieter. "Just leave him alone. He's young, and men can be foolish. Just walk away if you meet him again. You hear?"

"I hear. I will."

* * * * *

Lucille stood with her hand on her growing belly and smiled abstractedly.

"It's better now, Lucille, isn't it? With the baby, and George ..."

Marcella had been skirting around asking for weeks. Lucille was so excited when she told her the news of her pregnancy, but then it had become clear George didn't want the baby. He had no need, he said, of squalling babies at his time of life. Lucille had been devastated, but now she seemed less shaken, more centred.

"It's better. This is my baby, and she's going to love me for the rest of her life. Isn't that something?"

"I guess so, but won't George ..."

"Well George won't matter, will he? I'll have this little one."

Something Bigger

Lucille seemed sure. She seemed kinder, more open. They spoke about Mimi with less of the harshness Lucille had shown before. Marcella watched her friend, and wondered what it would be like to know you would be loved for the rest of your life like that.

Just then there was a noise from the hallway as the front door pushed open and George's voice called out, confident that someone would answer, someone waiting for his return. Marcella looked quickly at Lucille, who seemed as startled as she was, sitting up straighter, tense to the sound of his footsteps like a well-trained spaniel. He wasn't supposed to be there on Mondays. Marcella braced herself but was still unprepared for his expression when he recognised her, as though she were some creature, less than human, that didn't belong in his house. It flashed across his face, this revulsion, so even after it was replaced with a cold smile, she could not pretend she hadn't seen.

"Miss Coyle, isn't it? Good of you to call to my wife. Keeping her amused, were you? I don't see why, with this fine house, but she seems to reckon she needs amusement. Don't you Lucille?"

Lucille was pale and quiet, as though she'd been caught in some act of disobedience. Marcella was too stunned to respond. Vaughan stood, filling the doorway, letting the silence build between them.

"Well, thank you for coming, Miss Coyle. Don't let us keep you from your important work — you're a working gal, are you? You have work apart from that brother of yours?"

"Yes, I work in Loveman's, on 3rd." Marcella recovered her voice and mustered her dignity. "In the accounts department. I'm a bookkeeper."

"Well ain't that nice. I sure hope that works out for you, Miss Coyle. I'm sure you got to get along then."

116

Chapter Eight: 1917

He stepped aside a little, still standing too close to the door so she had to almost brush past him as she left. His physical presence made her angry. She turned back at Lucille to say goodbye, but she was looking away.

Back at the rectory she told Jimmy about the encounter, and immediately regretted it. It was exactly the kind of thing calculated to set him in a spin these days.

"Ah, keep clear of him, Siss. He's a hard-shell True American, not an ounce of compassion in him. He's not safe to be around, Lucille or no Lucille."

"Jimmy, what even is a True American? Vaughan just loves money. He doesn't care about being American or anything else."

"That's not what I mean, Siss. Don't you pay any attention at all to what goes on outside these walls? You must know about the True Americans? The Ku Klux Klan?"

She sighed. Jimmy was off now, on an unstoppable explanation.

"The Klan revival started in Atlanta. Isn't that where your friend is from? That Ashby girl? Anyway, they're supposed to be secret, just for men, white men, American-born, Protestant men. Nobody supposed to know who's in and who's out, but for a secret society, it sure knows how to make its presence felt."

"So what, Jimmy? Isn't that just like the Syrian Brotherhood, or the Ancient Order of Hibernians, or any other society. Like the ones you're in?"

"No, Siss. It's nothing at all like the Order. These aren't men to stand for something — they're not for the Irish or for the Syrians or even for the City. They're against — against education for the Black folks, or poor folks. Against Puerto Ricans and Catholics. Against different kinds of folks just moving in and getting on together. Against, us Siss. They call us 'un-American,' and that means anything they want it to mean. Anyone not like them. They're a bunch of old toads, with their robes and their masks and their whispers. Respectable enough on the outside, some of them, successful men with money or the look of money. Others are dirt-poor and desperate to follow something stronger than themselves. But the hatred ... trust me, Siss, you don't want anything to do with them."

He was getting angry just talking about it, so she let him finish and didn't interrupt. They didn't sound dangerous to her though, these men. Robes and masks! It was hard to imagine taking grown men seriously who indulged in that kind of thing. Still, she resolved to avoid the subject for a while. That and the war — two sure subjects to get him ranting. Birmingham seemed to love the war like it was a festival. There were banners on city buildings, full page ads in the newspapers. Young men were as excited as for a football game. Except for Jimmy, who was just angry. He said that America was fighting Britain's war. He said it was all about money, about boosting the "Magic City," a new name for Birmingham that he hated. He said it was about sending the unemployed and unemployable overseas and getting big steel contracts into the mills. And of course, work was good, but money, he said, was no reason for war. But he said these things only at home. It wasn't like him to be careful like that.

* * * * *

Chapter Eight: 1917

Bess was uncomfortable in her stiff collar. She wanted to go play with her boy cousins, but one look from her Momma stopped that thought dead in its tracks. She was fourteen now, supposed to be a young lady. So instead of playing, she sat at her Grandma's table, under the persimmon tree, listening to their whoops and hollers from the other side of the house. They sounded like they were having real fun. Bess was swinging her legs like a far smaller child, bored by the adult conversation around her, picking at the lace tablecloth. Her father sat stern at the head of the table, wearing his best dark suit, frowning at the empty chairs. The sounds of play stopped. Her Auntie Kay went to round her sons up from behind the small house. If they'd gone quiet, they were bound to be up to no good. Bess wondered what game they were playing. Bound to be more fun than being stuck at this table, too fancied up for its meagre picnic lunch, ice melting in the sweet tea.

"Stop that, child."

Her father's voice was almost a whisper, and she didn't notice at first that it was addressed to her. She looked up surprised.

"What? I ain't done nothing, Daddy."

Her mother moved quickly to pull her arm back from the table, and she realised she'd been picking at the lace tablecloth again. Her Grandma had made a real fuss for this Sunday lunch, laying out a lace cloth over a clean white sheet to fancy up the old table. Her fingers poking through the lace seemed to have found a hole in the cloth underneath, through which she could see the faded wood of the table.

"Stop it." Her Momma's voice was quiet too, almost a hiss.

Something Bigger

"But Ma, I didn't do nothing."

"What you got there, Bessie?" Her cousin Chad slipped into the seat beside her, laughing. She liked Chad. He was a year older than her, and had a way of talking to her parents like he wasn't afraid of them. "You tearing up Grandma's tablecloth?"

"The tablecloth's fine. That hole there in Grandma's sheet was there before I found it. I didn't make it."

Chad leaned down to look. Bess's father glared, but Chad acted like he didn't notice.

"I reckon you're right, Bessie. You didn't make that hole, did she, Uncle Abner? That ain't no bedsheet, is it? Those your old robes?"

"Don't you go talking about what you know nothing about, young man." Her Daddy's voice was low, but Chad didn't seem to see the danger in it. He laughed, surprised and delighted.

"It is, ain't it? It's one of your old robes! What've you done, Uncle Abner? You got new ones?"

Her father slammed down his fork and left the table just as Chad's mother arrived, a little breathless, with the smaller boys in tow.

"What's up with Abner? Ain't he going to say grace?"

"Bessie here found Uncle Abner's Klan robes, Momma. His old ones. Laid out here under the lace tablecloth."

"Klan robes? Daddy's not in no Klan!"

The silence that hung over the table told Bess she was wrong.

Her Grandma broke the silence.

"Nothin' wrong with the Klan, child. A lot of you kids would never have Christmas if it weren't for the brothers."

Chapter Eight: 1917

"But ..."

There was no more talking about it. Bess tried to think of all she'd heard about the Klan – dressing up in scary robes and burning crosses, burning out houses, and something they called lynching which she didn't want to think about. Could her Daddy be doing all that? He was back at the table now, more composed. They all sat and bowed their heads and he said grace – a longer than usual one, with new prayers she hadn't heard before. Head still bowed, she opened her eyes, and met that hole in the white fabric under the lace tablecloth, seeing the edge of a second one poking out from under the bowl of greens. Eyeholes for sure, staring back at her. She suddenly couldn't see anything else.

Later, her Daddy made his big announcement, how he was getting ordained, and going to be an official Methodist minister now. Her Grandma almost cried with pride, and he sat, basking in the admiration. They sat and drank lemonade for a long time before clearing the table. Her Grandma didn't want the meal to end, the cloth so pretty and white, a fine show for the neighbours.

* * * * *

After the picnic, Bess's mother, Ethel, was silent all the way back to the city, sitting up front on the mule cart as they made their way home. She had a range of silences, Abner had learned. It seemed like a game she played, where his part was to coax her into speech, so that when the argument blew up, as it always did, he would be the one to have started it. This silence had the feel of a long one. But this time he was going to just ignore her. That was the advice of his new friends, his new brothers. Don't start with her, Abner, they said. Don't pay her no mind. And it was working, by and large. But then there was Bessie. She used to be on his side in the game, but lately, things had changed. She was getting away from him somehow, even though she wasn't more than 14 years old. She was getting to be her own problem. His house was turning into a house of women, the two of them, and him. That wasn't right, a man in his own house. It wasn't proper for the woman to be at the head of the family, or to be playing her silence game until he was fit to scream, fit to hit out just to get a reaction. Just to see what her problem was, exactly, this time. But he had men now who understood. Good men. The finest kind of family men. Brothers who could tell him how to live. It made him feel a bit easier, teasing the mule with his switch, carrying his own silence to match hers.

Anyway, he wasn't rightly sure what was really bothering Ethel. Was it the way his old robe had been found? Or was it being in the brotherhood that bothered her? Because he wasn't going to argue about that. If she thought he was ashamed, she was just plain wrong. He had answers if she ever asked. "They asked me to join, what could I say?" That's what he'd say first. And then "I can't leave now." Or maybe "Someone's got to fight for this city." Mr. Vaughan told them all the things to say to anyone who didn't understand how fine a thing it was to belong. Folks thought sometimes it was to hide, that they met at night, or from shame they wore the hoods, like it was wrong. Folks thought that — not important people, just family. Just the folks that didn't know the brotherhood. The ones that didn't belong.

It was far from shame. It was power, if they only knew. That feeling — putting on the robes, standing

Chapter Eight: 1917

shoulder to shoulder with the finest men in town, all dressed the same. It was the most belonging he'd ever felt. When Charles Stone had dropped by his barbers the month before, asking if he'd join up, he hadn't needed persuading like other men. He hadn't needed to have it explained to him, how important it was for them to stand together, to put America first over all these negroes and Romans and Catholics and Frenchies moving up from Mobile. He'd known way down deep in his boots that this was the right thing for him to do. And the first time he'd gone up Kane's Hill, standing in the dark, looking out at the brothers and knowing he too looked like them, taller than usual with his stiff pointed hood, he felt a rush of rightness flowing through him. This was where he was supposed to be. This was standing for something real, robed in white like priests. Like wizards. Like men of power. All circling the fire, turning their backs on the dark, owning the night. He belonged to the finest group of men in the whole Magic City. The ones who made something out of nothing — planting their seeds in the fields or digging riches out from under the ground, making jobs for the God-fearing poor folks, going to service on Sundays. These were men who knew what was what and knew how things should be. They told the truth, and he was learning it, not the lies in the Birmingham Herald, but the real truth that the lying papers wouldn't print. He had reading to do now. Educating himself so he could help out in all the good work they were doing. He got to be part of it without even trying to join. They came to him. They asked him. It was an honour no woman could understand. He had no need to break Ethel's silence about this. Not tonight. Not if it was about brothers.

Something Bigger

When they'd meet in the daytime, barbers or lawyers, bankers or ministers or trolley car drivers – they'd know, by a look that they shared that memory of flickering power. The night mattered. The hoods and robes mattered. But the belonging lasted longer than the night. He had new customers now in his barbershop, some men who crossed half the town to come and have him shave them. He had a respectful nod, now, from the doorman at the bank. He'd never ask. Nobody ever asked if another man was in the Klan. You could assume, if the man was white, and upright, and not a filthy foreigner or a catholic. You could assume he was a true American. A brother.

People paid for this — hard earned money. Not just the monthly dues that he was happy, no, proud to pay. Folks paid ten dollars to join. Ten dollars, cash in. But he was asked. And there was another reason for him to be part of this. Now he was a minister, asked in there too, with a role in the courthouse as a marrying parson. He had no trouble there, not like others, no clerks trying to move him on. Only respect. And he got it for free. They weren't sitting back, waiting to decide if he could join or not, waiting to see the colour of his money. They wanted him. He mattered.

So he could let Ethel hold on to this silence as long as she pleased, really. He smiled to himself as he cracked the whip lightly over the mules, hurrying them back along the road to town. It was a grim stiff smile, and Ethel saw it. He made sure she did.

* * * * *

Only three weeks later, Marcella came home from work to find a hand-delivered note in the hallway, a small white card with two sentences.

Chapter Eight: 1917

Marcella,

Come when you can. News from France. Will has died.

Lucille

She read it twice. And then again, searching for something she must have missed in the space between the lines. And then she set out to Lucille's townhouse. The front door was already looped with a black satin ribbon. The maid let her in without a word, pointing to the library where the light was low, and Lucille was framed in the window, stiff in a low ladderback chair.

"Lucille?"

She didn't answer. She didn't move, even when Marcella put her hand on her shoulder, and bent into her line of sight. Her face was far too still, her eyes fixed but unfocused, her hands loose in her lap.

"Lucille ... I'm here, honey. I'm here, Lucille."

She didn't know what else to say. Lucille leaned into her shoulder. Her sobs were quiet at first then gasping until finally there were no tears left. Marcella just held her. When she finished crying, she looked up, meeting Marcella's eyes with a look of pure sorrow.

"Thanks, Cella. Thanks for coming."

"Of course I came, Luc. Of course I came. Where is George? Is he here?"

"I don't know where he is. He just heard the news and walked out. He never cared for Will. Or Will never cared for him. He's ... oh never mind. He's not important."

She was rocking a little, in the chair. Holding herself in her own arms now.

"They sent a man around with the news. A boy really. A young soldier. He came this morning. He said he had a message from the front. That's what they called it, Cella, and oh ..."

She was sobbing again. Marcella waited.

"Anyway, that's where Will was, at some place they call the front. The soldier said it was an accident. Some gun that wasn't supposed to be loaded, and explosives. He said Will died well. Imagine? Did you know there were different ways to die? I guess you can die badly. But not Will. He died well. He does everything well, doesn't he, Cella? He was born well – no trouble to Mother. He rode a horse well and went into law like a good boy, ready to move home, and live well. He was so young, Cella, the soldier who came. His face. He had lips like a girl, and I was just angry with him for being here in Birmingham, carrying bad news, instead of being out there in France getting killed for no reason like Will. Oh Cella, can you imagine me thinking that? He was just some poor young boy who turned up to my door, and I wished him dead instead of Will. Oh, what a thing."

She was silent for a while. For so long Marcella wondered if perhaps she should leave.

"What about your mother and father, Lucille? Do they know?"

"I sent Mother a note. Daddy is, well, he's not so clear in his head these days. She will have it by now, I expect. I sent it with Matthew – he's the best of the men working here. He will tell her properly. Not like that soldier – Cella, I swear he can't have been more than sixteen years old. At least he seemed like such a child. So yes, Matthew has gone to tell her. I don't know. I don't know what to do. She won't have anyone to talk to about it, not really. And there may not even be a funeral, Cella. They may not ... it was an explosion. There

Chapter Eight: 1917

were two of them who died. They may not, they may not find ..."

"Hush, Luc. Hush now. It's alright. Hush now, honey. It doesn't matter. That doesn't matter. You must get home to your mother now. That's all. You ..."

"But I can't, Cella. I really can't. I must stay here for George. He won't stand for me leaving now. He ..."

"Lucille Ashby. You get home and be with your Momma. She needs you more than George does, and you know it. You need her too. You two can look after each other for a while."

Marcella would always remember that she'd said this and wonder how much it mattered. That night, Lucille packed to leave, and George was not happy. Afterwards he would say he didn't forbid her from going. He would say he wanted to help. But it was true that Lucille was the one to order up a horse and buggy, and that she set out late with young Callum, the newest of the stable hands, to drive. Callum was blamed too, later, for driving too fast, for choosing the wrong horses. Lucille was blamed for being impetuous, for running out on her husband, as though that's what she was intending. Nobody blamed Marcella because nobody knew what she had said.

After the accident, when Lucille came out of hospital, half-recovered, settled back in the Ashby house in Georgia — when it was clear to everyone that there would be no baby — that's when Marcella blamed herself. Quietly, and every night, just before she slept. Over and over, for the hurt, for the pain, for the loss of the child, for the loss of some lightness and beauty in her friend. She went to spend time with her, thinking all the way along the road to the Ashby house of the accident, wondering at every turn if this were where

Something Bigger

it had happened. Mimi came down from New York for a while, bringing an awkwardness into the house that none of them could explain, as though everyone belonged there more than her, even Marcella. Mimi stayed for four days, perhaps two days too long, on the edge of crying for all that time, always a breath away from sobs. She was the only one in the Alice in Wonderland house showing any emotion of any kind. Mrs. Ashby held herself cold and stiff. Mr. Ashby didn't seem to understand much other than that Lucille was back. Sometimes he forgot she'd been away. Sometimes he went outside to the stable, calling Will. And Mimi, well, he had no idea who she was, and he kept asking, loud and sometimes querulous. "Who is that woman?" he'd say. "Who is that woman at our table?"

Lucille moved in a golden haze, like a mechanical doll. She wouldn't speak of the baby, or of George. She wouldn't speak of Will. She walked when they made her walk, talked about flowers and birds and nothing at all, as though they were all sixteen years old again. Mimi couldn't take it for too long, and after she returned to New York, Marcella also packed to go home. The day she left, a letter came from George, a short one that Lucille didn't share. Weeks passed, and Lucille stayed, as though on a holiday and then as though on a journey to the past, and then as though she had never left her childhood home. She sewed with her mother, cared for her father, helped with the decaying house, and settled herself back, shrinking her world to the front room, among her childhood toys and the silver-framed pictures of her family.

And then, three months later, she climbed onto a carriage sent by George, and let herself be carried back to Birmingham. She became again his beautiful wife. There was no more talk of a baby.

Chapter Nine

1917

Birmingham Age Herald, May 1917
KU-KLUX KLAN OFFERS ITS AID

I Mackey, exalted cyclops of the Robert E. Lee Klan No. 1 Knights of the Ku Klux Klan, issues the following statement of the Klan's offer of aid to the nation.

"The Knights of the Ku Klux Klan, a patriotic and fraternal organization instituted by our imperial wizard Col. W. J. Simmons of Atlanta, its charter bearing date December 4, 1915 and July 1, 1916, whose paramount features are pure patriotism and real clannishness. Its keynote is protection; protection to the country expressed in patriotism; protection to each other expressed in clannishness; protection to the home and family expressed by manhood.

Something Bigger

"Resolved as follows: that Robert E. Lee Klan No. 1, realm of Alabama, unanimously endorses the action of our President and his official family in regard to our relation with the imperial government of Germany, and realizing the graveness of the situation, do offer our services as a unit of 100 honorable and upright men to do services as home guard in the city of Birmingham, subject to call of the proper authorities, day and night."

Jimmy grew thinner, moving faster, and working harder as the war progressed. He wondered if he was compensating, taking on new projects and working himself to exhaustion, instead of really speaking his mind on the war. He hated how the war effort had become embedded in the city, with collections for the families of draftees, and all the adverts in the papers branded with the war effort. It was wrong, he'd say in private, to send young men to die, to enter a war so rich men could sell coal and steel to England, for the companies who were making most money to call their profiteering patriotism. But he had the sense to see the patriotism for a force to be reckoned with. Public parks were being turned into victory gardens. The local papers were filled with advice on how to support the war effort, how to feed a family on no money, how to be loyal, how to belong. The Klan were in on it too, offering to help the government, sometimes patrolling at night, causing prisoners who escaped to disappear. He was shaken, because he'd loved America since he landed, and he loved it still, the people, the mix of them, the open-handedness, the high blue sky, the possibilities. But this narrowing sense of what America might mean, and what it might not, made him less sure of his ground. Overnight, one weekday night, fliers were thrown on every front doorstep on the street warning of traitors, telling people to be vigilant, saying spies and people of low morals should leave or be dealt with. It wasn't signed, just the symbol of the local Klavern at the bottom corner of the page. The Klan weren't missing the opportunity to take power.

And yet, he thought, wasn't this what Ireland had done? Seen an opportunity while England was at war, taken the chance for nationalism? He wondered if there was a difference between the Irish nationalism he loved, and this closer one he feared? That was another reason to keep busy; it was a way of avoiding thoughts like that.

He wasn't the only one who didn't love the war. At dawn as he read his Morning Office outside on the rectory porch, and he often saw young couples coming stealthily next door, to the courthouse. At first a trickle, and then a stream, all young, urgent, bashful, coming to be married, perhaps because they were running away, or now, more likely, because married men were safer from the draft. If you could call these striplings men – barely shaving, half of them, holding their young girls by the hand like they were holding on to life. Jimmy saw another figure becoming regular on the courthouse veranda. A tall figure wearing a dark hat, and out of context it took him a while to recognise his barber from across 3rd Avenue. Old Man Stubbs, as Johanna called him. Jimmy watched him from the shadow of his porch seat. Abner Stubbs spent most of his time doing nothing, just leaning on the rail, sometimes smoking. And then a couple would hurry up the steps and he'd snap to life, presenting himself smiling in front of them. They'd talk for a bit in the early light, and then they'd follow him in the side door of the courthouse, emerging maybe ten minutes later looking lighter, making themselves scarce down the street, as Stubbs himself followed them out and took up his post again by the railing. He'd be there all morning, back in his barbershop in the afternoon. The more he watched, the more Jimmy wondered.

Curiosity brought him down there early one afternoon, as he had done often enough in the past. Stubbs stood outside his shop, under the awning, sharpening his blade. The sun made a hard, bright line on the sidewalk, so his face in the shadow was hard to see. He looked up as Jimmy came near but didn't move. Jimmy moved towards the door to open it.

"We're closed."

"Ah sure all I want is a trim, Mr. Stubbs. It's only 3pm."

"Not today, Father Coyle. Closed."

He drawled the word father, dragging it out in a way that was clearly mocking. Jimmy felt his blood rising but kept his voice low and calm.

"And why's that, Mr. Stubbs? What has you closed so early in the day?"

As he spoke another man approached from the south side of the street, and walked right to the door, which opened easily.

"Be right with you, Jed" said Stubbs, not breaking eye contact with Jimmy. "See, I'm busy. Can't fit you in right now. Don't have the time."

From inside the shop came the sound of low laughter, two or three men, listening. Stubbs didn't smile.

"I see you've less time for this, right enough, now you're closed in the mornings. You're busy at the court-

Chapter Nine: 1917

house. A new job, you've got?"

"Not so much a job. More what you'd say is a calling, I reckon. I've taken up cloth."

"Cloth?"

"You'd best be on your way, Father Coyle. I've no time to shave Catholics today."

"Oh, that's the problem, is it?"

Now Stubbs smiled, and turned away, drawing his whetstone over the razor, slowly honing the blade.

Jimmy had no choice but to turn away. He sought out Tony Brennan in the sacristy.

"He just ignored me, Tony. Just stood there, letting other customers in. And I've been going there on and off for years now."

"Leave it, Jimmy. If he's not shaving Catholics, he's not shaving Catholics. There's plenty of other places you can go."

"Yes, but why should I? What good is it to leave him in his bitterness? And what's this taking up cloth nonsense he's going on about?"

"The cloth, he means. He's found himself an out of town ministry and got himself ordained as a Methodist. That's where he's taking authority to marry those young couples. The marrying parson, they're calling him now since he's not got a church or a congregation."

"A minister is it? By dad. Well that's different then. I hadn't seen that in him."

"Seen what? It's just a living for him, James. A better one than barbering now with half the young men of the city gone to war."

"Ah you don't know that. Maybe he has a calling for it."

"What calling, James? He's just a barber who found a new trade."

Something Bigger

"It's something more he was all the same. Alright then. It seems I'll be needing a new barber."

Jimmy laughed. It was that quick, decisive laugh he had, the one he used to change the subject. He wasn't sure what to think. That was new for him. He didn't care for the feeling.

Next day Johanna came with the news that Jackson was being served draft papers even though he was married with a child. Jimmy went straight out the door to the courthouse. The official took his time coming up to the white, dusty counter, a broad, squat man with a smile that grew slowly when he recognised Jimmy.

"Father Coyle. What's up? Something urgent, I guess?"

"Kurt. Yes, urgent. What's this about drafting married men now? What happened to hardship cases?"

"Married men? So not you or one of your priests, then, Father." His tone was a little mocking. "No, we don't generally draft the married ones, least not if there's hardship. Not if they've children. You got a case?"

"Yes, I have a case, Kurt. This letter came to Jackson Clarence up in Longfield just yesterday, and ..."

"Longfield? You're here about a Negro man?"

"Yes. A man who is my cook's son. Married. With a young boy, mind."

"And he's a working man, this Negro?"

"He's working in the new school there. His wife, April, too, helping with the little ones. They're a good, upstanding couple."

"Ah, there's your problem, Father Coyle. His wife is working, you say? That means she ain't dependent on him."

"What are you saying?"

Chapter Nine: 1917

"If she's the one bringing home the dough, he ain't got no reason not to go fight. That's just how it is."

"But ..."

He slid the letter back to Jimmy, not breaking eye contact.

"You might want to check that out, Father Coyle. Check that out and come back to me."

Jimmy saw how the man's eyes had hardened. He'd seen that expression before, on officials dealing with others, but never with him. He was astonished more than offended by the hostility and left the office without a word. Back in rectory he looked for Johanna, but found Father Brennan first.

"He needs better work, Tony, and most of all better work than his wife. Immediately. Not just mornings now. What can he do, I wonder? I could make him a caretaker for the afternoons. We could pay him for that if we pay April less. We can make him the breadwinner, if it's breadwinners they're looking for. That should satisfy them."

"I don't understand it, James. He's a married man with a small son, and the whole city is heaving with volunteers. There's no shortage. I don't know why they picked on Jackson. And I don't know what's got you so riled up about this?"

"Ah, I don't know. It was the way he looked at me. I mean it was Kurt in the office. How long have I known him? Weren't we regulars at the games before the war started? But he looked at me, Tony, like he was looking across a barricade instead of a counter."

"You're a bit rattled, James."

"I am. I am. But we'll fix this. I'll fix this."

It was easily enough fixed in the end. Jackson was appointed to coach football and teach music in the af-

Something Bigger

ternoons at the Longfield school. April was to earn a bit less. Another visit to the courthouse and Jackson's draft was rescinded. Johanna was beaming, singing to herself in the kitchen, and Jimmy felt easier, back in control. He stepped out to the shady side of the porch, a little early that evening, and read his Office on the porch swing. He wrote some notes for a Sunday sermon that was almost finished. He found himself losing concentration, but not in his usual distracted way of having too much to do. He felt content. He lit a cigar, and sat back on the swing seat, watching people passing. Young mothers passed, holding small children by the hand. A young lad on a bicycle slowed outside the rectory, slipping off the pedals but righting himself, and then carrying on. A little music drifted from across the road. Marcella's latest adopted cat crept onto the porch from the Church side and stretched out near his feet, not looking for food or attention, just basking in the warmth from the wooden boards. Jimmy scratched him, between his ears. Captain. She always called them Captain. He felt slowed down and easy in the evening light. The city seemed gentle and easy. He breathed the still air, thinking this was like calm after a storm, or the calm before one. He must have dozed off, because the next thing he remembered was Marcella coming in the gate, struggling with a bag she hadn't left with that morning. He knew right away by her downcast walk what had happened.

She'd lost her job, she said, as though it was something she had carelessly mislaid. As though it was her fault, rather than something that was taken away from her. Her boss hadn't given a reason, but then, he didn't really have to. She'd overheard enough conversations through the flimsy partition of her office, and Jimmy

had said often enough that all over the city, businesses employing Catholics were being boycotted by the
Klan. Her boss could hardly look her in the eye as he
held out her final paycheck. She had raised her chin
and waited, not wanting to take it until he looked up
and met her gaze. But he waited longer. She reached
out and took the money, trying to be curt and strong,
trying hard to look like Fran or Jimmy, and then she
had walked out the door carrying her few things and
her dignity. It was only when she was back at the rectory, shaking, trying to smile and pretend not to be sorry that she felt like breaking down. Jimmy said not to
worry, there would be no shortage of things she could
help at right there in St. Paul's. Jimmy said hush, Alan-
na, hush, using her mother's pet name for her, making
her cry properly. Jimmy said to take her time, that it
would all be for the best. Wouldn't it be handier for
her not having to cross town in the morning? And yes,
she agreed, it would. He said it wasn't as if they needed the extra money, not really, though of course she
knew they did. Prices kept rising, and she couldn't be
sure she'd enough put by already to take them both to
Ireland, if this war ever ended, if the city ever got back
to normal.

Because it wasn't normal now. That became clearer to her in the following days, with time on her hands
to read the papers and watch the streets. The Klan,
it was reported, was busier than ever burning crosses outside the city limits, holding mass rallies in their
spook-like robes. There was a lynching almost every
week — some young Black man picked up on suspicion, who'd escape or get released from his holding
cell in the middle of the night, and be dragged away
by a crowd of men and hanged. The last one she'd

read about, the report said a thousand men had been involved. A thousand men, here in Birmingham, and this a secret society? She'd found herself watching the men who passed, wondering who was in that group, and who was out. It seemed like they had to be one or the other. The mailman smiled as he always did when he dropped letters on the porch, and she wondered what the smile meant, and hated that she wondered.

Every man in Birmingham seemed to have to belong to something. It wasn't just the Klan. Even Jimmy had his Knights of Columbus and the Ancient Order of Hibernians, the Syrian Brotherhood, and a dozen other organisations. Maybe at heart he was a joiner? Maybe they all were, more and more with this uncertainty of war, with half the young men gone and more signing up all the time. She didn't think she was a joiner, not really. She didn't need to join into something more than she had. She knew what mattered: her and Jimmy, Johanna. Carlo? Maybe. Fran? For certain. Tommy? Tommy meant home and future and getting to Ireland one day to see what might be left there. He mattered for sure. Maybe her job wasn't important, or the Klan. Maybe it was only belonging that mattered, finding people to be with, like Jimmy now. She'd work with him. So now she was losing money, and Fran would surely say it was a step back, away from her independent life. But what good had that life done her? Scrimping and saving, and she had still not found her way home.

She threw herself into parish work, and to her surprise, she was good at it. In time she grew to love it, both helping and leading, organising women's groups, new school committees, Legion of Mary women's Sodality groups. She kept accounts, her bookkeeping skills proving useful. She applied for naturalisation.

Chapter Nine: 1917

Jimmy said it was best for her, that it would put a stop to the accusations of Roman Catholic disloyalty and let her become American officially. She swore allegiance to her new country without a second thought, easily renouncing the loyalty she was supposed to have had before to the British King. She felt no loss. She had never felt British, she realised, only Irish, and even that was more of an idea than a place, with no passport to hold. When she thought of Ireland, she thought only of Rockfield and Athlone, small places where people struggled to make a living, to get an education or a husband, or a ticket to a new life in a new place. She couldn't imagine a country beyond that tight parish boundary. She couldn't imagine it being spacious enough to hold a government and a flag. Despite what Fran wrote in her letters about the aftermath of the rebellion, the rise in Irish patriotism seemed almost imaginary to Marcella.

She had called to Lucille only once more, the day after she'd been let go from Loveman's, arriving earlier than usual without giving her customary notice. She wanted to tell her what had happened as soon as she could. Looking back, she wondered what she had been expecting: a friend to console her? Someone to spend time with now that she had no job to go to? The maid saw her in, and she waited in the library. It always reminded her of sitting in the convent parlour to see Sr. Levinus when they were in trouble of some kind. She shivered a little at the memory and drew herself up straight in the chair. She waited a long time before Lucille opened the door, her long white skirt and loose blouse looking elegant as ever. Everything always looked well on Lucille, Marcella thought, until she saw her face. She was wearing too much powder and rouge, and it was streaked to the side of her face as though she'd applied it in haste just now. She walked steadily enough to her chair in the window, but her voice was bright and brittle as glass.

"Cella! What a lovely surprise. What brings you around?"

Marcella realised she was staring. Her friend looked more than thin. She looked frail.

"What's wrong, Lucille?"

"Nothing. I'm fine. And you?"

"Lucille, don't put me off like that. Are you ill?"

Lucille's hand went to the side of her face, and for a moment she appeared as though she were going to cry. When Cella reached out to her, though, she flinched, and lifted her chin.

"I'm fine, but you, you poor thing, how are you? George told me you lost your place in Loveman's."

"George told you? How would George know? I only found out myself yesterday."

Lucille paused a little too long before going on, her eyes startled.

"Oh, I don't know. Georgie knows most things, I guess, that go on in this town. He told me before he left for Virginia. He and the Lovemans go back a long way, of course. They do a lot of business together. It's a shame about your job. I wonder what happened? Did they tell you?"

Lucille had her smile back, sweet and cold as ice cream. Marcella stared, her mind racing, not liking the thoughts that came pouring in. She would not respond. She forced herself to sit and let Lucille babble. She made herself wait until she could trust herself to stand and walk steadily to the door. She mustered a smile and left without saying she never planned to come back. After that, she simply stopped calling. Gradually, over only a few months, they all but abandoned whatever friendship had held them together. Sometimes Marcella wondered if Lucille felt as bad about that as she did.

Instead, she spent more time with Carlo, who had changed his mind about going to war, and had somehow avoided being drafted. They went to the movies most Thursday evenings to watch stories on the screen that had nothing to do with fighting, loyalty or loss. After the movie, they'd walk down Third 3rd Street, a handsome couple reflected in the dark shop windows, often stopping off along the way home for an ice cream on warm nights. He always ordered for both of them. He always paid. She found herself looking at him in a new way as if weighing him. He could be cold, but considerate. He was steady, and not unkind. Was that enough? He seemed stronger since the war had started, and more closed. He had a new plan most weeks, always about money, but finally he had one that was serious.

"You're going to work for George Vaughan? Carlo Moretti, how could you?"

"Why not? What's wrong with old Georgie? He likes me. And he's a man who can get things done."

"What things? Don't you care about what he thinks of Catholics? What he says about us in his papers? Don't you care about what he says about Jimmy?"

"Oh Jimmy. Well, he's not part of the deal, honey. This is about me and my big shot. And being Catholic ain't something you can't change. You know that. Hell, even his wife knew that. And she knew how to get ahead, didn't she?"

"That's not the point. Don't you care what George believes? Jimmy says he's in the True Americans, and that's as bad as the Klan, he says."

Something Bigger

"What do you know about the Klan, Cella? They're the only game in town right now. Where do you think I'm going to get work? Up at Ironton they're only taking on poor folk for digging and Klan members for managing. Same at Spalding Mine, and up on Red Mountain. Now Vaughan owns everything from the mine, to the plant that buys the ore to make pig iron, to the steel mills, and the newspapers that write about it. And ..."

"And he'd like to own the people who make it too. You want to be one of them, Carlo?"

"Yes, Cella, I'm happy to be one of them. Because the only other thing I can be around here is poor. Don't you see that? I got a chance to join the Nathan Bedford Forrest Klavern. They've asked. They're gonna let me in. And once I'm in, I'm in."

"The Klan? But ..."

"But nothing. Cella, You may not like George and his good old boys. But this is their city now. There's one train moving here. You can get on it, or get out of the way. And you can't tell me who to talk to, or who to work for either. This is a big shot for me."

"Fine. Do what you want, Carlo. Do as you please. Just don't expect me to hang around with one of Georgie Vaughan's running boys. What's he getting you to do anyway? Bootlegging liquor to dry states, no doubt. His delivery boy, that's what you'll be."

She didn't mean to be so hurtful, but she couldn't help herself. The confidence in Carlo's voice, his certainty and ambition, all seemed ugly to her. Maybe it had always been ugly. She wondered how she hadn't noticed before.

Carlo wasn't angry. He sat back, folded his arms, and watched her, with no emotion to read on his face.

Chapter Nine: 1917

"So that's what you think, is it Cella? That's what you expect of me? To be a delivery boy? "

"No, that's not the point. That's not what I said."

"Isn't it?"

He sounded calm, like a stranger. She felt angry and wanted to go home.

"I'm going to work for George Vaughan, Cella. I'm going to work hard for him. We're going to make a whole new fortune between us. And I don't think you'll have any part of it, not because I don't care for you, because I do. I always did. You know I care for you. But you just can't, can you?"

"Can't what?"

"You can't just accept how things work in the real world. You got to tie everything up in knots with bringing in religion, and who's done what all to some other person who doesn't even matter. You have to make everything about something more complicated than it is."

"No, I ..."

"No nothing. It's true. That's the difference between you and the woman who'll marry me. That's the difference between you, Cella Coyle, and women who end up happy."

She pushed back her chair and stood up. He sat back and let her. Let her walk right out the door into the night; let her walk home alone. She was too angry for tears. Too angry for words. The street was quiet — only one man walking the same direction as her on the other side of the street, carrying a bag low in his hand. He was walking slowly with his head up, watching the streetlights, so she was sure he didn't even see her as she overtook him on the other side of the street. She went straight to her bedroom and wept.

* * * * *

Something Bigger

Third Avenue was almost deserted, and Abner Stubbs was almost home. The night was chill, and he missed the warmth of his robe, tucked in the bottom of his bag. He entertained the idea of slipping it on, walking solo down Third in the middle of the street, walking tall, robed and hidden. Nobody would challenge him. The folks around here, they knew to stay indoors with their doors locked and their lights off, living like the mice and rats they really were. The street was all his at night, his and his brothers, and that was as it should be. It was sweet. He should be tired, but he wasn't, with some kind of victory pumping in his veins. That's how it was, always, the night of a fire.

He slowed as he came close to his own front door, reluctant to end the night. He liked the emptiness of the street, the pools of bright from streetlights, just for him — nobody else on the long sidewalk. Most houses were darkened, but there was a lamp burning in the front room of the priests' house. Abner imagined him in there, the priest, writing more lies. He stopped in a shadow across the street and watched for a while. Nothing moved except a stray cat on the front porch, creeping, sizing up something small in the bushes. Abner could see its eyes all bright from the window light. Who knew what all went on in that rectory, in that church? Maybe all the stories he'd heard were true. For sure, they were trouble.

But not for long. The Klavern had trained men now, fresh back from the war who would know what to do when the time came. Men who wouldn't hesitate. But Vaughan said they shouldn't be complacent, 'cause there were trained men on the other side too. Romanists, and dark-skinned soldiers who got their passports for fighting, and now acted like True Americans. They were starting to walk up his end of town now, wanting to come to American churches. Wanting to take what didn't rightly belong to them. Vaughan was right — their granddaddies didn't build this city to give it away. It belonged to them and their families, and if it came to it, they would fight. But those people, there were so many of them, more coming all the time. Vaughan was an educated man. A rich successful man and he knew sooner or later they'd start looking around and think they could just take charge. Vaughan had said it just that evening. "We better start getting tough and we better start getting vigilant, and we better start using our heads or we're not gonna have a city, folks." Abner was ready. That's what the brotherhood was for. Soon, they'd take their city back and clean it up. Pretty soon now, they'd better watch out.

Up his own stairs, he didn't bother to be quiet. If his boots woke Ethel, no harm. Bessie was in her own room, and he looked at her closed door, imagining her in there, sleeping like a baby doll, safe because he was protecting her. She was a good girl. He saw her some evenings from the courthouse, dawdling home from school, walking on her own, not like those flirty convent girls parading themselves up to the ice cream parlour to meet boys. His Bessie was not like them. She was smarter than the others. Smarter than him, maybe. Quick little thing, that's why she ain't got no friends. Nobody to keep up with her lightning mind. She was like him that way, but not like him too.

When he was her age, he'd been scrabbling for his next meal every day for two years, living in doss houses and doorways and church halls. He was nothing. His Daddy was so mean, he upped and left him when his Momma died. Nobody was going to treat him that way.

Something Bigger

He was mean sober, but stupid drunk. That made it easy to get away. Staying away was harder, empty nights on dark streets, trying to be a big man, when really, he was a skinny kid with no credentials. Bess was never going to struggle like that. She was going to have a real good life. She was going to stay in school, learn her books and get a fine job in a fancy office. She'd marry a man who'd drive a good car and work with his brain. And Abner and Ethel, they'd be set in a good family then, settled in this city. They'd have tickets to the Christmas mixers and Ethel would shop in Loveman's. Abner would wear a fine suit with black patent shoes and maybe get elevated in the Klan. They were going to have respect.

Bess was a good girl, steady and smart. Pretty, though. She was getting way too pretty for a child. She didn't know it yet, but Abner could see she was getting looked at. He watched her sometimes pass the courthouse, bimbling home on the shady side of 3rd, and every time he was glad she was on her own. The day he saw her with a boy, he thought, well, that'll be a day he'll want to forget. She was his little girl, and he wasn't about to give her up anytime soon. Being her father, that was something. Her father, and a brother in the brotherhood. A protector. The Klan protects, he thought. It's what they were for. And they weren't going to be stopped.

Chapter Ten

1918

Birmingham Age Herald, September 1918
SLACKERS WARNED BY KU KLUX KLAN
100 Men Silently March Through Streets Of Montgomery, Scattering Warnings

Montgomery, September 21 – For the first time in 42 years, the Ku Klux Klan passed through the streets of Montgomery tonight distributing warnings to slackers, immoral women and spies, if perchance there be any there. Garbed in white, with black head dress and occupying 18 automobiles, 75 to 100 men silently appeared early tonight, traversing the principal thoroughfares, and as they passed scattered this warning printed in red letters:

"Work, fight or get out. No slackers allowed in Montgomery. We protect good women – bad ones must go. When the Red Cross and Y.M.C.A. call, be sure you answer. Have you bought your pro-rata of Liberty Bonds and War Savings Stamps?

Something Bigger

You can't be a slacker in any way and live happily in Montgomery. If there is a German spy in Montgomery County, he will be properly handled. This is a warning and final notice. Do your duty."

Summer of 1918 stretched into fall, still full of tension and unrest. Both Jimmy and Marcella scoured the papers for news from Europe, for any sign of an end to the war. When the Carpathia was torpedoed close to the coast of Ireland, Marcella shivered at the news. This was the ship that had rescued passengers from the Titanic, and had seemed like a symbol of hope, now lying at the bottom of the sea. Letters from home were infrequent now. One from Fran made her smile, in spite of the tone, she could hear her sister's voice so clearly in it.

> Crancam
> Rockfield
> Athlone
> Ireland

Dear Marcella,

This will be a short one, but I had to write after your last letter. Will you cop yourself on, girl. What are you doing, breaking up with what sounds like a good man there, that Carlo fella, and you not getting any younger? Do you think you can wait forever? I waited long enough, and if I had my time over, I wouldn't have. I know the war is dragging on, and I don't know if you've been waiting for some boy you like to come back from it, or what kind of nonsense is going on in your head, but start your life now, Siss. Don't wait.

Now — I've done my giving out to you. I hope you

take it well. I'm your big sister, and even if I haven't seen you in all these years, it's still my job to look out for you. Take care of yourself there, and of that brother of ours. Let him not be meddling in things that aren't his business. And come home now, soon, as soon things settle down, won't you? You've yet to meet my sturdy son, let alone baby Elizabeth.

With more love than you could guess,
Fran

Closer to home, the hectic war effort brought the Klan to the forefront of life in the city, gaining some respect as they organised community patrols, and still feared as stories of lynchings grew in the daily papers. Eventually the interminable summer ended, the air cooled and smog hung over Third Street like a layer of grimy steam. Marcella longed for the sea, and fresh air away from the smoky city. She thought about the green emptiness of winter fields in Ireland and how it seemed perpetually out of reach.

A case of Spanish Influenza appeared in nearby Huntsville, and then it seemed to spread like gossip through the thick air. People began to wear masks over their faces, to stay home. All Jimmy's meetings were cancelled. The streets thinned out and emptied. In October, all the theatres and churches in the state were closed, by order of the Governor. Immediately, Jimmy approached The Birmingham News, and they offered him a regular column, to keep in touch with his congregation. At first he published only sermons, but moved on to full descriptions of the order of the Mass, explaining the sacraments, the importance of communion. Marcella watched him typing it all out in his study, now and then staring out the window looking for a perfect phrase. She loved him in those moments more, she realised, than when he was actually preaching. His sermons were more gentle. He wrote about peace in the midst of war, about people putting aside their differences, and though they could not congregate, how they could come together for the common good. Marcella would bring tea to his table, loving the quick smile he would give her without speaking, the simple intimacy of it. Sometimes he'd read her a sentence, trying out how it sounded, and she'd tell him when it was too long or too pompous. He learned to laugh at himself more, with her. They laughed together, and she could hardly ever remember what it was they found so funny. People were afraid of influenza, but in her heart, Marcella knew there were things about this time that she would look back on and love.

Then, in November, war ended, suddenly and forever. A giddy sense of optimism seemed to infect everyone, and for a few golden days, the city seemed united in it. All the labour of scrimping and stretching seemed at an end. The boys would be home soon. Newspapers proclaimed victory and peace. Jazz bands began to play again in the small places on 2nd Avenue, and the Lyric opened again three times a week. Marcella wondered about finding work again, paid work outside the parish, although the rectory was busy, and Jimmy seemed to need her. It seemed like the start of new things, with the return of young men to the city, and of peace. Jimmy made ambitious plans, and for once, Marcella was with him.

But the euphoria of those early days passed, and she realised that some things hadn't changed — she was still unable to get work in Loveman's despite her qualifications;, still a Catholic, still shunned. Most importantly, the Klan were still here too. In fact, they led a victory parade right through the city — hundreds of men in white robes, walking in two long columns in single file, all with their faces covered. She watched from the shelter of Jimmy's study. Several of the men turned their hooded faces towards the rectory as they passed. She felt the threat like heat.

The war coming to an end was forcing her closer to a decision. Could she live in Birmingham, with no work of her own, and those men in charge of the city? Or could she leave her brother alone, to move to a place as small as Rockfield, to a boy she hadn't seen in fourteen years? Mary Catherine in her letters wrote about soldiers in Athlone, fresh back from the war and swaggering. She talked about going to dances at the Ritz, wherever that was. It was hard to imagine a place called the Ritz in Athlone, which seemed to have faded in her memory to shades of grey. Marcella wondered if Mary Catherine would have mentioned Tommy if she caught sight of him. She imagined him changed like the returning soldiers were in Birmingham, uniformed heroes with money in their pockets. She imagined his face more chiselled, his eyes still laughing and blue, and him going to the Ritz, dancing with anyone he chose. She watched the mail for letters from him, wondering if she still mattered to him. She knew he still mattered to her.

Finally, the mailman brought a letter with tight, unfamiliar handwriting and an English stamp smudged by an illegible postmark. Fearful, she opened it right away in the hallway. There was no address at the top.

Something Bigger

Dear Marcella,

You won't be expecting this letter or recognise the writing. My mate Harry is writing for me – he's better at it. You always found it hard to read my writing, and your Da had a hard job teaching me to begin with, remember? But my hand is sort of broken up now and I can't hold a pen yet, so Harry is doing me this favour.

I'm in a hospital in England, but don't feel sorry for me, Cella, because this is the best place I've been since this war started. I have a bed, and food, and lots of pretty nurses, though none as pretty as you. Or as pretty as I remember you – how many years is it now? Are you coming home soon?

I am. Going home, that is. My hand is not good enough to work a gun anymore, they say, and my leg isn't right either so I'm sort of useless to them now. They're to send a batch of us over to Ireland out of this place very soon, so please God I'll be home by Christmas. My mother will be delighted. I'll be glad too, I think. Glad to have left war behind me, at least. I don't know what I'll do when I'm home, now I can't be a soldier. My leg's not so bad, but it's not right. My walk is not right, but I could work on a farm if I can get work. I can't write proper with the hand. Maybe I can learn to use my left hand again. Remember how your Da made us all write with our right hands? I wish he hadn't tried now.

So, I suppose, Cella, what I'm saying is, I'll be home. So when you can, come and find me. I'll be wanting to see you. I've been thinking about you most days and wondering when we might meet again. I'd like to see you home. I don't have much to offer, but I can keep your place like it used to be, if you're coming back. And we can have a life there. Are you coming back?

Thinking of you always,
Tommy B.

She read it twice. "Thinking of you." Not "love," though love seemed there between the lines. The envelope didn't look fresh, and there was no way to tell how long it had taken to get here. He might even be back in Ireland by now, home and safe but not swaggering and dancing as she had thought. She could picture him in her head, speaking the letter to his friend in some quiet corner of an army hospital ward. She could imagine the light on his soft hair, and it made her smile inside. She folded the letter carefully, and put it by her bed, not away in the bundle with the others. In the following days, she kept going back to it, trying to peel all she could from the thin blue pages. She wondered what he would do, back in Rockfield. She wondered how it would be for him, to go back after all he'd seen, or for anyone to go back to those small fields and houses, having seen a bit of the world?

Finally, she wrote to him at his home place in Ireland, saying she was glad he was well and home, saying she needed a little more time, three years or four, to help Jimmy. They were young still, after all. Not yet thirty. He wrote back, to her surprise, saying yes, more time would give them a chance to make a good start. He had plans, he said, to make his home a place she could be proud of. All she felt was relief at not having to decide. Rockfield was a memory now, fading as fast as that dream she still sometimes had of her father in the classroom, almost turning around. She wanted to go home. She wanted to see Fran, and her mother again, and Tommy – to see what he was like now, how they might be together, but it made her afraid, the idea of leaving the rectory. The life she had here was a good one, wasn't it? If she left, what if she could never come back?

* * * * *

Dear Diary

Sorry I ain't written more. I been busy. Exciting times, diary, that's what Daddy says. We been in a war, and we won. We fought people far away in Europe. Not all of 'em, just the bad ones. Everyone here around Daddy's barbershop talks about it all the time. They love it, love how strong America is. They sit and smoke and chew tobacco and talk about it all day long.

I don't see no excitement in the war. I still got school, and that's a dull as it ever was. But I got two secrets that are way more exciting than any war. First one is, been to that Catholic church, St. Paul's. I been so often now, I can walk right in without even being scared, and slip up the back stairs. There's a balcony up there, all steps and shadows. I sit in the cool, under the roof, and watch the ladies come and go with their beads and their candles. I look down at the tops of their hats and headscarves, and they don't even know I'm there. Sometimes I think about dropping pennies on their heads. I like how it smells, all fine and polished. I don't pray none. It ain't my place for praying, but it's peaceful, and I like a place of my own after school before I go home. The ladies are mostly like the ladies at our church, but some are fine and fancy, and some ain't even white. They don't stay long. Sometimes they move around the church, praying up at pictures on the wall, like what Momma calls idols. Sometimes they line up in a pew and take turns stepping into another room. Sometimes they kneel down on their own for a while or light a candle. They sure love candles.

Daddy says they're no good, those Catholics, but they look pretty ordinary to me. Momma says evil wears a mask, so maybe they're right. Daddy knows about masks. So does Momma. I seen her washing that new robe he got last month, the hood all white and ghostly. She don't try to hide it from me no more. Just made me promise not to tell.

And the other secret, I met a boy! His name's Diego and he's a whole lot older than me. 25 or something, he won't exactly say. He's kind. He's been in the war and he's sweet and handsome. He came to our house to hang wallpaper for Daddy, and he worked just as slow as could because he's noticed me, and he says I'm the prettiest thing he's ever seen. Nobody said that to me before. He's asked if I'd go with him on a date, but I know that can't happen. Momma would like to have a fit. Daddy would kill him, and then kill me, like as not. But that's OK. I just like that he asked.

I told my friend Becky and she says he's too old. I reckon she's jealous. She thinks I'm too young, but I'm not. I'm fifteen. Momma was fifteen when she met Daddy; she told me so herself. I'm plenty old enough to have a beau. He's handsome and steady, and he's been all over the world. He used to live way up north in Boston, he said, and he was born far away, in Puerto Rico. He was in Europe in the war, but he doesn't like to talk about that much. He brings me little things most days, a hair clip, or candy. He brought me this pen. It's brass and steel and shiny.

Something Bigger

Momma's calling for me to get ready for church. Our church – the one I pray in, not the one I play in. heh – I like that. That's what Miss Carter would like to call "a turn of phrase." I'm getting good at writing. Daddy ain't coming to church, it's just Momma and me. Maybe that's cause he's a minister himself now. He spends more time out of the house now than he used to, and I like that. He's gone most evenings to some meeting, that brotherhood of his. I ain't going to write about that. I don't like it, but it's better that he's gone.

I still got to come in the barbershop to sweep the floor up, most days even though I'm not a little kid any more for doing chores like that. I don't like it there like I used to. I don't like how the men look at me. Specially I don't like Brad Harbeson, though I won't have to worry about him no more. He's the worst. He smiles at me real cold and looks me up and down like I'm something he might buy. It all started a month ago. I was petting his old dog. He's a sweet old dog, half blind, and he follows Brad Harbeson everywhere. I reckon he's the only thing that loves that man. Anyway, I was hunched down there, petting just at the doorway, and I didn't see Mr. Harbeson had finished his shave and came up behind me. He reached down for the dog's collar, and he pushed his hand right down my blouse — right there at the side of the street, so quick nobody saw. And he looked at me with that awful grin of his, and he winked. Then he started reaching out for me, whenever he could. Pinching and squeezing past me real slow. One time he told me, real quiet, that I'd be in some trouble with my Daddy if he thought I was flirting with him so. That's true. I hate him, but I can't tell.

Chapter Ten: 1918

So today, when he came in, I went in the kitchen and got Momma's carving knife, and I snuck into the bathroom and cut up my arm some. Not deep, but enough blood so it looked pretty bad. Then I just went out to where that old dog was lying in the shade, and rubbed him a little, and then screamed fit to bring the house down. Daddy was there like a shot. I cried like I was bit, cried like a little baby. And sure enough, Brad Harbeson got mad, like I knew he would. Started calling me a liar, saying his old dog wouldn't hurt a fly. Then he and Daddy got to fighting and my Daddy kicked him right out onto the street, told him not to show his face again. Then it was my turn to smile at him so nobody saw, a real sweet smile, so he knew what I done. Dog might be killed, Daddy says. It's a shame. He was a sweet old dog. Just a dog, though. Old Harbeson won't have nothing or nobody then.

Daddy was all riled after that, all evening long. He's still angry, that cold angry he gets sometimes. I gotta stay out of his way for a while.

Momma's calling me again. Gotta run.

Bess

Chapter Eleven

1920

Birmingham Age Herald, April 1920

**LEGION COMMANDER REFUTES
CHARGES OF POLITICS ABOUT DE
VALERA'S PROPOSED VISIT**

**Ex-soldiers, led by wounded officers,
were unanimous in expressing their
distaste for appearance here of man
who took sides with the Huns**

* * * * *

Crancam
Rockfield
Athlone
Ireland
February 1920

Dear Jimmy and Marcella,

Is it true what we heard? That Eamon de Valera himself is to visit ye there? Martin heard it from one of the Cumann lads. If it's true, be sure to take a photo and send it home. Martin would be proud to hang it on our wall. Marcella, make sure to get Jimmy to do this. It would be a great souvenir for us here. Mother would be proud of it. Well there's not much can make her prouder of Jimmy, but this is something she'd surely hold on to.

Not that everyone feels the same around here. The Duffys have no time for de Valera, but they were always troublesome. They'd rather fight, Martin says, than settle down and make a country. We don't see as much of them as we used to. We don't see as much of many of the neighbours. This new flag we have seems to be dividing the place. That lad you used to be friendly with, Tommy Banahan, is another one. He called by last week when I was out feeding the hens. Wouldn't come in. Knows he'd not be welcome here, I suppose, what with him having taken the shilling and fought for the British. He was asking for you again, asking when you were coming home. I ran him out of the place, Siss, and I was sorry after, but I haven't the patience for him always calling, like a stray pup, as if one day he'd find you here. He's not right in the head since the war, God love him, and I don't know what gives him the idea he can ask after you.

But mind now, get that photograph for us. It will be something for our children to have. Some piece of history.

With love,
Your sister, Fran

* * * * *

The visit of Eamon de Valera to Birmingham was the biggest news that had hit the Catholic Church in years. Marcella would always remember Jimmy breaking the news to her, asking her to guess who was coming to visit. He looked so pleased with himself. Like he'd won a prize. It made her pulse race.

"Is it Fran? Is Fran coming, Jimmy?"

His smile slipped a little.

"No, not Fran, Siss. I guess just not our visitor, really. More for the whole city, but we're the ones to organise it. Go on, guess?"

She guessed wildly: Count John McCormack? President Wilson? It turned out to be a man she'd never even heard of. Eamon de Valera, fresh from the Irish rebellion to a whirlwind tour of the US, calling himself the president of a new republic.

"Why's he coming here? Isn't the rebellion long over?"

"It's only beginning, Siss. Only the start of it. And this man, Dev, is the one to lead it now."

"I thought they shot them all."

"Not them all. You can't kill an idea, and that kind of a sacrifice has an effect. Didn't it birth something bigger than anyone could have imagined?"

That wasn't a line of talk Marcella wanted to go down. There'd be no use starting Jimmy talking about honour and sacrifice, and the meaning of things any fool could tell were hopeless.

"Alright, but why here, Jimmy? Why Birmingham?"

"Why not, Siss? Aren't we the biggest Irish Catholic community in the South?"

"But, wait. He's raising money, is it? Is that it?"

"Ah shush with your talk of money. Of course he's raising money, with the country new and penniless. He needs dollars, but that's not the important thing. He's coming here, to our church, to this house. He'll not be staying, but he will visit us, and in barely three weeks! Won't it be grand?"

Chapter Eleven: 1920

She didn't see cause for his excitement, but she liked to see him excited, losing that guarded, haunted look she'd been getting used to lately. He rattled on with his plans.

"We need to do this together, Siss. I can get the Hibernians organised, and we can work on having a rally. I need you to get the women behind it. They're the ones who hold the purse-strings, and if they decide that de Valera is worth an investment, we can make this the star of his whole tour."

"So, it is about money then?"

"Ah no. Not at all, Siss. But money counts too."

Jimmy was pacing up and down, bubbling up ideas. She could see how much this meant to him, how it brought everything together for him, all the themes that ran through his poetry: faith, Ireland, America, all intersecting for once. She stopped talking about money, and tried to ignore the way the day was shaping up to be all about donations. It would be just one day after all. Eamon de Valera would arrive by train in the late morning, have lunch in the rectory and meet some schoolchildren and a women's Sodality, and that evening there would be a rally – how those men loved a rally – and then he would be off again with no harm done.

Once news of the visit became public, Marcella read about de Valera in all the papers every day. There were some who welcomed him, Jimmy, and others, but most of the space was given to angry meetings of the city leaders, and proposals to ban him from coming, from holding a parade, from speaking in public. They said he was a traitor, an enemy of their British allies, a man who would end the relationship between the US and Britain and wreck the market for coal and steel. Marcella couldn't see how one man could do that. There were letters here and there from other Irishmen, who said he wasn't really Irish, not really a hero, not even a martyr to the rebellion, having used his American citizenship, they said, to get clear of the firing squad. Esther Gavin, recently widowed and now a stalwart of the women's Sodality, was in that camp, and whispered about it urgently to Marcella when Jimmy couldn't hear. Mrs. Gavin was a whisperer at the best of times, always calling her over with the crook of her finger to ask a question or make a sharp observation about another parishioner, adding more weight to her gossip by lowering her voice, making Marcella lean in to listen.

"We should have nothing to do with that young pup."

She was helping to wash the good china for the visit, at risk of breaking it, muttering over the sink. Marcella ignored her in the hope she would stop.

"Not even Irish – a name like that. What's anyone called de Valera doing thinking he might lead a country like Ireland? Down in Mexico, he should be."

The cups were getting rattled around the sink, in danger of being chipped, so Marcella tried to calm her, parroting what she'd heard Jimmy say. "But sure what's Irish, Mrs. Gavin? Isn't the country only free a wet week?"

"We're Irish, Miss Coyle, and well you know it. We were born there. He was not. Simple as that."

"What matter where he was born? Amn't I American now, and I not born here?"

"You're not all that American, Miss Coyle. Not American enough to hold your job now, were you?"

As soon as she said it, Mrs. Gavin's hand flew to

her mouth and she was all apologies, but the remark stung just the same. They finished the work in silence. Marcella knew she was right. She wasn't American enough for Loveman's, in spite of her citizenship. She was always going to be outside that circle. But who was Mrs. Gavin to remind her of that? Maybe it was only that annoyance that led Marcella to seek out Johanna, a move always sure to irritate the likes of Esther Gavin. She found her out in the back yard hanging laundry and put her proposal to her at once.

"Johanna, I wanted to ask you. Do you think Jackson would bring down his schoolboys to meet President de Valera when he comes? They could do a guard of honour at the station, just a little one. It wouldn't take more than half an hour. What do you say?"

Johanna looked unimpressed. She bent to lift the basket of clothes pegs. Thinking.

"Why no, Miss Cella. I don't see that's fitting. That de Valera man, he's here for the Irish, ain't he? What call does Jackson have to get mixed up in that?"

It had only been a whim, but now she was being opposed, Marcella didn't want to let it go.

"Not just the Irish, Johanna. Isn't he coming to see St. Paul's, and all that Jimmy's doing here? That includes the school in Longfield. Wouldn't it be fine for him to see all that's being built here? See the young boys getting an education? It would sure make Jimmy proud."

Johanna remained stubbornly noncommittal, so she brought the idea to Jimmy, who loved it.

"This might be the best idea you've had in months, Siss. It wouldn't be right for him to come here and meet only Irish people. Now he'll see what's possible, how you can build up something for everyone in only a few years."

Something Bigger

Johanna never warmed to the plan, but Marcella was delighted when she saw Jackson coming up the front path to discuss arrangements with Jimmy. That would show Mrs. Gavin who was and who wasn't Irish enough.

As the visit grew closer, editorials in the newspapers intensified, and grew more personal about St. Paul's and everyone associated with the church. De Valera was called a crook, a liar, traitor to his King, a jumped-up, fast-talking conman who wanted to whip up the poor for power and money. A typical Irish Catholic in other words. Jimmy wrote a few letters in response, patiently at first, and then scathingly. After a while, the anonymous editorials and letters began to focus on him personally. The Menace was a local paper – a rag, Jimmy called it – that was popular among the secret societies. They devoted pages to the issue of de Valera, and the way Catholics were coming out to meet an enemy of America's friend. It seemed to vindicate them in some way. See, they said, these people are not real Americans. James Coyle shows it, with his Irish loyalty as well as his Catholic loyalty to Rome. Marcella wished Jimmy would stop writing back. It only seemed to feed them. She wondered what they had to be so angry about, now the war was long over.

"It's not anger, Siss. It's just politics. Sure, the people reading these letters don't know it, and maybe not all those writing know what's going on either. But the owners do, Georgie Vaughan, all his set of peanut politicians. They're making a fortune from their mills and mines. The last thing they want is their workers fresh home from the war, lifting their heads and getting together to demand fair play. Easier to keep them hating something like they hated Germany in the war. This month, with de Valera coming, it's us. It'll be someone else after that. Dev isn't what they hate. Hope's what they hate. We've nothing to worry about."

Marcella wondered what kind of man Eamon de Valera could be to trigger such passion. She couldn't wait to meet him. Still, when Jimmy went to meet the train, she waited at the rectory. Johanna persuaded her.

"It's only like to be trouble, Miss Cella. You're best waiting here with me."

So she and Johanna never got to see Jackson waiting on the platform with his honour guard of ten-year-old boys. They didn't see the watchfulness in his eyes, the way the street around the station filled with loitering men, all white, many focused on the little troop of boys whose shirts were scrubbed white as an ad for Sunlight Soap. Jimmy saw, but distracted as he was by the approaching train, just put his hand on Jackson's shoulder approvingly as he passed him by in his eagerness to meet the party from Ireland. When he stepped off the train, de Valera hardly seemed to notice the waiting children, and Jackson was left alone to shepherd them home. He ignored the taunts that began to follow him as a small group of men broke off from the main crowd and tracked him up 1st Avenue as he made his way back towards Longfield. Around 13th St. they gave up and began to hang back, shouting out a final threat. Jackson was shaking when he reached home, not from fear, but anger. He'd said nothing. He'd let those men call him names no man should hear, in front of his boys, and he'd said nothing for their safety's sake. He'd brought them up there to see this important Irishman. He'd told them all about him, about how he cared about their school, but then this tall white man had just swept past the boys like they were nothing. And Father Coyle had let it all happen. He'd let them stand there for nothing. He'd left him alone on the platform with his boys. For nothing. The wrongness of it built inside him like steam in an engine.

Back at the rectory, de Valera took the porch steps two at a time, effortless, stooped to shake Marcella's hand, nodded at Mrs. Gavin and the gaggle of church ladies, ignored Johanna. He was tall, but not handsome, thin but powerful, and he was charm itself over lunch, complimenting the food, turning Mrs. Gavin into a giggling girl. He knew some people from Rockfield, or at least he mentioned the right names. He talked about the school there as though he remembered her father, although when she thought about it, she felt it was unlikely. His laugh was easy but not too loud. If it weren't for the way he kept glancing up at the men who came with him as if waiting for some signal, it would feel as though he were just a friend from home, with all the time in the world to talk about old people in the old country. His voice – that was the one thing that didn't fit. Too high and thin. Reedy, like a professor, or a bishop. An indoor voice. Not one for action.

Jimmy hovered around him like a moth, seeming taller in his presence, flushed with the importance of this visit, this big man in his city, in his house, and later in his church where de Valera went to light a candle.

"If you'd have told me, Eamon, I'd have arranged something for you here. A service, you know. The nuns ..."

There was just enough lingering over the 'Eamon' to show Marcella how much it meant to Jimmy to use the first name.

"Now Father Coyle, I don't want any fuss. I only want to say a prayer."

Chapter Eleven: 1920

He made his way up the side aisle, as if he were ordinary, straight to the bank of flickering candles at the picture of Our Lady of Perpetual Help, green and gold like the banner of the Ancient Order of Hibernians that was already being unfolded outside. He knelt for a long time, his straight back casting a long shadow on the terracotta tiles. Marcella watched from the back pews, calmed as always by the marble peace of the church. She wondered what prayers he was saying, and then wondered why she cared. He quietly asked Jimmy for confession and spent no more than a minute in the box. When he came out, he was business and action, striding out the day-lit doorway with his mind in the future. Jimmy fell in beside him and they joined the men outside, marching to a meeting at the Jefferson Theatre as the light began to fade.

Marcella followed after with Mrs. Gavin and the Sodality women. At first there was no real hint of trouble. The crowds that lined the street seemed friendly; women whose children were too small for the main event had gathered over the road, wearing their Sunday Mass clothes to watch the men pass by. Closer to the theatre, little knots of men gathered on corners, threadbare suits and flat caps, arms folded, watching in silence. Closer again, the crowd thickened, and the mood darkened. There was a grim set in the men's faces, and no children now among the people on the sidewalks, fewer women. The men were not all Irish, or even what passed for Irish in Alabama. They were not there to applaud. Marcella found herself wishing they'd taken a carriage instead of walking, though the distance was short. She had never felt afraid on these streets before. This was home, after all, the word in her head triggering her usual ache for that other place, the damp green place. But she'd lived longer in this hot, hungry town, longer without the cradling familiarity of the little cottage, and her Mother and Fran. This was home now, this city, those strange looks from the milling crowd, her walking behind her brother.

She held one end of the women's Sodality banner, feeling as though they were actors with each street corner a stage, each streetlight a spotlight. Jefferson Theatre was teeming, but there were seats reserved for women on a side balcony. President de Valera stepped up on the stage, and she watched as he transformed before her eyes from ascetic to politician, raising his arms in full flight as though conducting an orchestra, his voice stronger now, carrying over the crowd, radiating conviction. There was a practiced air about his speech, words he'd said before, she felt, full of three-part rhetorical flourishes: nationalism, pragmatism, pride; the spirit of Ireland, her young men and her young women. She leaned over the balcony rail and saw he had captured the crowd in the stalls. Hardly a face was not turned on him. She thought she saw Jackson standing in a side aisle, intently watching, but the crowd shifted, and she couldn't be sure.

Just once, from the back, came shouting, a chant of "Take him out" that threatened to boil over into violence. Burly men moved down towards the back door, forming a kind of a wall. De Valera stopped speaking until the chanting died down, and then addressed himself to the protestors, playing a patriotic card.

"The republic of Ireland has a right to ask the people of the United States for their help. Every time in the last 100 years that the American flag has been in danger, true sons of old Ireland have been the first to defend it. Irish blood has flowed in every battle that the United States ever fought. Today should the flag of this country be endangered, every man in Ireland would be ready to fight, and die for it, proud that he had the chance."

Marcella wondered if that were so, thinking of how Tommy had fought for a flag, not from pride but from poverty. She saw Jackson again, certain this time that it was him. He seemed to be alone, arms folded, standing near the back door in a small cluster of Black women and men, some of whom she recognised from church. They were getting attention from the protesting group, just for being there, she supposed, in this white crowd.

"When the war broke out, Irish citizens volunteered for service in the British army because England promised that she was fighting for the rights of small nations, and it was by winning the war that Ireland hoped to win her freedom. And when the war was over, she forgot. Her promises to Ireland were scraps of paper. Ireland was a squeezed lemon, cast aside. It is your privilege, it is your right and it is your duty to say what side of this question you are on. Whether you stand with England, the imperial autocracy, or stand for the freedom of Ireland, the only white nation on earth still in the bonds of political slavery."

A white nation? She glanced involuntarily at Jackson and saw him flinch, then turn to leave.

On stage, de Valera was unfolding a flag, a tricolor of green, white and orange, to a chorus of cheers and jeers. He waved it over his head, and Marcella looked at it, blankly. Was this Ireland now? Was this what we had to show for it all?

Afterwards, it was straight to the railway station and de Valera and his entourage were waved on a train

169

and away. Jimmy and Marcella walked home together, the streets emptying around them like the end of a carnival. Jimmy strolled as though it were a Sunday afternoon, swinging his brass-topped cane, his hat in his other hand and the flag, a parting gift, draped over his forearm like a waiter's cloth. He was talking and talking, going over and over the details of the day. She half listened. He remembered the good things, the kind words from Eamon as he loved to call him, the letter from his bishop that was read before the speeches, the size of the crowd. Not the heckles or threats, the malevolent glares from that cluster of men near the back. As they approached the rectory, he stopped, then placed his arm on her shoulder as they crossed the road. He didn't say why. He didn't mention the man standing there under the streetlight, watching for their return. She looked back quickly and saw Stubbs. She knew his shape as he slouched back up past the church and home. She shivered but told herself it was only because of the night air. Still, she felt his eyes in the small of her back as she walked up the porch steps with her brother.

Jimmy took down the whiskey bottle that was only ever opened at Christmas and poured himself a dram. He laid the flag out over the back of the sofa, and sat back, admiring it, still talking, talking, as though he would never stop. He was so happy. Years later she would remember him this way, leaning back on the high-winged armchair with his collar loosened, running his hand through his hair, relaxed, saying over and over how well it all came together, and how easy it all was, in the end.

Late as it was, Marcella was buoyed up by his happiness, and could not sleep. Instead she wrote home,

Chapter Eleven: 1920

to both Fran and Tommy, describing the highlights of the visit. She put those letters aside, so she could add newspaper cuttings later, and she made up extra details in a longer letter to their mother. In this account, she played a bigger part, organising a choir of schoolchildren, spending more time in conversation with the great man himself. She signed that letter, as always, from the two of them, sending love from Jimmy as well as from herself. It was satisfying, in a way, to rewrite the day this way.

It was late when she finished, and she padded barefoot through the half-dark kitchen for a drink of water. Standing at the back window she saw something move in the backyard and the screen door burst open. Johanna rushed in, her face stiff, mouth twisted down and tears brimming in her eyes, but not quite falling. She was breathing heavily, as though she had been running. Surely she couldn't have run all the way from Longfield?

Marcella pulled up a chair, and eased Johanna into it, handing her the glass of water she'd just filled. She waited while Johanna's breathing subsided. Johanna stared at the glass in her hands. It was clearly an effort to compose herself, and still when she raised her head to meet Marcella's eyes, her expression was accusatory.

"Jackson" she said at last. "He's gone. They came and took him. April come around and told me, and she's gone now too, her and the little one, back to her Momma. Safer for her. They're fixing to wait there, until ... Jackson won't go back there. It ain't safe, but he might come here, when he gets away. This is where he might come."

"Who, Johanna? Who's taken him?"

"Those good old boys, Miss Cella. Came right after dark to my boy's house. Dozens of them, April said. Men on horses, and some only boys as far as she could see under their robes. Skinny little boys."

Marcella went to hug her, but Johanna's body was rigid and unyielding.

"I'll get Jimmy. He'll sort it out."

She wondered later, in the long times she had for wondering, if she really had believed herself then, that Jimmy would be able to sort it out, or if she was just running away from Johanna's frightening stiff grief. Jimmy strode in, tousled from sleep but apparently not disturbed by the strangeness of Johanna's glassy eyes, this impossible story she had about Jackson. He left with her, taking the automobile, to drive her safely home.

He returned, looking shaken, as it was getting bright outside. Marcella made a pot of coffee, and they sat together in the front study. There was no sign of him explaining, so Marcella had to ask.

"What's happening, Jimmy? Where's Jackson?"

"I don't know, Siss. We'll have to ask around. We might need to ask your friend, what's her name, Lucille? I might need to talk to that husband of hers."

"Vaughan? But why ...?"

"He'll know. Him or people close to him. Jackson's not at the courthouse, or the police station, so ..."

She wanted to ask more but sensed it would be pointless for now. They drank their coffee together without talking. After a while, Jimmy picked up a pen and pad and began to write. Marcella watched the familiar, silent intensity come into his face, addressing the page as though it were a person, as though he were explaining something urgent. He didn't look helpless or lost when he wrote. She wondered why he wrote instead of talking to her. 'It's ridiculous to be jealous of

Chapter Eleven: 1920

pen and paper, Cella', she told herself, but she watched all the same as the room grew light, and Jimmy seemed restored before her eyes, filling pages with his looping cursive. She didn't care what he was writing. He was coming back to himself and that was good. He was not talking to her, and that was not. She sipped her cold coffee, said nothing, and watched.

An awkward exchange with Lucille led to a brief arranged meeting in the Tutwiler Hotel between Jimmy and one of Vaughan's foremen from the mine. A day or two later in the front study, Marcella stood in the doorway watching Johanna sitting very still in the visitor's chair while Jimmy talked quick and low.

Jackson had run, Jimmy said. He'd survived the mob, heading to the centre of town, hiding in yards and doorways, until he was arrested days later all the way over in Anniston. The police claimed he'd been angry. He'd been trouble. A quick court session convicted him of resisting arrest, and he was right away bonded, leased to a mine. Now, thanks to meeting Vaughan, they knew where he was, but could do nothing to save him.

"It would have been easier, Johanna, in the prisons. We could have seen about the law. But in the mines, he's under the owners and Vaughan ..."

Marcella had hardly ever heard him falter like that. Johanna just sat, waiting for silence.

"You haven't lost him, Johanna. It will be a few years. He'll be back to you."

"Will he, Father?"

"He will. He will to be sure. He's a fit, strong young man."

"There's lots of ways, Father. Lots of ways of losing them you love. Underground, that's a slow way, but it's a sure one."

Something Bigger

Jimmy had no answer. Johanna pushed herself up from the chair and walked out of the study, brushing past Marcella without a word. Marcella stayed. Jimmy looked so lost; she didn't want to leave him alone.

Later, unable to sleep, she took down a letter received from Tommy a few days earlier. It was more serious than usual, asking about de Valera, and if Marcella believed in him, asking not when, but straight out whether or not she would be coming home. She'd been skirting around commitment for a year now. She took out her notepaper, and wrote the shortest of letters, saying, she needed another few years. A little more time now that Jimmy needed her. She described what had happened to Jackson, said he wouldn't understand, that nobody at home ever could. That she hardly understood it herself, all this fear and hate. Still, she wrote, she was all the family Jimmy had, now, and she'd need to stay just a few more years.

She wished she could have been honest. She knew now she was never going home. She signed the letter, not writing "love." She wrote "yours."

She sealed it and left it for mailing in the hallway, finally drifting off to sleep late into the night.

Some weeks later came a report that Jackson had run again, and this time had gotten clean away. Not shot, though there had been bullets to dodge as he escaped the mine with two other men. Not recaptured either. But gone. Johanna seemed to take some comfort in the news. Some warmth came back into her relationships at the rectory: not enough for her to sing in the kitchen, but enough for her to smile, sometimes even with a little warmth. Enough for Jimmy to be able to talk to her again about Longfield, not enough for

Chapter Eleven: 1920

Marcella to enjoy her company again in the slow evenings.

Marcella wondered if it was true, this story? Had Jackson really escaped? Was he out there, somewhere? Or was the truth simpler and darker than that?

Chapter Twelve

1920

The fire was slow to take. Marcella supposed the wood was wet after the storm. She thought they'd have planned for that. She thought they'd be prepared, all those important men. It made her less afraid, that they would forget something so obvious as storm-soaked wood. Maybe there were other things they hadn't counted on. Maybe they were not so powerful after all. She hoped it was true, because looking down from their vantage point, if they were half as powerful as they seemed to think they were, the whole city was in some trouble.

Jimmy was not afraid, she could tell. He always whistled when he was afraid, hummed when he was happy, and on the drive up here, he had done neither. He and Tony stood near her, beside the automobile, just in the shadow of the trees. They were back far enough not to be seen, and the Alabama night was soft and close, like a blanket. Anyway, the men were not looking for them. They were not looking towards

Chapter Twelve: 1920

them. They were all in a huddle, like cattle in a field, looking inward at the long torches they were trying to light. Tony stepped back, snapped a twig, and jumped. He was on edge. He'd never been comfortable away from 3rd St. When he spoke, it was barely above a whisper.

"I don't think we should be here, James."

"This is part of our job, Tony. What good's a priest who never sees his people except on Sunday?"

"These aren't our people."

"They're people, Tony. All people are our people."

Jimmy's voice was not loud, but it was hearty. He'd been acting upbeat ever since he took this notion. He had driven too fast out of town and up Kane's Hill. The automobile lurched on the muddy road, and Marcella feared they'd slide into the trees. It was only as they reached the crest of the hill that he slowed and turned off the headlights, eased them in to this gap in the trees where they could look down on the valley.

Tony was trying a new tack.

"This is no place for a woman, James."

"Marcella is fine. And she needs to see this. She needs to know what we're dealing with."

Marcella didn't like being talked about as though she wasn't there, like some child who should be quiet and let the priests talk. Jimmy leaned back on the hood and Marcella stepped forward, listening through the discord of crickets and frogs to a shuffling, stamping noise rising from the hollow beneath them. A smell of earth mixed with the thick green air of the forest. And then fire leapt up, suddenly, from a dozen or so long torches. The men spread themselves wider into a thin, moving circle. The valley was small, but it panned out there like a theatre. No surprise then, that they would make it their stage. Now that the circle had opened up, there seemed to be more of them, maybe a hundred, not talking, not singing, just shuffling round. Perhaps every tenth man held a torch, and they all held them low, pointing to the centre. The circling figures looked darker on the side of the watchers, lit from the torches in the centre, casting long pointed shadows towards them. On the far side of the circle, Marcella could see them more clearly, mostly wearing white robes, some tied with rope, but here and there a red belt, and one man covered head to toe in bright green robes, standing close to the centre as the others wheeled around him. It occurred to her suddenly that they might not all be men. How would you know, under those hoods? Then one began a call and response, like a novena call. For God. For Country. For Race. For Klan. They began to a repetitive chant that was not quite speaking, not quite singing. It sounded deep and dark.

Tony lifted the binoculars and scanned the crowd and the dark spaces behind them.

"No. They've got nobody there, James."

He passed the binoculars to Jimmy, and when he was done looking, Marcella could see his tension easing.

"Good. Here, Siss, take these. Look at what they do."

Marcella took the binoculars and focused on the circle of men. She was sure they were men now, because of the voices and their shoes under the long robes: mostly black boots, some brown, mostly scuffed. The man in the green robes had shoes that were shiny and black, like a banker or an attorney. The wrong shoes for a field like this; they were shoes for managing, not for working. She wondered why he chose them to come here. Did he wear them because he liked them? Did he want to show the others that he owned no work boots? He barked out a command and the dozen or so holding torches stepped forward into the centre, and dipped their flames low, to ignite a pyre topped by a tall cross. This wood was thin, but it went up quickly. She saw it was wrapped in rags and thought they must be soaked in gasoline. Was she wrong about them not being prepared? Were they stronger than she thought after all? The men were moving in two groups now: the larger group a wide circle, and the dozen or so torchbearers forming a smaller ring, close to the centre. This inner circle, alert to some unspoken signal, threw their torches down as one at the burning cross and stepped back in unison, arms stretched wide in a gesture that looked as though they were disclaiming something. They stepped slowly backwards, outwards, to be absorbed into the main circle, never taking their eyes off the flame. She wondered what the expression was on their hidden faces. She wondered why they hid their faces when there was nobody there but themselves.

Jimmy put his hand on her shoulder. Kindly now. "Will we get home, then, Siss?"

When he fired up the automobile, the gears locked, making a screeching noise that seemed to tear open the night. She didn't look down to see if heads turned towards them, and they didn't wait to hear if the chanting stopped. They reversed off the bluff, turning on the automobile lights as soon as they were back over the hill. Jimmy was driving too fast again. A few miles before the edge of town, he turned abruptly down a side road, cut the engine and the lights. They waited in the dark. Marcella's heartbeat seemed to her like the loudest thing in the automobile. She realised she'd been holding her breath and forced herself to exhale, inhale, exhale. Minutes passed. Nobody came following them. They turned back onto the road and drove more slowly the long way home. Nobody spoke until they were back in the rectory.

Inside the back door, Johanna was waiting on a kitchen chair. She stood when Jimmy came in, saying nothing, just letting the question hang there. Jimmy shook his head, and her shoulders slumped. Marcella wasn't sure if she was relieved or disappointed. She used to know Johanna so much better. Or at least she had thought she did. Tony crossed to the church where evening confessions were already late. Marcella followed her brother to his office where he sat back in his wing-back chair.

"Well, Siss. What do you think?"

"There's more of them than I thought. But I still don't see what brings them up to the middle of no-where in the middle of the night, chanting and singing around a fire like that. And not just a fire. What has them burning crosses?"

"If all they did was burn a cross, if nobody ever disappeared from Longfield in the middle of the night and never came home, then we wouldn't worry about the Klan too much, would we?"

"Is that what you were looking for, with the binoc-ulars? Jackson?"

Jimmy was quiet for a while. She saw how tired he looked.

"Maybe, one of these nights it will be him. And if it is, it would be as well to be there, wouldn't it?"

She wanted to ask what he would have done if Jackson had been there; what he could possibly have done that wouldn't get them all killed, but his voice was flat and defeated. When Jimmy went out to join Tony at confessions, she sat in his room with only his desk lamp on. She wasn't sure how to feel, exactly. She didn't like what she'd seen, but she was glad to have gone. She was glad he had brought her. The chair was still warm from him, and the house was quiet. She used to sit in his chair sometimes when she came to the rectory first, when this study seemed bigger to a child of fourteen. She'd coveted this chair then, she saw now, for the authority of it. She used to want to be able to do what Jimmy did, or failing that, to be the one who helped him. To be important in his world.

From the street outside, she could hear low voices, passing in the half dark between streetlights. The porch was dark and empty. She used to sit out there too, all the time, even late into the night, watching people pass. She didn't do that so much anymore. She could, she thought. Perhaps she should, just to claim it. Just so as not to be afraid. But instead, she sat in the shelter of Jimmy's wing-back chair where she knew she was invisible from the outside, inhaling the remnant of his pipe smoke. Those men around the fire, that sound they had made was frightening. She'd expected whooping and hollering and noise, but that low, purposeful chanting was worse, and now she filled up with quiet familiar sounds to wash it out of her head: the ticking clock, the creaking, contracting boards of the house. Her hands were empty in her lap and her head was laid back against the chair, too full to move. She sat and waited for peace to wash over her. It took a while, but finally it came.

* * * * *

In 1920, Birmingham was exploding. Money flowed. Someone had put a sign up at the Railroad

Something Bigger

Station welcoming newcomers to "The Magic City," making official the nickname the city had held for so long. You could almost hear fortunes being made on the wide streets, with flash new motorcars and new department stores opening to supply the fashionable young rich, and young men with their families flowing in to feed the steel mills and the mines. The city grew hectic, with an edge to it that sometimes made Marcella uneasy. She often walked by Loveman's, and saw it was thriving, but she knew better than to ask for her job back.

As the city grew, so did the churches, and Jimmy's way of partnering with different communities of Catholics led to a dozen or more churches going up all over town. He worked closely with Johanna on a church-raising project in Longfield, enjoying the time this gave him to spend with her. The two of them driving together scandalised Sodality women like Esther Gavin, but they both liked it. Johanna found it easy to talk when they sat side by side, both looking forward. Jimmy did too, opening up easily to Johanna about things he couldn't discuss with Marcella or Tony. Their work went well. Johanna was a natural organiser, knowing who to talk to, how to talk to them. And similar work went on, all over the city; Catholic schools and churches, orphanages and convents sprouted up not only in Longfield, but among the Italians, Syrians, the new, poor Irish. Catholics became more prosperous, more visible. Not everyone was happy about that. Catholics were a mixed lot — Italians, Syrians, Irish — but they had some things in common that a lot of people didn't like. They drank and played golf on Sundays. They had big families. They built schools to raise their children in their own faith. They were

Chapter Twelve: 1920

different. They were soaking up resources, people said. They were changing the city. In March, a pastor from the First Baptist church preached a sermon covered by the local papers which he titled "Romanism vs Americanism." To a packed church, he explained that Catholics, even those born in America, or those who had taken up citizenship, could never be seen as real Americans. Their loyalty would always be to Rome. It was rumoured, he said, that they stored guns under their churches.

"Some people say they are training armies in secret — these Knights of Columbus, the order of Hibernians. Some people say they are almost ready to take up arms. I don't know, but if that's true, we better be careful, or we'll lose our city. Some of them aren't even white, and their services aren't in English, but Latin, a language nobody understands but themselves. How can they be trusted?"

These reports angered Jimmy far too much, Johanna thought.

"Why do you fuss about it, Father? What harm can one old bigot do?"

"What harm? This is how it starts, Johanna. Words matter. More than most people know."

"It's just foolish talk."

"He's talking for a reason. He's talking to make us an enemy, so he sounds like a friend to everyone else. It's not hard to get a mob going around here. You know."

"I do know."

Jimmy was ashamed, hearing himself preaching to Johanna about mobs. But he couldn't let it go, and wrote to the paper next day, quickly, sardonically, parodying the style of his critic. "Oh, we Catholics, what frightful monstrous traitors we are, to be sure. What furtive, deep-dyed, deadly, diabolical, damnable plotters against America, the land we profess to love." He dismantled the arguments with satire, but that didn't bring an end to it. Instead it fanned the flames of a war of words in the local press. Protestants had better wake up, the editorials said, or they'd find themselves strangers in their own land, victims of the Romanist plan to turn America Catholic. They only way to counter it, another said, was with true blue, red-blooded Americanism. James Coyle was not just a hyphenated American, they wrote, Irish-American, with Irish coming first, but a bad one, who wanted nothing less than to establish his own power here right in the middle of their city.

Jimmy changed tack, and wrote more seriously, answering every letter and article in the papers systematically. "The church is not a political machine," he wrote, "but an institution founded by Christ for the salvation of men's souls." At this, some other church leaders came out to support him, while others took him aside to give him advice. The Presbyterian leader cautioned him to be more moderate for his own sake.

"Ignore those men, James. They don't speak for most churchgoers. As you answer them, you give them a platform."

Some of his parishioners agreed. They didn't like to read what was written about Catholics, and it seemed to them that the more Jimmy wrote, the more it grew. Marcella was proud of him, but she didn't like it either. Despite herself, she read what he wrote, and read the vitriolic replies. Jimmy grew more cautious for a while, but following one particularly colourful account of Catholic practices, he set out to end it, once and for all. In a letter to the local paper, he listed all the charges that were being made about Catholics – that they worshiped idols and were forbidden to read the bible; that all priests were issued with guns, and stored munitions in their churches; that they sought to overturn public schools and control American politics; that they kidnapped young women and locked them up in convents; that they were more dangerous than Black people because the Jim Crow laws didn't apply to them; that they stole babies just to baptise them; that they all planned to have at least a dozen of their own, to breed themselves into a majority and change the whole country to suit their beliefs. Most of all, that they were disloyal, taking their orders from a foreign pope in Rome. Jimmy set out the allegations and challenged anyone to prove them, offering a reward of one thousand US Dollars, a small fortune put up by a parishioner who had come into money, but didn't want his name known.

A local physician, Dr. Orion Theophilus Dozier took on the challenge. He already wrote for The Menace, and published his own pamphlets and poems which he circulated through a group he had founded called the Regents of the White Shield, a small and secretive group, sworn to protect the supremacy of the white race in the South. Dr. Dozier responded not in the newspaper but in a book entitled "Response of Doctor O.T. Dozier to Priest James E. Coyle, pastor, St. Paul's Roman Catholic Church, Birmingham, Alabama." He wrote that in opposing freemasons, the Catholic church was in fact opposing America. He quoted liberally from canon law and Catholic doctrine on the rule of bishops. He wrote in the vilest terms about the prospect of priests who were not white being allowed to minister in convents. He said he was sure that some Catholics were good people, but all priests were enemies of the country, the flag, and America. He called Jimmy "Mr. Coyle" throughout the book. It was intended to enrage, and it succeeded. Men from the parish formed small delegations to the rectory. Some wanted Jimmy to respond more forcibly; most wanted him to stop responding altogether, and let the whole thing die out.

Marcella could see Jimmy's name rising in the city. Sometimes in a store or a café, she'd overhear another customer discussing the Catholic problem. They were foreign, weren't they? Roman? Rome was further away than even Chicago. And in this war America had just won, whose side was Rome on? Whose side were the Irish on, if they were fighting England? Who could be trusted?

When people thought she couldn't hear, nobody called her brother Jimmy or James. It was either "that wonderful Father Coyle," or "that uppity priest." Someone said there was talk of a bomb to be placed in the church. Someone said he was going to be taken care of, one of these nights. When she brought these threats home to him, Jimmy agreed to step up security around the church, but he still wrote, day and night, on notepaper borrowed from the railway office, or a music school, or the doctor's office. If it wasn't letters to the newspaper, it was sermons, or what Marcella called his glory poems, all written with a pounding pentameter beat. He wrote about faith, the Red, White and Blue, the green fields of Erin, ever unfree. God, America, Ireland, the same three themes always, relentless, like a train. He sent his verses quickly for publication in the papers, or poetry magazines, or anywhere at all that would print them. Then he barely read them, already moved on to the next thing. He walked tall and fast as ever, faster maybe, striding up the path, taking the front steps two at a time. In a curious way, he seemed happy, full of sarcastic wit to his critics, driven and full. He kept his smile sharp, and his voice strong. It was only at night that Marcella could see the strain as he sat reading or writing, up lit by his desk lamp. At rest, his face looked older now.

When he was late home from meetings, she didn't worry, not really. She just found it easier to stay awake, listening, until she'd hear his key in the lock and know he was home safe. At such times she sometimes got up for a drink of water and found herself humming just to break the silence, a tune whose name she didn't remember, an old one, from home. She'd hum it over and over, wishing she remembered the words, counting the verses until he got back. Sometimes Jimmy hummed it too, when he was busy with something around the church. And she liked to hear him sing because it meant he was easy in his mind.

Into all of this, in April, exploded two letters from home.

Tommy's letter came on paper that looked like it had been torn from a child's school copy, with no address at the top. No date.

Dear Cella,

How are you all doing there in the big city? I suppose it's grand. I can't imagine it, not really, though your letters are great to have. I have enjoyed them. I've read them over so much, sometimes I've felt I was there with you. I loved how you wrote about all the small things you saw and did. I loved you writing about Dev. It's still hard to believe he came to call on you.

Something Bigger

The long fellow, as they call him, has half the country whipped up into revolution. I suppose your brother will love that.

I can't imagine what it would be like to meet Dev, what you might say to a man like that. Well, he wouldn't meet with me anyway, and I on the wrong side of the war, as it turned out. I didn't intend to be wrong. I only joined up to try to make something out of myself — to make something for both of us. I thought with the barracks in town, I could have a soldier's life, and we could have a place to live together down by the broad river. I often walk there now. There's a path along the far side that runs under the bridge, and you can look over at the married men's quarters, that long terrace that runs down to the water. I see clothes hanging out there some days, Cella. Shirts and vests and dresses and small baby wrappings, and sometimes I imagine that everything went different, and that we got there, to a small place we could be together. It wouldn't have had to be Rockfield. I know your world got too big for Rockfield. But it's too late for all of that now.

I'm sorry I couldn't make it work for us. You're all I wanted, Cella. You know that, don't you? You knew that? But I'm not afraid. If you can't get one thing, you get something else, isn't that it? I'm not afraid.

I hope you get what you wanted out there in Alabama. I used to think what you wanted was me, or that I could be part of it, whatever it was. But it was something else, I think, all along. Something I can't see from here.

You mean the world to me, Cella. I'm sorry.
Your Tommy.

She put the letter down. Her hand was shaking so she could hardly read enough to make sense of

Chapter Twelve: 1920

the strange, unsettling words. She felt her face grow stiff with something like fear. Numb, she reached for the other envelope. Fran's letter was a long one, written over several days and she breathed in deeply, and picked it up, getting lost in the first few pages of blessedly mundane news of children, farm and family. Then Fran wrote about a group of RIC who called to the house, with guns, demanding to see Martin.

"And he barked it out: 'Where's your husband? I give you three minutes to fetch him.'"

One of them searched the house, called the others in to look at that picture you sent me of yourself and Eamon de Valera. They were very interested in that alright, but they didn't break it or anything. Two more raided the outhouses and took all the eggs they could find. I was mostly trying to keep the children quiet. When they came to where Martin was, they took the pony by the head, turned him on the road and being fully armed, forced him and the Duffys as well to cart stones to repair the bridges blown up by the IRA. And them hardly talking to us since the rebellion, but it made no difference to these lads. They kept their guns on them all the time. Martin didn't know whether they'd be shot or not, even if they did the work, but they knew they'd be shot if they didn't. I just waited. I didn't know if he'd be coming back or not. We don't know what's going to happen from one day to another, or how long we'll be alive; the shootings and ambushes are coming nearer to us. We have no heart to do anything except just our day's work.

This is what they call freedom now, Jimmy. This is what they're waving that new flag for. All the young men of the parish are taking sides and fighting now. Fighting these new men, these Black & Tans. That's what they call them, because they have no right uniforms, not like the British army, but only wear a bit of this and a bit of that. And if they're not fighting the Black & Tans, they're fighting each other. Some families are hardly speaking. The Deegans are the worst of them — two brothers there, and they live together. They work the fields together. They walk together to Mass, but don't speak. It's not right."

She stopped reading to try to imagine men with guns in a place as quiet as Rockfield. She was imagining them in white robes, until she corrected herself. She read on.

"But sure, we'll keep going. It's all we can do. I'll finish and post this letter now, as there is no more news. Oh, you remember Tommy Banahan? Little Tommy with the limp? You and him used to be very great with each other when you were young, weren't you? He died last week. He fell into the Shannon, they said, on the far side, over from the temperance hall, after being at a meeting. Well, it's not like him to be in the temperance hall, but who knows? He hasn't been right since he came back from the war. Ah, he's been very odd. Up walking the fields, talking to himself. Hanging around the post office in town — not going to Mrs Harney in the local place, but all the way in to Athlone to do his business. But hasn't Mrs. Harney a niece working in the town office, so she knew well he was going there — buying stamps for America. He used to be drinking on his own, they say, early in the day. He's living alone now since his mother passed. Or he was. Michael Callaghan at the funeral Mass said Tommy had been telling him that you might be home to him. I told him he must be mistaken, that you wouldn't be coming home for a scrap like that. Sure you wouldn't, Siss?

With best wishes from everyone here.

Your loving sister,

Fran

Little Tommy with the limp. Imagine him being known that way? Tommy with the laughing eyes; Tommy that could make everyone laugh at school. Tommy who decorated his homework with pencilled birds. Tommy who was gathering his money to make a start, who went to war, promising he'd be thinking of her, who got hurt and who was waiting for her. Until now. She could imagine the place where Tommy fell. She knew the spot just across the bridge, beside the Royal Bank of Ireland, with the shadow of the barrack wall stretching across the river, the dark water shimmering, slick as an eel. He had no business down there, except watching the married men's quarters on the far side. She could see him standing on the edge of the cool, relieving dark, not noticed by anyone passing over the bridge. She could see the whole thing in her head. She remembered Mary Catherine writing about him walking nearby. Now she knew for sure he was walking alone all that time, and then he fell. Just slipped on the bank.

But he wasn't a faller, Tommy. There was nothing accidental about him. He made mistakes often, but he always made a choice, brave or foolish or both. Like going to war. She wondered how it would have been if they had all stayed, and just let things drift? She wondered what it meant to say he was "not right in the head." Sure that could mean anything at all, and now there was nobody to tell her what he was like for those last few months. Tommy, the hair-puller, the charmer, the loyal, the sketcher, the British solider. Not a faller though. No. He didn't fall. Whatever he did, he chose to do.

She realised now the whole town must hold such stories. That she had never really understood her father's life or her mother's, not knowing the landscape they grew up in, and seeing everything through the imperfect lens of the child she was. The same with Fran. The same with Jimmy. Could anyone know anybody really? Would anybody ever know her?

She went to her room, took down her best writing paper, and wrote to Tommy one more time.

"I'm not going back. I want to see you, Tommy. I wanted to see you, and Fran and her babies. I wanted to see home, all the places that mean things to me, but they are few, and I know for you it's all been overwritten by new memories.

I'm too old and too tired to start to understand all that. I'm going to stay here. I will write to Fran, and oh I wish I could still write to you. I love you. You know I love you? You knew? But I'm not going back. Now, I wish you were here. I wish you could come, and we could be somewhere like New York that means nothing to me and nothing to you, and we could sit in some empty place and drink a cocktail and look at each other across the table, your blue eyes, and try to make sense of our lives."

The note was short, but it took a long time to write. Then she picked it up along with a rose that was dying in the stone planter outside the front door. Lacking a fireplace to burn them, she laid them in the kitchen sink, turned on the water, and watched the ink swirl and fade until there was nothing left to read, just some

Chapter Twelve: 1920

pale pink petals floating on the darkened water. She stood there shivering for a long time.

She read his letter again, his question. What was it, after all, that had kept her here? What was it that she wanted, that she'd never bothered to articulate to herself? It was time she stopped drifting. It was the least she could do, to honour Tommy, to maybe be able to answer him in time.

She stepped out the back of the rectory and crossed to the church.

The women were in early for confession. They came before the priests, to do a round or two of the stations of the cross before settling in, in a queue outside the confessional, kneeling forward piously in their blue and pink coats. Marcella knew them well by now, knew them to be good women for the most part. Most were willing to pitch in to help other people. Some of them were kind. She wondered what they had to confess. Did they just come because it was the First Friday, or had they been saving shame to bring along and be absolved?

The line was always longest outside Jimmy's box, and while you could take that as a sign he was popular, Marcella knew it was mostly because he was quick. He listened. Never asked questions, fired out a penance and gave absolution for whatever list they've recited to him. Marcella always went to Tony. It would have been impossible to confess to her brother.

She had her standard list: a little pride, a bit of impatience, some anger. She had found ways to make a confession that didn't give too much away, but still got at the truth. It had to be true, or what was the point? She'd say, "I felt pride," instead of "I was upset that Jimmy didn't recognise all the good work I've done with those new Sodality ladies up in St. Francis, getting them to do things properly." "Felt pride" was all Tony needed to hear. Or she'd say, "I showed anger to another," and that would cover it, without showing him the mess behind those words.

Now, she had more to add, more to quickly code. More regret. What was it that had kept her from Tommy all these years? Was she ashamed of him? Did she want more than he could offer? Did she want too much? Was it really all just pride? And why could she not have been honest in that last letter she sent him. Was that lies, to say she needed only a few years more? She sought out forgiveness in the place she knew she would receive it. Latin absolution, words she didn't understand, as soothing as the sound of a train carrying her away. Tony never asked her for details, though she knew he did with other penitents. He liked to tease things out with them, to find the root of their trouble. He was happiest in the confessional, Marcella thought, listening in the dark, ministering to one person at a time instead of holding a whole congregation in his hand as Jimmy did at the pulpit. Maybe that's why they were such good friends, having each found what they wanted to do, and being able to do it together.

She was back to Tommy's question again. What was it that she wanted? As she queued, she wondered if she were a priest, which kind of priest would she be? She didn't think she could work like Tony, locked in a dark confessional. She liked to be free, in some way, coming and going when she pleased. But she couldn't hold a room like Jimmy. She didn't have his way of spinning words. Still, people talked to her, and sometimes she could help them. "If I were a priest," she thought, "I'd be like Tony, but in the open, not the dark. If I were a priest, and not only a priest's sister."

Chapter Twelve: 1920

She waited her turn for Tony and told him about being angry. And proud. And telling a lie. She said her five Hail Marys and three Our Fathers and then she really did feel a little better. She had made mistakes. She had expected too much, been too dismissive, judged Tommy too harshly. She would become better now, more kind and braver. She would find a way to minister to people. She slipped into the side chapel, and lit a candle for Tommy, a candle for Jackson, and watched the flickering shadows they cast, finding no words to form prayers.

Lifting her head, she saw the girl skulking in the shadow of the side aisle on the Blessed Mother side, kneeling in behind a pillar. She was a skinny little thing even though up close, she looked older than her age. Strange how her shape was a child, but the eyes and that full, pouting mouth almost made a woman of her. Marcella knew her on sight and watched as she slipped up two more rows, and oh, she was kneeling now by the women in the queue for Jimmy's confessional. What could she be thinking?

Marcella was up and on her feet before taking time to think, and Bess saw her before she got to her pew. Later Marcella was glad of that. Otherwise she didn't know what she'd have said in front of half the altar society, kneeling there. Bess caught Marcella's intent in her walk, or maybe it was showing in her face, because she slipped out the end and walked ahead of her, into the side chapel at the back where they talked in fierce whispers.

"Bessie Stubbs. What do you think you're doing here? This is confession, a sacrament. It's not for the likes of you."

"Ain't it? Don't anyone have the right to come in here and talk to a priest?"

Something Bigger

"Confession's not for talking, Bess."

Marcella stopped short, hearing her own anger, hearing how wrong it sounded, and she fresh from forgiveness. She stopped. Started again, talking half to herself.

"Ah, how were you to know it's a sacrament? What do you know about anything? It's not a place to just show up and talk, Bess. What brought you in here to begin with?"

"I been here before, Miss Coyle. I just never talked to a priest. That's all I want to do."

"Well it's just not right, Bess, to walk in like that."

"I gotta learn, Miss Coyle. You can't stop me learning."

They sat together, talking at cross purposes. It seemed unlikely that Bess was only looking to learn, but then Marcella wondered if she was able to judge what was best for this girl? She'd been wrong about Tommy, about how she felt about him, about what he could do. Her mind abruptly ran far away from the still air of the church, to a small schoolroom, chalk-dust hanging in the air, something just out of reach of her memory, and Tommy's eyes, smiling at her. It hurt, so she jerked her mind back to the cold pew, the shuffle of people moving along the row towards the confessional, and the tick-tock of high heels as Louise Pettigro sashayed back down to the door, her business done. Bess's eyes were on her. Marcella could see hunger there, and she made a quick decision.

"Don't come here again, Bess. We'll find some other place to talk. I'll send you some message, and we'll talk properly then."

Bess nodded and left. Marcella stayed on in the cool of the side chapel, her mind racing. Something was not right here. She almost felt she should go back

Chapter Twelve: 1920

to Tony, get absolution again. But this time she didn't know what she could confess. It wasn't anger, or pride. It wasn't spite, but not far off. There was something in her that was glad to chase the girl out of the church, and that was a part of herself she didn't trust. She made a promise then, silently, though she wasn't sure if it was to God or to herself, to find a way to talk to this troublesome girl, to give her the benefit of whatever doubt she could find in her heart.

Chapter Thirteen

1921

Birmingham Age Herald, April 1921

**FATHER COYLE SEES
COMING SETTLEMENT OF
EUROPE'S TRIALS**

Father Coyle's Views

**The World War has left the world
fight-weary, financially bankrupt, cyn-
ically mistrustful and bereft of those
ideals that people were wont to laud in
the days before. And no peace, this of
course is a truism, save a peace founded on justice will last or endure.**

Johanna came alone to church on Sunday. April
didn't care to come downtown. That was OK. It might
not have been safe to take her little one here to St.
Paul's. Jackson used to come with her, and it was still
hard to get used to walking without him on a Sunday
morning. That had been one of their best times, walk-

ing down from Longfield together, him all smart and spruced up. They'd talk so much: maybe something he'd read that week, or the school, or the war, or the steel mills and what all they were doing. They'd talk about the big things, not just children and food and weather. She had nobody to talk to like that now.

Except, sometimes the Father. Sometimes. He reminded her of Jackson then. When he'd drive her home, looking right ahead, the straightness of his back. Maybe that's why she kept coming to St. Paul's on Sunday, walking all the way downtown and taking her place in the back pews.

Jackson used to say they oughtn't to sit in the back, but that didn't bother her. They never sat together anyway – him on the right side with the men, the Sacred Heart side as they called it; she on the Blessed Mother side, under the balcony, right under the green window of St. Patrick. Father wore green too this morning. He sang the psalm, off kilter like always. He read the gospel slow. She liked to hear him read. It was that passage from Luke about loving your enemy, not just your friends. Johanna was never sure about that one. She didn't know she could love those men who took Jackson.

James closed the book, and the congregation settled back to listen to him preach.

"The Gospel of Luke tells us to give — give to all who ask. Give and it will be given unto you. You all know that verse. But that last part, waiting to have it given unto you, that's not the reason to give."

There were still stragglers coming in the back door. Johanna didn't turn to look at them, though she could feel them staring. Some folks, she knew, didn't like that she came in here. Other churches in the city were segregated — a church for Black folks, a church for whites, a church for Syrians. Johanna didn't like the burning feeling of being stared at. She looked up at the Father again.

"You all know, we are facing need, not only in our parish of St. Paul's, but in our sister parishes. There are people in this city who are doing great work, working for themselves, but you can help."

He was talking about Longfield now, talking about the church they were building there. They had talked together about how a little more money from this part of town could move that along.

"They're raising churches, building schools, serving the Lord in a hundred ways and we can be a part of it if we can find it in our hearts to give. But there's a better reason still, to give. Now, you've given, in this congregation, generously. You've cleared all the debt that was on this fine church when I came here. You've repaired the rectory and provided well for all of us priests. But there is more to giving than paying a bill here and there."

Johanna stole a glance back towards the door. It was men who were standing there, though there were seats up the front. It was always men. They were shuffling cause the sermon was too long for them. Some of them looked like they wanted to go outside and smoke. She wished they would. She looked for a little too long, and one caught her eye and glared at her. She tilted up her head and turned back to the front.

"Here's why we must give. To give is to renounce our claim on the world. To give is to connect us to something bigger than ourselves, to find our purpose and commit to it. But you have to give enough."

Johanna fumbled in her pockets for her offering.

Chapter Thirteen: 1921

She didn't see any of those straggler men doing the same.

"I'm not going to stand here and tell you what enough is. You know the Lord valued the widow's mite more than the Pharisee's gold. You have to give enough so you notice, so it changes you. You have to give just a little more than you think you can."

She looked back again to check those men out and saw another latecomer, standing in the shadow of the pillar. That Stubbs girl. What was she doing there, gazing up at the altar like she was searching for something she lost?

"When you give, you get outside yourself and your own cares. I'm not just talking about the offering plate, or about money. Give more time to someone. Give more of your talent, more of yourself. Give what you have and then try to give more. Give until it hurts. Only then is there sacrifice."

Fr. James stepped down from the pulpit and it seemed to Johanna that the congregation exhaled. He held them all when he preached. They sat up straight and listened. She looked back again, and Bess Stubbs was gone. Whatever had brought her here, it was no good. She'd felt that since the first day she saw her. Those pretty blue eyes, so wide and so serious. That mouth all set down at the corners. Not satisfied, that's how she looked to Johanna. Never going to be satisfied. Johanna saw how she could smile, lighting up her face like sunshine, and how the smile fell off her face like a mask when she looked away. She never tried that kind of thing on Johanna, so she wasn't fooled.

The offering plate went around slowly, and she could tell it was a good collection. She was glad for the project in Longfield. She wasn't so sure about sacrifice.

Something Bigger

She wondered if anyone there, any of the well-dressed ladies up front, say, knew about the kind of sacrifice April and she knew. She didn't know that the Father did either – what had he ever given up? Still, there was something steady about him, about being able to come to St. Paul's and hear him. It made her feel safe, like one day she would walk in here with Jackson again. And if there ever was news about Jackson, she felt it would make its way to St. Paul's like a dog coming home to be fed. One day. Until then, she'd come to church, and give what she could, though already she knew, she had given more than enough.

* * * * *

Marcella knew it was risky to go near Stubbs's barbershop. There were many reasons why it was no place for her — a woman, a Catholic, a Coyle — but she had made her mind up to find Bess, and this was the only place she knew she might be. She had dreamed all night of Tommy, sweet Tommy and him slipping into the river at night. She needed action to push that image out of her head. She needed to do something, anything at all that was her own idea, so she would feel she was doing more than drifting along in her brother's shadow. So she set off walking down 3rd without much of a plan. She thought she might glance in the doorway of the barbershop, and see if Bess was there, maybe catch her eye, but there was such a glare from the sun that all she could see from the sidewalk was a bright oblong of tiled floor lit up from the doorway, and the rest of the shop in shadow. She kept walking, and once past the window she stopped, close to the wall, pretending there was a problem with her parasol, fidgeting with it and listening to the growl of men's voices from inside.

Chapter Thirteen: 1921

"Someone's gonna have to knock the hell out of that big mouth. Next time we see him, we may have to kill him."

"There's other ways to silence a man. Easier ways than that, Jed. We can scare his mouth shut. Easy."

"Not him. He thinks he's something special. Anyway, he's got too many ways to agitate, papers and pulpit."

"Papers don't matter none, you know that. All they print is lies anyway. You know that. 'Cept Mr. Vaughan's papers and The Menace. All the rest is fake."

"Sure, they're fake, Abe, but folks read'em. And plenty of folks go along to his Catholic services, and they fill up that church of his Sundays, and just sit there, letting him spout his lies at them ..."

She realised they were talking about Jimmy, and must have gasped audibly, because the silence that fell was sudden and thick. She looked up to see Abner Stubbs filling the doorway, just watching her. It took more courage than she knew she had to turn and face him.

"Evenin' Miss Coyle." His shadow fell at her feet as he stepped out of the barbershop. She looked up from his black scuffed boots to his face. He was standing too close to her, closer than he ought. She could smell his cheap cologne and even a little sweat, dried into his shirt. He was taller than she thought he would be. Taller than Jimmy, maybe. For a barber, his hair had too much oil, and some of it had soaked into the side of his collar, staining it. His hair was slicked to one side, like older men did to hide a bald patch. His voice was cold.

"Mister Stubbs. Good day to you."

"What can we do for you today, Miss?"

Something Bigger

That pause before the "Miss," it felt like an insult somehow. She fought the urge to walk away.

"I wondered if Bess were here, Mr. Stubbs? I would like to visit with her."

They locked eyes for what seems like a long time. There was something in there that didn't match his stern face. Something not so controlled, like fear or excitement. She found herself straightening her back, becoming as tall as she could. She knew he wouldn't answer her, about Bess, but she didn't want to turn away and come back the way she had come. It was oddly exciting to stand there, looking up at this man, feeling like she was facing him down.

One of the men in the shop broke the spell, coughing a rattling smoker's cough. It seemed to bring him back to some kind of control, and he smiled with just his mouth, turning to go back inside.

"You take care, little lady. These streets ain't safe, you know."

"Safe enough for law-abiding people, Mr. Stubbs."

Marcella smiled too, as cold and sweet as she could and she walked slowly, only a little way past the door, and slipped into the shadow of next door's awning. Berry's Fancy Goods was closed for lunch, and the streets were quiet in the noonday heat. The lines of light and shadow were hard, and she knew she couldn't be seen here.

That man coughed again, a rattling, phlegmy cough that went on for too long and took too much effort. Whoever he was, he was sicker than he knew. When the cough subsided, he started right in to grousing.

"She's got a nerve, calling round here like that, as if she's got a right."

"What call's she got, visiting with your girl, Abe?"

Chapter Thirteen: 1921

"Well, she ain't the only one coming sniffing around after little Bessie, is she?"

That was a new voice, thin and reedy. You could hear a grin in his tone, like he thought all the men would laugh with him. Instead there was a silence that would deafen you if you knew how to hear it. Which he didn't, it seems, because he persisted.

"Yep, I reckon there'll be plenty more to come calling."

"Shut up, Joe."

"And they ain't all right-standing folks either, is they? Why one of 'em ..."

"Joe. That's enough."

"One of 'em done call around last night, didn't he?"

"What's that you say, Joe?"

Stubbs's voice should have warned him, coming slow as treacle. Like a fool, the man continued.

"Come on now. Ain't you all seen that wallpaper-hangin' Mexican hanging around? He ain't here for a shave, is he? He's come calling for what he can see, what sweet thing he might ..."

There was a crash, like a chair falling, and a man was flung physically out the door. Marcella pressed herself deeper into the shadowy doorway. Stubbs stepped out into the light, his open razor in his hand. A small man was scrabbling on his back like a cockroach, edging away into the street, dangerously into the path of oncoming horses. The few people on the sidewalk stopped to stare making a small circle of onlookers and Marcella took the chance to step quickly out behind them, not turning back for the raised voices, the slamming door. She walked all the way around the block to avoid passing back that way.

When she got home, she was shaking. She had

an idea now why Bess seemed so urgent, so much in need.

* * * * *

Marcella didn't really like Bess. Perhaps she had never liked her, but now she had made a promise that she couldn't seem to drop. Then there was that curious tie between her and the haughty child, that little woollen bunny rabbit from years ago, the fear she'd been unkind to her. There was more there than curiosity and boredom at work; it was time she followed through on something. She was so busy with parish work now, even Jimmy called her a powerhouse. Work was soothing, easier than thinking. It saved her from missing the long letters she used to write to Tommy. She had bought a journal, as a replacement, but found it hard to begin. It sat on the dressing table in her bedroom like an accusation. It was easier to be busy, so she worked harder than she had before, organising donation drives, drawing up rosters for church decoration, flower arranging, hospital visits and food runs. She set up two new Sodalities and a care group for the orphanage. In between, she went calling on local houses. She called it "visiting the sick," but in fact no sickness was required. She knocked on doors to see who might need a food parcel, help with school, or to join in a women's group. This part of the work was the best for her. It felt openly useful.

It was also the part of her work that gave her a story for what she did. The very next day after calling to the barbershop, she went out in the evening and knocked on the wrong door. Or so she told herself afterwards and told everyone else too. The wrong door, as though it were a mistake. As though she hadn't intended to get there, sooner or later. She'd been watching Bess Stubbs pass the rectory for days now, watching her dawdling home from school in the late afternoon and sidling in the back of the church as though nobody could see. Marcella also watched her father on the courthouse veranda, next door to the Rectory. She saw him waiting in the shade by the front door, or smoking on the steps while the sun shifted his shadow around. She saw young couples come by, uncertain and a little lost, he could see the hesitancy in them, the scrubbed-up, worn-down shoes of the men, the skinned-back hair of the girls, all too young. Stubbs would straighten up and break a smile out on his stern face. He'd offer a smoke, sometimes, and what do you know, he had a minister's licence and a pocket full of brass rings so they could do the wedding just right there and then. He'd wave them inside like he owned the place, and they'd be out the door again in ten minutes. Jimmy told her "the marrying parson" wasn't just what others called him, that he used that name himself now, like a badge of honour.

Sometimes Bess was early, and she'd hurry past without looking up but Marcella worried that he would see her. She saw that he watched as Bess passed the courthouse, but she'd be out of his sight when she went around the corner, and that was always how far she walked before darting across the road and disappearing into the church. She saw Stubbs watching the side of the rectory too, sometimes. On a long hot day, he'd stare with a face like stone. It seemed to Marcella that he hated the place. Like it was personal. Surely Bess knew how crazy it was for her to visit the church, so close to him? That afternoon, Marcella saw her step out of the church, quick as a fox, and cross the block to her own house. She let herself in with a key, so she had to be home alone. It was time. Calling to her was no accident.

Something Bigger

As soon as she knocked on the faded blue door, Marcella began to regret it. She looked quickly up and down the street. Although she saw nobody she knew, anyone at all might see her here and wonder what she was doing waiting to get into the Stubbs house. That stern-faced old crone crossing the side street; the delivery boy who just cycled past. Any one of them could tell Abner Stubbs. She was about to move away when the door opened without warning and she found herself eye to eye with Bess. Recognition flashed across the girl's face, and she stood quickly aside for Marcella to come in.

The house was almost empty. Marcella had been visiting poor places all week, but this was not what she expected. Two chairs flanked a table covered by a grimy oilcloth. The walls had no pictures, just one small chipped mirror tacked to the inside of the front door. And yet there stood Bess, with her perfect hair, her immaculate collar, her tight beauty looking completely out of place.

"Can we talk, Bess?"

"Not here, Miss Coyle. Not now. Momma will be home soon. I can't talk now."

"But you want to?"

"I need to. You know that."

The expression on her face: it took Marcella a while to read it. Fear.

"Come around to the rectory then, Bess. Call in this time tomorrow afternoon to the back door, and we can talk."

The offer was quickly made, sounding thoughtless. Marcella slipped out and was home before her heartbeat slowed to normal.

* * * * *

Chapter Thirteen: 1921

Dear Diary,

Guess who called around today? That Catholic lady from the priest's house. Miss Coyle. She called right to our house, and asked me around to the rectory, any time at all. Maybe she's smarter than I thought. Maybe she can help.

I'm fixing to go. Momma would die if she knew. Daddy would kill me, like as not. He came home yesterday so angry; he couldn't even talk. Don't know what was bugging him so. We had to eat without a sound, just for him. I went to bed early to get out of the room. I hate when he's like that, raving on about people who are ruining his life. Most of the time, that's Catholics and Father Coyle. Imagine – just imagine how red in the face he'd get if he thought I'd been invited around there for afternoon tea?

Daddy thinks I'm still his little girl. He's wrong. He'll see. Like Brer Rabbit, I can be a trickster. I can get my way in secret if I can't get it all out in the open. I'll get myself away from him and Momma both. Just watch me, Diary.

* * * * *

Next afternoon, Bess hesitated at the rectory gate long enough for one quick glance to the courtroom steps. Then she opened the latch and walked right around to the back of the rectory, as though she'd done it a thousand times. Marcella felt a thrill. She had made this happen. Bess was standing outside the screen door, and she gestured for her to come in. They smiled at each other, as Bess stepped across the threshold, looking at one another with open expressions, each seeming happy to see the other.

Something Bigger

"Sit down, Bess. Sit right down. Let me get you something to drink."

And that is how it began. Sweet tea and listening, while Bess talked. She told her first about finishing up in school, about a song she'd learned, a new dress. She spoke like a book review, and Marcella was impatient until she realised she'd learned this talk by heart like a prepared speech. She sipped her drink so slowly the ice all melted. They both seemed to want the light and trivial talk to last a while, before getting serious. Marcella didn't say much. She watched with concentration, as though a half wild animal were consenting to be tamed. They didn't talk about what Bess had asked for, in the church. Instead, Marcella lent her a book she'd read as a teenager, a blue bonnet for a date, as though they were friends. And then when Bess learned that Jimmy was out, they arranged for her to call again at the same time the following week, when they would all three meet, and they could talk. Marcella walked her around the side of the house, and watched her leave, squaring her shoulders a little in the shadow of the church then stepping quickly out on the street. She was humming to herself as she came back in the screen door, unprepared for Johanna, standing as though she'd been there all along, left hand on hip, right palm flat on the table, head to one side, quizzical.

"Just what do you think you're doing, Child, having that Stubbs girl around here?"

"What do you mean, Johanna? She just called."

"She just called? She just called. Seventeen years living on this street and now she just up and decides to call round for sweet tea? Come on, Miss Cella, I know you asked her. Now I'm asking you – just what do you think you're doing? Don't you know who she is?"

Marcella flushed.

Chapter Thirteen: 1921

"Yes, Johanna. Yes, I know who she is. Do you? Have you ever spoken to her? Or are you just judging her by that mean old father of hers. She's a scared, smart girl who needs a friend. She doesn't have a sister. She has no one to ..."

"Is that what you think, Miss Cella? You think that little scrap of a thing can be like a sister to you? A play doll for you to play with?"

"No. A friend, I said."

"No good will come of this, mark my words. No good. No. What would the Good Father think if he knew?"

"Matter of fact, Johanna, Jimmy does know. And he approves. He's very happy about it. So if you have a problem, I suggest you take it up with him."

The lie slipped out easily. It couldn't be put back. It had its effect though. Johanna stopped, mid-stream, and there was no more about it. As soon as Jimmy got home, she made for his study. She needed to tell him before he heard from anyone else.

"Really! Really, Siss? She just called in cold, just like that?" He didn't seem as perturbed by the news as she'd expected.

"I wonder what she wants?"

"Well nothing, I think."

"Ah now Siss. You know she wants something, or she wouldn't be here. Well, we'll see in time, I guess. I can't see good coming of it, but if she's going to call, she'll call. Just be careful, Siss."

The next morning, Jimmy left for two days of meetings in Mobile. Marcella saw him off at the railway station and walked back towards the rectory feeling bereft. She had come to realise since getting the news about Tommy, that Jimmy was her anchor now. There was a poem she had learned at school, perhaps even from her father, about a man who had gone mad and lived in the trees, talking to the birds. The only line she remembered went "unsettled, panicky, astray." That's how she felt. She imagined how it would be if Jimmy were on a train going north instead of south, the two of them together, heading for New York to catch a ship to Ireland. She could picture the slow boat trip, time for them both to walk around the deck, to talk and let the sky do its magic, changing from blue to grey, easing them into a damp island way of thinking so that by the time they'd get to Cork they'd be thinking like Irish people again. Jimmy would be so excited to go, to see the country free, if only he could peel himself away from whatever it is that held him so tightly to parish work. She could picture Fran and her brood waiting for them both at the station in Athlone. Mother would be made up to have her prodigal son returned. Then she realised she had placed Tommy in the picture too, awkward at first, grown manly and distant. That meant none of it was real. None of that could happen.

Instead, Jimmy was gone south, to spend the day arguing with the Bishop and while he was away, even for a day, nothing would get done. Nobody could make even the smallest decision without him. When he was gone, she could see most clearly that he was the centre of all of their worlds.

Then Bess called, unexpectedly, ducking in the side gate like a thief and appearing on the back porch. She stood there, in silhouette, waiting for the screen door to open to her.

"He's not here, Bess. He's in Mobile for a few days."

"I know, Miss Coyle. It's you I wanted to talk to if you got time?"

Marcella looked at her sharply, pleased and suddenly gratified. Bess looked back with real warmth in those blue eyes of hers.

"Why sure, Bessie. Come on in."

Bess sat, and spoke slowly. Marcella could see that like the first time she called, she had prepared her words, so she sat back a little in the kitchen chair, to let her talk.

"It's about what I said, Miss Coyle."

"About you turning Catholic?"

"That and more. I need to explain, and I need your advice. You know I've been walking out with this fine man. He's a serious man with a good trade and an American passport he got from fighting in the War. He's a Catholic man. And he's asked me... he asked me ..."

"Yes, Bess?" Marcella's voice was soft, almost a whisper. "What has he asked you, girl?"

"Miss Coyle, he's been and asked me to marry him. What am I to do? He wants us to marry right away, now I'm coming of age, and move to Chicago so we can start a new life up North. I think I want to. I'm going to need to get away from Daddy, so maybe this is the way? We could be happy, couldn't we? We could have a good life. Do you think so, Miss Coyle?"

"You say this man is a Catholic? Does your mother know? Do you love him, Bess?"

"Momma don't know a thing. But he loves me. I'm sure of that. He loved me, he said, from the first time he came to our house to hang paper for Daddy. He loves me for sure, like no one ever has before. Oh, and he's handsome, Miss Cella. The softest brown eyes, and a face like a film star."

"But you, Bess? Do you love him?"

"I can't be sure, Miss Cella. That's what I wanted

to ask you. How do I know? He's quiet. He's kind. He's been nothing but good to me. He makes me feel safe. Is that love?"

Marcella wondered what to say. What did she know of love? She thought of Mimi, who from her latest letter was living with a new man in New York, and of the chill between Lucille and George Vaughan, and her sticking with him still. She thought of her own long nights, and the memory of Carlo, and his voice in her head repeating what he had said about the difference between her and women who ended up happy.

Then she thought of Tommy. There was a kind of suppressed excitement coming off Bess like steam. She didn't look trapped or bullied. She looked free and open, with that full, downturned mouth and those wide, clear eyes. What would she be waiting for if she waited? Who else was ever going to come along to brave the wrath of Old Man Stubbs? Who would want to be the young man dating his daughter? Whoever this suitor was, he had courage, and that was something. But there again, Stubbs was her father. Surely that should still mean something. Should a father be side-lined like this by his own daughter.

"Bess, what would your father say?"

"He can't know. If he knew, there'd be trouble and that's a fact."

"Don't you think he has a right to know? You're his daughter. His only child. I'm sure he has plans for you."

"Plans? My Daddy ain't like that. He never wants anything for anyone else. You know him, Miss Coyle?"

"Well, yes, I know him. Or I've seen him."

"Well then you know, Miss Coyle. My Daddy's what's known around here as a good man. He's a minister. He works in the courthouse. He's on Howdy terms with the mayor. He's a good man. Anyone will tell you that. You can't fight a man like that."

Bess's left index finger was absently rubbing a small, fading bruise that Marcella hadn't noticed before, just below her right eye.

"What are you saying, Bess?"

"I'm saying he looks like a good man, so that's who he'll always be, no matter what he does. Can't you see, Miss Coyle? Momma and I ain't no match for that. He's the man out there in public. He's the one that's known in this city. We never had a friend between us, Momma and me. You're the only friend I've ever made in this town, Miss Cella."

"What happened to your eye?"

"What do you think? I didn't walk into no door if that's what you're thinking. I didn't fall down no stairs or get into a fight. What do you think? "

Bess seemed older when she spoke like this. The bruise was sharp and dark. They were both quiet for a long time, and then she spoke again.

"Daddy has his rules, Miss Coyle. Good rules for good living. Hard to argue with that. But rules are made to be broken, and Momma and me, we break them all the time without trying. You should see the way he lights up when we break a rule, almost like he's happy. He gets his chance then to lay down the law, to unbuckle his belt, and that buckle's sharp."

"You can't stand for that, Bess. You and your Momma, you know you should tell someone."

"Who exactly are we going to tell, in this city? His church? His Klan? His friends at the Courthouse? Who'd believe us? And even if they did, there's no good in believing, if you don't do nothing about it?

Those Klan brothers, they're never going to let anything be done about this."

"But ..."

"But nothing, Miss Cella. Nothing. That's what's going to change if I stay here in this city. I need out, Miss Cella. I need out fast."

Outside a dog somewhere in the distance began to bark, and then stopped.

"Do you want this, Bess? That's the question. Is this what you want? A wedding?"

"Yes, Miss Cella. I want a life. Something more than this life. I got a chance just now."

Tommy came suddenly into Marcella's mind, his laughing eyes, his young face, the older way she'd pictured him from his wartime letter, an older version still, limping by the Shannon river, a boy who wanted a chance. She turned to Bess.

"Then take your chance, Bess. And may it work out for the best."

"Oh Miss Coyle, thank you. You'll talk to the Father for me? I'll go and turn Catholic to make this all go right. That's what Diego says. He wants a proper church wedding, and Father Coyle to do the marriage. And won't you be my witness? When we get married, I mean? I'll need a maid of honour. Would you be mine?"

"Why sure, Bess." Marcella's throat thickened with unexpected emotion. "I'll talk to him as soon as he comes back. I'll set it all in order for you. It's the least I can do."

* * * * *

Abner Stubbs sat that night at the head of his table reading The Menace while Ethel prepared dinner.

216

Chapter Thirteen: 1921

Bess set the table around him. He ignored her, intent on the tightly printed paragraphs, squinting over the longer sentences. Ethel laid out the food, waited a minute, maybe two, and then asked, keeping her voice light:

"Honey, couldn't you put that aside for a little, just while we eat? Or why don't you tell us some of the news you read there so we can all share it?"

As soon as she spoke, she regretted it, Bess recognised the way her mother's smile slipped for a second before she put it on again. Her Daddy dropped the newspaper onto the floor and attacked his dinner, not meeting either of their eyes. Angry again, so early in the evening. Something seething in him, like boiling water that could hiss out. When he did speak, it was in a low, edgy tone.

"News. Well, there's news from our own street here in this paper. That priest, that Coyle man, it says right here he got himself a flag, and hung it up the front of his church there, back last month. Not even an American flag. Irish, he claimed it was, and you know it says right here that Ireland ain't even a country, don't even have a flag. Who knows what traitorous lies they're telling in that church? They tried to break England, and next thing you know they'll be trying to break America ..."

He talked and talked, and Bess kept her eyes on her food. She hadn't seen any flag in the church, but then she hadn't really been looking for one. Maybe it was there somewhere. The meat was tough and full of gristle. She felt a little sick but wasn't going to leave any food on the plate to get his attention. She waited for a lull.

Something Bigger

"Daddy, there's a school trip Thursday. Over to Bessemer. It's not gonna cost anything. Can I go along? It will mean being late home."

"What trip, Bessie?" Her Momma's voice was sharp. Did she suspect? "You never mentioned no trip. Who all is going?"

"Let her be, Ethel. You can't stop schoolin'. Sure, Bessie, you can go, but be sure to come right home after, you hear?"

"Thanks Daddy." Bess smiled him a little girl smile and didn't meet her mother's eye. She could hardly wait to get up to her room, write the note to Diego to say Thursday would be a good day. She would not be expected home until late, and they could make plans. She could hardly wait, but she did. She cut her meat and chewed slowly. By now she had learned that some things took patience.

Chapter Fourteen

1921

All morning the sky had been steel, hanging over the city like a hot roof. Marcella sat and sewed in the shade. She wrote the same letter to Fran, and Mother, and Mimi. She made the same jokes in each one. She wished she could write to Tommy and thought again about the journal she had lost so long ago, and her new one, waiting on the dresser. She would start it that week, she resolved. She had drunk far too much sweet, cold tea in the hot, still air and now her head was jangling and her throat was dry. This storm better break soon, she thought.

Walking inside, she saw Jimmy at his desk, writing too, but faster than her. More focused, with his cool drink warming, neglected beside him. He never seemed to get tired of writing and working, but headachey and cross as she was, she was tired of seeing it. Tired of watching him wear himself out like this. It had been years now.

Something Bigger

"Jimmy, leave off your letters. Can't you keep your preaching for the pulpit?"

"Ah Siss. Sure you know not everyone comes in the door of the church."

"Can you take a break? Could we not go drive somewhere together just for fun, for a change? Or even just sit outside and talk like we used to?"

"When did we used to do that, Siss?"

He was joking. She knew that. And because he didn't lift his head, he didn't see he had hurt her. Because it was true — when had they ever had time to sit and talk? Not that she could remember. She felt tired, though she hadn't done any work to speak of all day. Why had she thought she could be a help to him at this work of his? Because that's what it was — his work, not hers. His church. She saw it clearly, now.

"Jimmy?"

He took a while to look up, he when he saw her serious face, he put his pen down, waiting.

"It's about Bessie Stubbs."

* * * * *

"You're serious, James? You're really thinking of doing this?"

"I'm surprised myself, Tony, but yes. I am."

"How? How could it be a good idea for you to marry Stubbs's daughter right here in St. Paul's?"

"Well, isn't it what we do when people need marrying? Why wouldn't I do this?"

"Because it's a sham, James."

"You can't know that. She's Catholic now, right enough. I talked to them up at St. Michael's and Anthony says she's sincere. I'm not going to doubt her faith. Why would we deny her?"

Chapter Fourteen: 1921

"Because it's dangerous, James. For everyone. Because ... you don't need me to tell you this ... you know who her father is."

"Abner Stubbs is no threat. Isn't he a man of the cloth now?"

"Not our cloth."

"Ah now, enough of that. He's a Minister, Tony."

"Even if he is, you know he's in the Klan. Can you imagine what they'll do with this? You won't just be some uppity priest. You'll be interfering where it's personal, as far as they're concerned."

"So what, Tony. Should I just do nothing? Stand back and let some other man take it on?"

"Yes. Yes, James, that's exactly what you should do. Let them get married in Chicago if they like."

"They can't do that. It wouldn't be right for them to travel up there together and they not man and wife. And anyway, this has come to me to do. Isn't it time I did something that wasn't safe?"

"Aren't you always doing things that aren't safe?"

"Only with words! Look, I didn't fight in the war. I didn't fight in 1916. I didn't go home and take a side in what came after that in Ireland. I stayed here and wrote and talked, and that seemed fine. But now? You know there are families here who have given young men. There are young men in Ireland who looked past what's safe and saw what was possible. Maybe it's not a time to play safe. It's a time to be brave, to not let things pass us. This is only a marriage, and I'm going to do it."

"But that's different. There's no war on now."

"Is there not?"

Tony stared at him for a long time.

"Right. We'll do it then. But we'll be careful and choose our time and get the pair of them out of here as soon as we can, off to safety. I'll be with you."

Something Bigger

"No, Tony. Thank you, but I'll do this one. This is mine."

"Well, yours then. But I'll be nearby all the same. You can't stop that."

* * * * *

August 7, 1921

This will be the last page of my diary. I've had you so long, little green notebook, and I've written so little. But this is the end. It's the end of my life in this house, as a girl life at home, as a little girl, with Daddy telling me how I should act and what I should do and what I should think. I'm done with all that now, and I'll soon be married to a Catholic boy.

I'll be a married woman soon, so nobody can tell me how to behave. 'Cept Diego, I guess, but he's not that kind of man.

I love that he has no family. I'll be his and he'll be mine and nobody can tell us what's what. It's going to be so sweet. I'm going to grow my nails out long like a church lady. I'll be a church lady in my own church, not Momma's or Daddy's. I wish Momma could be there, but she'd be so mad if she knew what I was planning. Best she stays. We'll be in a new city, and I'll make Diego buy black shoes just for Sunday and keep them polished so you can see them gleam. I'll wear something simple to Mass every week. Nothing trashy, but still a little style. We'll walk in a little late to church, so folks can see us walking up. I'll have a green cloche hat, not too bright, and I'll keep my eyes down. Demure. That's what I'll be. That's the word.

The Catholics will be our new friends. They'll be pleased to welcome us, wherever the church is, and

Chapter Fourteen: 1921

soon maybe we'll have a baby and when we do, surely then Daddy will be happy again? Momma will be so happy she'll cry, and Daddy'll be glad to be a Grand-daddy, and he'll see sense and maybe get the son he wanted all these years. Momma will sure be glad. Maybe then we can start coming home again, maybe even going to St. Paul's. I'll make a proper gentleman of Diego. New shoes. New shirts for Sunday. Maybe an automobile of our own one day. It's going to be a life.

Goodbye, Diary. You've been my friend since I was young, but I'm grown now and ready to begin my own life. A fine sweet life it's gonna be. I'm gonna leave you here, with my kid things, my rag toys, and my too-small shoes. I'm leaving you. I'm leaving everything.

Ain't nobody can stop me.

* * * * *

Marcella stood in the shadow of the sacristy door-way, watching her brother on the altar in the darkening church, missal in hand, green vestments over a white alb echoing the colours in the stained-glass window behind. Diego looked tall, stiff, a little sinister in the flickering candlelight. He was older than Marcella had expected. Harder. She struggled to see the kindness in him that Bess had described. Bess herself looked like a child in a green lace dress she had borrowed from Marcella half an hour before. Like a child play-ing dress up, a child who had just got what she want-ed from an unwilling parent. She held a tight spray of white roses from the rectory garden, her hands a little twisted, finding the smooth places between the thorns.

Jimmy was speaking very low and fast, speeding through the words like a prayer said to himself instead of a marriage ceremony. He kept his eyes fixed on the gold-edged pages of the missal, never once glancing up at the back door of the church. Marcella did though. Her glance flickered up there every few minutes. There was, after all, a reason for holding this ceremony with the church lights turned off, for this haste, for the way Jimmy insisted she and Tony stand back, even though they were witnesses, in the shelter of the sacristy doorway. Perhaps Johanna had a point, with her trepidation and warnings about the foolishness of all of this. She wouldn't come into the church. Instead she sat on the back porch of the rectory, mending, watching the sacristy door for their return.

Despite the rush, the ceremony seemed interminable. Diego's grinning clumsiness in placing the plain gold ring on Bess's hand was jarring. It was far too big for her finger, and Marcella wondered who had bought it? Was it Diego? Had he never looked at Bess's tiny hands? Bess held it in place with her thumb, still smiling, still pleased, still the girl who got the prize.

The candles in the back of the church flickered, as though there was a draught. As though the side door had opened for a moment. Marcella stared into the dark nave. Was that a deeper shadow to the left of the doorway? A person? She blinked and it was gone. Her imagination again.

They finished the vows abruptly, and Jimmy gave what could pass for a smile, and strode into the sacristy, busying himself, putting away his vestments and missal. The couple stood by the altar, awkward and waiting, and then followed when they realised there was nothing to wait for: no congregation, no congratulations, no well-wishers. Marcella found that words had deserted her. She wanted to talk to Bess alone. She wanted to wish her luck, to say goodbye, to say she

Chapter Fourteen: 1921

was brave. She tried to convey in a look what couldn't be said aloud, but Bess was hanging off Diego's arm like a first timer at The Lyric, like the debutante she nearly was, and she couldn't catch her eye. For his part, Diego looked serious almost to the point of anger, his hands folded together across his waistcoat buttons as in a formal photograph. His fingers interlocked, and his knuckles a little white. He had dirt under some of his nails, and she noticed that one thumb was clubbed a little, curving forwards at the top. She realised she disliked him. Which was unfair, because they'd hardly spoken, but there it was.

There were no photographs. Marcella had earlier brought the camera to the sacristy for that very purpose, but now, with this rushed, tense feel to events, and her dislike for Diego rising, she forgot. What she forgot was not the camera, she realised later, but the warm impulse that might have led to her taking some pictures of the smiling bride, coaxing perhaps a smile from Diego's taut face, convincing Jimmy to stand behind them. Instead those quiet moments went unrecorded. When Jimmy was ready, they walked out the side door to the rectory yard, with awkward gaps between their sentences. After a quick goodbye, Diego and Bess were gone out the gate to 3rd St and into the evening traffic. Marcella filled a saucer with scraps for Captain, and left it on the front porch, where the cat would come creeping later. She stepped past Johanna, into the kitchen and leaned forward over the sink, filling a glass of cold water. Jimmy's voice drifted in the open window as he talked to Tony Brennan. He didn't light his pipe, and so she knew he would not be staying there on the back porch. Their low voices were broken by Jimmy's quick, forced laughter.

Something Bigger

"Where are you going?"

"Out on the front porch, Tony, like always. To say my prayers."

"Would you not ... would you not sit around the side tonight, James? Just for the quiet?"

A pause.

"Out of sight, is it? No call for that. Isn't it grand now, they got away with no trouble?"

"I'll join you, James."

His laugh again. That quick one.

"Do that, Tony. Later. Give me a while to read my Office first, and then we can talk. I was thinking we should head to Mobile one of these days, you and me. We might meet the Bishop, make some new plans."

"Jimmy?" She called out the window. But he was gone already. She could hear him whistling as he disappeared around the side of the rectory, heading towards the street. She let the water overflow her glass, swirling down the drain. She felt exhausted.

"They've done it then?"

Johanna's voice came from the doorway behind her and Marcella could picture her arms folded in a study of disapproval. She straightened her back and folded up the corners of her mouth before turning.

"Yes. All done and dusted and they're away already, no time to drop in."

"Small mercies. Nothing but trouble, that Stubbs girl."

"Well now they're wed and gone. That's the end of it."

She picked up her novel from the kitchen table and moved to the back room, her walk as stiff as her voice. Johanna fussed around, seeming unwilling to finish up for the day. The evening sunlight was sooth-

Chapter Fourteen: 1921

ing, and despite her jangling nerves, the novel began to absorb her.

So that's where she was, lost in that fictional world when they heard the unmistakable sound of gunshots, and the crash of something falling against the front window of the house. She ran. She went running up the hallway, running for the front door. Johanna tried to stop her, tried to physically catch her.

"Stop, Miss Cella, stop. That's a gun, Cella. Come back."

But she would not be held. She ran, and as she ran, she screamed.

Part II

Chapter Fifteen

1921

I was screaming, they told me later, I who am so quiet about the house. I was screaming and they heard me in the street, in the store across the street. I don't remember any scream. I remember silence and slow motion: a catch of low sunlight as I burst through the front door; Jimmy lying in an awkward, impossible way, bulky and helpless, his legs folded over, and him staring up at the porch roof like he could see something there. I was kneeling beside him and looked up there myself, expecting what? I saw nothing. But then I saw Stubbs, standing right there on the porch steps looking down on me. I was so shocked that it took me a few seconds to even see the gun in his hand. He lifted it, pointed it towards me. His lips were curving down, and his eyes were shining way too bright. He looked right at me, then he lowered the gun, turned, and walked away, calm as a sunny day. He latched the rectory gate after himself, quietly and carefully, as if he were a well-mannered neighbour, visiting a friend. He looked back just once, right into my eyes again and his face looked empty now, eyes wide and he was breathing very fast. He walked slowly up to the courthouse with his gun hanging loose in his hand, all out in the open. Seeing the shape of him slouching up the street seemed to jerk back a half memory of Jimmy and me, and now I want to cry. Now I believe I screamed. Johanna's voice behind me:

"How did he know? How did he know so soon?"

Jimmy was still breathing — chest heaving, and I suppose that breath made a sound, but I can't hear him breathing in the movie reel that still plays in my head. He was just lying there, his blood spreading like bathwater all over the porch. So much blood. I remember wondering how we were going to gather it and get it back into him, how we were going to fix him now that he looked so broken. I held his hand, but he didn't squeeze back. He didn't shake off his glassy trance, and the light in his eyes started fading, I think, or maybe it was my eyes that were blurred because I was crying then. I must have been. I held his head on my knees. Johanna was crying behind me, going "How did he know? How did he know so soon?" over and over. Father Tony put on a stole and started blessing Jimmy, giving him the last rites, chrism on his thumb, marking his forehead. Police appeared. It was suddenly a crowd.

I moved back out of the way, kneeling on the blood-wet boards of the porch. Tony didn't close Jimmy's eyes, and I thought to myself, that's good. He's not ready to close his eyes. I thought that made a difference. Men bundled Jimmy on to a stretcher. I don't remember then if he was breathing those effortful,

Chapter Fifteen: 1921

heaving breaths like before. They hurried out the gate with him — ran to the ambulance, and it tore away up 3rd. Tony followed in Jimmy's automobile.

The ambulance didn't come back. It took only an hour for Tony to return. I was still sitting there. Johanna had made me sweet tea, made me drink it. As soon as Tony got out of the automobile, I knew from the way there was no rush on him, the way he wasn't quick to meet my eyes. I knew then.

I wrote all these things down. I am starting this journal today. I never wrote anything before, except letters to Tommy and made up letters to Mother, and both of them seemed real to me. But now, in case I forget, I'm writing so as to leave a record. I'm writing for Jimmy. In case I die and leave nothing behind.

* * * * *

His blood rinsed easily off my hands, swirling pale down the ceramic sink, but it lodged around my thumbnail, so I had to scrub it free. It reminded me of my uncle's hand, long ago in Ireland. It was a big dinner – Sunday it must have been – and he'd come from a lambing. I remember him reaching for milk across the dark table, that blood under his nails, congealed. That memory must have been what made me sick. Before I knew it, I had thrown up in the sink. When I washed it away, my thumb was clean again, pink from scrubbing. I regret it now, that loss of his blood, washed down the drain, useless.

* * * * *

I need to write home. I need to tell them. I thought I'd need to organise this whole funeral undertaking. Funny, that's what we used to call them at home — undertakers. They'd be the ones to call. Here they call them morticians, like beauticians for dead people, no help to the living. I thought it would be me who would need to do this, to be the grown up one now, but it turns out no, it all gets done. The parish does it. The bishop. The other priests. There's a machine that cranks into life without me, and it has nothing to do with me, really. I don't choose hymns, or readings. I don't choose anything. Except for family, and telling them, that's my job.

So I go to the post office to send a cable to Fran. I am at the counter before I have words. I don't know what to say, so I just say what happened.

"JIMMY SHOT. PASSED AWAY 11th. FUNERAL 13th. RIP. WILL WRITE TOMORROW. MARCELLA."

It's twelve words, but really it just needed two. Jimmy died. Everything else is detail. I send it to Fran – I can't bring myself to tell Mother.

* * * * *

I'm sitting in my room with the light off. Outside the window the church looms over me in the dark, with lights on inside so the stained-glass windows are bright like Christmas paper. They're working in there, the men. It's nine at night, but they're clearing out the sacristy, sorting out the records, and they've left the lights on in the main church. I sit and imagine how the shadows fall. I think of slipping in, going up to the balcony where I used to go hide when I was a child, but they might see me, all these new priests that are swarming about to help Tony, and they'd worry, or wonder, or ask why. And there's no reason why, of course. I've no reason to ever go back there again.

Chapter Fifteen: 1921

This is my last night in the rectory. I've already packed all my things, except what I need for morning in a new black trunk with brass hinges. I'd have loved that trunk last week. I'd have seen some beauty in it, but after all it's just a box to carry me away from here. Carry off the pieces of my life to a new place. I'm not sorry to be leaving. It's too sudden, of course. A week ago this was home – the longest home I've ever known, the house I thought I could call mine forever – but without Jimmy, what's the point? And of course, without Jimmy I can't stay, even if I wanted to. I've no connection now to this whole thing we built here, him and me, no tie to this church. I'm nobody's sister now.

So I sit and watch the stained-glass that's lit by the steady electric light of men working. I don't want to write home again, though I know Fran will want to know about the funeral. And what a funeral it was — "One hell of a funeral, Siss," Jimmy would have said. I can hear his voice in my head. He sounds well.

I should be tired. I've been up since six. I slept a little last night, which was good. But today was so long. Such a long three-act play, this funeral. I'll write to Fran after all and tell her. She'll want to know.

Two days ago, they brought him back from the mortician's. Young men with pale faces, they were, looking fearful for some reason, as if I were fierce, as if I could threaten them in their clean black suits and their too-clean nails and their blonde hair and their youth, their living skin. Was I scowling at them? I suppose I was. Maybe they deserved it for being alive and young as they carried in the coffin into his small study, the room at the front, only just in the window from the swing seat where he was killed. They carried him like he was furniture, angling in the door, working out the best way to navigate the hall, shuffling their feet on the tiles. It must have been heavy, that big oak box.

"We'll set it up here," the shorter one said.

They set the lid leaning against the wall, and then they called us in, me and the Sodality women. Not Johanna. Mrs. Gavin hung back at the doorway, but I couldn't wait to get in, to see him again. His desk was gone, so the room looked wrong, as if everything was facing in the wrong direction. They'd put the coffin on the low table from the front office, and he was just lying there, as cold as marble, his hands locked around a black rosary beads that wasn't even his. His face was clean except for the wound, and the silk ruffled up at the side of his head, just up past his ears, so you couldn't see where the back of his head was all blown away. At least you couldn't see it if you hadn't seen it, as I had, on the bleached boards of the porch the day before. Was it really only then?

They'd talked about leaving the coffin closed – a closed casket, they called it. I wasn't having that. I might have had no voice but for this, no, they weren't closing that lid until we had a chance to say goodbye, and anyway, I wanted people to see what had been done to his beautiful head. But in the end, the damage was hidden. They'd fixed him up, their morticians. His eyes were closed and peaceful in a way that made him look plastic, like a good amateur painting, or one of those waxworks. It caught some likeness but it wasn't him. His mouth was all wrong, twisted up at one corner, in a sort of a sardonic smile that I never saw on him in my life.

Still, I was glad to be close to him there. I never wanted to leave, even for food, though they made me eat. They took me out sometimes. Johanna took me

Chapter Fifteen: 1921

outside into the back yard where I could be alone and eat. I didn't want to talk to anyone else, but I could stand to be with her. She was warm and tolerated silence. Mostly I stayed beside Jimmy, standing there watching his face. Touching his marble hands now and then. Watching his silence and peace. Soaking it up, this strange, pale version of my brother. This very still Jimmy; this silent one. I had no words for it. I stood and looked at him. Wondering what had become of the other Jimmy, the one I loved so much.

I stood like the still point of a wheel and all around me was change and movement. Women came and sat in tidy rows under the window. Priests passed through by the dozen, each one leading a new blessing, a new rosary, a sorrowful mystery. Men called, awkward or important, never both. They'd pass the coffin real quick, bless themselves, then stay outside on the porch or the thin grass of the front yard, smoking big cigars or cheap tobacco.

Thousands of people streamed through the rectory all morning, dressed and ready, it seemed, for some occasion. Like a church social. Mrs. Gavin sat crying to herself in this room or that, waited on by a team of women making food, making endless tea. In the back scullery was Johanna, not singing, moving slow and shell-shocked, but still moving. Oh, bless Johanna for her great presence. She never tried to say the right thing or squeeze another tear out of me. She was just there, beside me when I needed her, letting me be quiet. Letting me cry without making a fuss about it. Women arrived with pies and casseroles. Others came in their Sunday best, bossy and bright, taking their place in the parlour, as they started calling the big office. I don't know why they called it that. Perhaps because it gave these women a place to sit. It became a female place when they went in and sat around the walls with that sense of entitlement, like their status was growing every minute longer they sat. Mrs. Quigley was there, that busty woman from the choir, sitting in Jimmy's high-backed armchair, holding on to it like a public office. The Pettigro girls strutted through. It wasn't his place anymore. None of this house is now, as far as I can see. They wiped him out, filling the space with their chatter and noise, the scent of their cologne lingering even today. I found it hard to go in there. It used to be his place, for him and his friends to argue and plan, a place full of loose ideas, cigar smoke, dangers and possibilities. But then his papers were boxed up and put away; a dark cloth thrown over the mirror and the room filled with women, buxom and bound, crooning like hens on a perch.

Others came quietly. The shabby ones, the dark-clad, the ones with bad shoes or no shoes. They came late, under cover of darkness to the back door and wouldn't enter the house. They were met there by Johanna, and sometimes by me, if I was out in the back yard. Oh bless Johanna again. These were the co-loured women, the ones who made the walk by night from down below 17th Street, a journey not without dangers. They know there are men who stand with Stubbs. These women were hard to see, dark in the night, and they brought a little food, maybe cornbread, or lemonade. One young woman brought flowers. A tight little bunch of them. Wild ones, I think, by their thin stems and quick-fading petals. They were dead before they got to us, but she held them like treasure, like delicate orchids. She was tired and hot, and looked like she had come far. Still she wouldn't take anything, not even a drink of water. She said she wanted to leave the flowers, for the father, and then she turned and was gone. I don't know why I remember her so clearly. There were many who came like that, many women with gifts; but there was something about her, something personal and driven. She came not like the women in the front room, for her neighbours, or to be seen. She came for herself. Like a pilgrimage. I never heard her name, and Johanna didn't know her. Still she's the one I remember.

Men came too, but none of them came alone. Twos and threes, fours and fives. The Ancient Order of Hibernians with their green ties and their Sunday best every day for three days of funeral. The Syrian Brotherhood in small uneasy numbers. They wouldn't take the whiskey that was being passed around, poured from a teapot into china cups, as if that would fool anyone. Good whiskey too, they said. Irish, of course. Who knew, though? With it coming from a teapot like that, you could have given them anything. They'd have thought it a vintage year.

The men who smoked made the porch their place, so the smoke seeped in the wooden walls and the cracks around the window and perfumed up the air in the room where he lay. I thought, this is going to make my clothes smell of smoke. And his – he's going to his grave in a shroud that reeks of cigar smoke. And that was a funny idea, but I didn't smile. I wanted to tell him, though. I wanted to tell him all the small things, all that day and the next, all the long night. The way people were talking about him, remembering the good things, laughing about his singing, telling stories that showed how well they knew him or how little. The men were so switched on. Making connections, and as the night went on and the whiskey took hold, talking money and mines, boosting their businesses, laughing too loud about things that had nothing to do with Jimmy. Not that they called him Jimmy. It was all Father Coyle, or Father James, or even James – this from people who'd hardly ever used his first name. It made me a little angry, now and then, but then I'd hear his voice in my head, full of laughter, going 'Now Siss, you have to let them have their day'. Like I said, he sounded well.

There was fear as well as laughter. A woman in the hallway whispering to Tony "Father Brennan, are we safe here? Is it safe this morning?" Those women, the fearful ones, all their focus was on Stubbs. Talking about him as if he were the one who mattered. The reporters were the same, hanging around the edge of the crowd, trying to see who there knew Stubbs, getting people to talk about what made him do it, who he was, all about his miserable life. Jimmy didn't seem to interest them at all, he who had been so central to all they wrote before, whose place this was, or used to be. It was as if there had been a game of musical chairs, like we used to play long ago, but this time Jimmy was the one caught off guard when the music stopped, with no place to be, no more moves in the game. There were many new priests: young men from Mobile and Georgia. Older ones, sounding Irish, who knew my name. Staccato Italians. Thin Black priests from New York. None of them humming or whistling. None of them taking the porch steps two at a time. None of them Jimmy.

And then, that second night, we started on the goodbyes, closing the coffin, and carrying him out of the rectory a few short steps to the church. There were far too many men who wanted to form a guard of

Chapter Fifteen: 1921

honour; far too many to carry the coffin. The church was packed, and the street was teeming. It must have been a short service – I don't remember it much. I just remember handshakes, endless strangers saying they were sorry for my troubles if they were Irish, giving me their sympathies if they were not, or shaking my hand and moving on with no words. So many hands – big clammy ones, thin dry ones, some limp, some firm. Endless. Staring at me glassy-eyed or peering into me as if they were looking for something. "How is she, the sister?" their eyes said. And later they could talk about it. Judge my grief. Judge my lack of tears. Speculate on what might lie before me now.

And then we all walked out of the church and left him there – his tallness and his laughter stretched in that box in the dim-lit side aisle. All his ideas and plans, all the memories of the two of us, all that light in his pale blue eyes, the speed of his walk, the swish of his cassock, the half-smile he wore when he considered an idea, the way he hummed when he was happy, and whistled, well he whistled only sometimes. Not often. The way he always wanted more for me, for Longfield, for Ireland, for someone that was part of some "us" in his mind. I left all that in a dark oak box and walked out into the heat of the evening. I didn't want to leave but they made me, the kind women from the Altar Society. Men from the Ancient Order of the Hibernians were gathering in clumps outside, making plans to stay up in shifts all night.

"What are they doing, Emily?" I asked the girl tasked with bringing me home. She was a child of about sixteen.

"They're waiting, Miss Coyle. Waiting for Klansmen. They're gonna kill them if they come. Or fight them anyways. They're gonna keep the church stand-ing."

And I thought, what a waste. What a waste of time, standing out there, when they could be home with their families. I hoped no Klansmen would come. I hoped nobody else would get killed. Even him. Even Stubbs. Then I remembered he was safe anyway – hid-den away in the county jail, sleeping, I guessed, like a baby. That made my eyes hot again. The men outside the church began to remind me of him, their heated voices, the tension in the way they stood. I wanted to tell them to go home, and I heard him again, his voice in my head sounding more tired now.

'Leave them be, Siss. They need something to do. If they don't have Klansmen to think about, they'll have to face up to bigger things.'

When I was walking up the path to the porch, I saw it had been scrubbed, just those boards where he bled. Even when I saw the clean patch that will take so long to fade; even then I didn't cry. I slept that night –last night? Yes, that was only yesterday. This morning I woke early and dressed in the darkest clothes I had. I put on my black pillbox hat with a veil. Not new, but I'd never worn it. I bought it years and years ago on a whim, out shopping with Lucille back when we were friends to go shopping together. There was a far nicer one in green, I remember, but she said black is classic, and with your brother being a priest, you never know when you'll need a respectable black hat for church. So sure enough, Lucille is right. Finally.

At the Mass, there were so many priests, there was hardly room for people. Afterwards, we walked to the graveyard which they call a cemetery, behind the horse-drawn hearse. His casket was just a box now. A prop,

Chapter Fifteen: 1921

like a wooden house-front in a parish play, there to set the scene. I don't remember the graveyard. There were thousands of people there, they said. Tens of thousands maybe. I was there. I must have seen them lowering Jimmy into the ground. Esther Gavin says we both left white roses on the top. It must be true. Like I said, I don't remember. I remember us all walking out the gates, and a squall gusted up so the priests in their cassocks hunched forward, battling the wind like women walking the shore road in Galway, years ago when I was small. Old women all in black with their head-scarves billowing. Why should I remember that now?

Then it was over. Bess never came. I don't know why I thought she would, but I did. I wondered where she was, herself and Diego? Chicago or New York, I supposed. That's where everyone seems to go. Like Jackson, like as not. Like Mimi. Up north to a place with no past and no old, bitter loyalties. I don't know how I feel about Bess now. I hope it was worth it for her. There had better be some good to come from it. Something to make it not just a foolish waste.

Lucille called, late and missing the funeral, but she did come. We sat together in my room. I couldn't entertain her on the porch. She tried to talk about the old days, our schooldays, the beaus we had or imagined, but it rang hollow. Look at us, the pair of us. Those plans we had to be friends forever. Are we friends now, I wonder? It's not easy to tell. Lucille said she'd read in the paper that the news that Bess had married a Catholic must have driven her father insane. She said her mother had screamed at reporters "Could you blame him? We've endured so much from the whole terrible Catholic question!" She said the papers reported that Bess was back in Birmingham the day of the funeral, sitting in a café on 5th and 20th, dressed in bright blue. I wonder if she was wearing that hat I gave her. I could see here at a low table, laughing like ice in a glass. I wonder why Lucille had told me those things, knowing how they would make me feel. I wonder why she pretended she'd read them in the papers, when I know she must have heard all this at home, from that hateful, gloating man she had married. I am too tired to wonder for long.

Now I'm ready to leave this house that isn't mine anymore. I don't think I will miss it at all. Apart from Johanna, I've nobody left here. Oh Johanna, how I loved her, and now there's hardly a word between us. Still, something of whatever was holding us apart has broken. She's the one apart from Jimmy, it turns out, that I loved, and I think she may have loved him too, in her way. We hardly talk now, but we look at each other, in the eyes, and we see each other almost like we used to.

I am lost, more than I ever have been. I feel unanchored in this small white room, present but cut adrift. I could stay, Tony said, working in the parish. I could get rooms nearby. But I don't care to. I don't want to grieve in the spotlight, pinned in the gaze of those sharp-eyed church ladies. And I couldn't bear to go to Mass here and see someone else on his pulpit. It's too much to ask of me. Even at the funeral it seemed wrong not to have Jimmy up there, presiding. I sat in the front, in the mourner's pew, tugging at my sleeves, dragging the hem up into my palm, pinning it under my thumb like I was trying to protect my blue-veined wrist. Protecting that blood that seeped back to my heart, making no sound.

'Don't mind, Siss', he said.

Chapter Fifteen: 1921

Who am I, really, now? If I'm not the priest's sister, what can I be around here? Jimmy was all energy and movement, and now he's fixed like a photograph. Father Coyle. The late Father Coyle. He's a hero, the women say. A martyr, the bishop said in his sermon. A fool, the papers write. Everyone has a view about him. But I never knew I'd be alone like this.

I'll be fine. I think I will. Even if I am not, I won't be told how to feel or how to be by those widowed women or those self-important men. And I don't care for parish work now. Lucille says it's not hard to get work in department stores. She says if I want to stay, that even though it's years since I worked in Loveman's, they would have me back, she says, in a heartbeat. I wonder how she knows. I know again it's her husband. In a heartbeat, I decide to leave.

Tony understands, or at least he is not displeased I don't want to stay. He said I could go to Mobile, a more beautiful town, gentler and more courteous. "The Bishop will look after you there, Marcella." I don't care to work with any Bishop. I was never doing it for the church. I was working with Jimmy. With him gone, what does any of it matter. There is a kindness in Tony calling me Marcella. Everyone else calls me Miss Coyle. Nobody calls me Siss. I suppose I must go to Mobile.

Jimmy agrees. 'Go on, Siss, Get out of this house. Otherwise you'll have Esther Gavin haunting you of an evening. You know you will.'

It's true. Esther is dreary, more than ever since her husband died. Yesterday, she crept up on me in the church like a wraith, and said we could sit together at Mass now, if I wanted. Like I'd want to stand with her down the back of the church while some new man reads the gospel too fast or too slow. Or sit with her in her front room on a long evening and keep her company. No. I won't be her widow sister or whatever it is she wants. I am not like her. I barely knew her before and now she's all around me like a moth, enveloping me in her creeping grief. She can't tell me what to feel or who to be. She was born to wear black but me? I don't know, maybe, but not yet. I can't be widowed before I'm wed, can I?

I never thought I wouldn't feel at home here. I never thought I wouldn't feel safe. But here I am looking around the room I've lived in since I was fourteen, the stupid shelf with its stupid river stone brought from Rockfield, letters from home and tattered Brer Rabbit books. What am I supposed to do with all that? Where am I to go with these ragged things? I grab an empty chocolate box, and pile in all the small keepsakes, the things that used to mean something, and stow it away under my folded clothes in that big black trunk.

The house doesn't sound right tonight. Its boards creak differently. There's a breeze pulling at my curtains that I don't think was there before. It's not that I'm afraid. I wouldn't say I'm afraid, but I don't feel safe. He's not here. He won't be here again.

I'm leaving Birmingham, this get-ahead city, these well-armed, hard-shell men with all their hate and fear, these braggarts and bigots. It gets darker, and I see they've turned out the lights inside the church. The stained-glass windows are reversed now. From here they are small panes of dark, but I know if I was inside, the thin light of the street would be colouring them in, making the pictures glow. That's what it would look like, if there were anyone left inside to see.

* * * * *

Chapter Fifteen: 1921

61 Ramble St.
Mobile, Alabama
September 15, 1921

Dear Fran,

How are you? I'm sorry I never asked, in my last letter, about you, or the babies, or Martin. I'm so sorry. Are things better in Ireland yet? Are you safe? I'm sorry, Fran. I was all caught up here, in what happened, and I wasn't able to ask. I hope you are safe. I hope Mother is well.

You see my new address on this letter. I have moved down to Mobile, and will be here for some time, I think. You can still write to the rectory for now. Tony Brennan, Father Brennan, he keeps any letters for me and sends them on. They come mostly from Mother.

I came here after the funeral to meet the Bishop. Mother would die of pride if she knew. Everyone said he would find me a place, and sure enough, he sent for me. What a strange man. His hands were cold and dry, and his eyes were troubled when we met, not with sympathy or sorrow, but as though I made him nervous for some reason. He could hardly meet my eye, and couldn't wait to get me out his door. His secretary gave me the name of this boarding house, and I share a room there now. The diocese has paid for a month. It's fine. I know I will get work, but I haven't looked yet. I can't bring myself to get worked up about things like that. The bishop offered to find me a place in a church school, but I could tell his heart wasn't in it, and I didn't want it. I don't know why, but it felt good to refuse. That was something, at least, that I could do. I don't know why I embarrassed him so, or why

Something Bigger

I wouldn't take his help. It wasn't his fault, what had happened. Anyway, work in a department store is easy to find, or I can get work as a bookkeeper again. I was always good with figures, Jimmy used to say. That's what he used to say.

They're putting him on trial. Stubbs, I mean, the man who killed Jimmy. They say I may be called as a witness. It seems so unnecessary. He shot Jimmy, and then he confessed. Half a dozen people saw him do it. I don't know why they need a trial at all, but I am happy to be a witness, and see him convicted. No. Happy isn't the right word. It just feels right to me.

I will write properly later, Fran. I only wanted to let you know that the trial is coming up, and like I say, I hope you are well, and that you and the family are safe. I will write again to Mother, as we agreed. You might let me know if she is happy with the letters.

All my love, Fran,
Marcella

And then I write to Mother, and I tell her all about our days, Jimmy and me. I talk about how he has taken up golf, and how bad he is at it. I talk about his car, what an excellent driver he has become. I describe his new poems as they are published in the local paper, and a reading he will give at the Tutwiler hotel, how half the city are coming, how even the people outside our congregation, the Protestants, as Mother calls them all, will be there to admire his words. I'm surprised at how easy it is to keep making things up, to write about this life we're not actually sharing. I imagine it so easily, and it hardly makes me cry at all.

Chapter Sixteen

1921

Birmingham Age Herald, October, 1921
STUBBS CASE IN COURT TODAY

Indications are that the trial of the Rev. Abner R. Stubbs, charged with the killing of Father James E. Coyle of St. Paul's Catholic church, will consume the entire week and possibly extend over into the following week.

The trial is scheduled to be taken up in the criminal division of the circuit court this morning with 74 witnesses summoned for the state and 103 for the defense.

It was rumored at a late hour last night that Mrs. Bess Rivera, daughter of the accused minister, had been seen alighting from a south-bound train in the outlying suburbs of the city. Word was received in the latter part of last week that Mrs. Rivera would arrive from Loretto, Tenn., this morning in order to testify at the trial of her father.

Something Bigger

The judge is getting tired. He takes off his spectacles and rubs his eyes. His hands are thick and marked with brown liver spots. The heavy tortoiseshell frame on his glasses is cracked and the left eyeglass is a little loose, pitched forward out of kilter with the right one. The glass is scratched too, like he let it fall, or he kept it in a pocket with his money. Why doesn't he get a new pair? It makes him look so vulnerable, those broken spectacles and his reddened, watery eyes. I forget for a minute that this is the man who'll decide what to do with Stubbs, and who looks more and more like a weak man, not the power of the law. Without his spectacles his face looks open, like a child woken in the middle of the night, or an old man who has walked into the wrong room. He looks tired, not in control.

Hugo Black is just the opposite. The most expensive defence lawyer the Klan could find. He's young, mesmerising. His authority comes from something other than age. His sharp-cut suit makes him look presidential. It fits like it was made for him, or he for it. I guess it was, actually, made for him. The trousers are pressed to an edge that could cut paper, and the white kerchief in his top pocket is immaculate. He looks like the shape of power in its natural form, but I know better. I saw him this morning. I came early, before the crowds, to avoid the reporters who are still interested in me, the sister. So the courthouse was more or less deserted when I came out of the ladies' cloakroom. He stood maybe thirty feet away, half turned away from me, looking out the window at the end of the courthouse corridor. He didn't hear me. He must have thought he was alone. He looked small in front of that big arched window. His jacket was unbuttoned. I saw him reach into an inside pocket and pull out a different handkerchief, loose and creased, yellowing. He shook it out over the windowsill, as though it might have held crumbs. Like Charlie Chaplin almost, on a park bench. And then he folded it in half and in half again, real slow, and used it to mop his brow. Then he shook it again, and replaced it, patting down his pocket so the bulge didn't show. Now I know what he holds inside that suit. That white pocket handkerchief is just part of his costume, not to be used. Knowing that helps me. Maybe I'm the only one who can see that he's pretending here, just playing his part in the game. Nothing he says needs to be real.

He says plenty, though. He's off now on a story about history. His own personal history, his down-home simple family, his hard work at law school, how it is part of the history of this proud state. I find my mind wandering. All day yesterday I sat by the back wall, and I could just look away if I wanted. I could even slip outside. But today, I am right in the thick of it. In the dock as a witness, though to tell the truth it was all far too late by the time I came on the scene. I saw nothing except my brother dying and his killer, calm as a pet cat. I answer questions by the prosecution and then it is the turn of Hugo Black to ask whatever he wants, if he ever gets to the end of this interminable story. I watch the juror nearest to me. Is he the foreman? I'm not sure. His thumb is tiny and waisted like an egg-timer, manicured like a girl's. There is an artery at the side of his neck that keeps pulsing under the skin. It's not very noticeable. Perhaps he doesn't know about it himself, but now that I've seen it, I can't keep my eyes off it. That's his life there, throbbing for all to see. That's his heartbeat, which he still gets to hold. His ordinary life. His blood all safe inside his body. I lift my eyes to his, and am surprised to see him staring at me, as though he were waiting. I realise the court is silent. Was there a question?

"I will repeat the question, Miss Coyle." He lingers over our surname, making it sound like oil. Not like it should.

"Isn't it true that you heard raised voices? That these are what made you come on to the porch?"

"No. There were no raised voices."

The calm in my own voice makes it sound remote to me. I see myself on the dock as though I'm in a play too, like Hugo (the Ringmaster) Black. I see myself small and neat, costumed and under control. As it should be. As he would have wanted. I turn to Hugo Black with a calm that should have frightened him. It would have, if he knew what was going on inside my head. He is fussing with his notes, looking busy and efficient for the jury. They are all men, of course. All white. All looking a bit like Old Man Stubbs. All Klan members, I suppose. Seems like every other man in Birmingham is a Klan member now. I look at them as though from a great distance. I watch them like a movie, as though they can't see me. They are watching someone else: some woman in the dock, wearing black with a white lace collar. Some bereaved Catholic. They can't see me, really. They can't see how I am clenched up inside. I don't smile. I don't cry. I am a good sister.

"Isn't it true, then, Miss Coyle, that you were in a back room. A long way from the porch, and so you would not have heard the two men arguing?"

"No, it is not."

"But isn't it a long way, Miss Coyle, from where you sat to where your brother and the Reverend Stubbs were talking?"

Chapter Sixteen: 1921

At the mention of his name, he looks up, old man Stubbs. Looks not at me, but at Hugo Black, like a man looking at his boss, or a dog at his owner. Like he's awaiting orders or something. All I can see is his belt buckle. I'd never noticed it before. A big silver buckle with a ghost holding a long flag. No, not a ghost, but a figure in ghostly robes. I think of what Bess told me, and it straightens my back a little more.

"No, Mr Black. They were not talking. Our home is small, and the walls are thin. I heard no voices because they did not speak."

"Miss Coyle, would you say your brother and Reverend Stubbs were friends?"

"Friends? No. I would not say that."

"You'd say your brother harboured an enmity towards Reverend Stubbs then?"

"No, Mr. Black. My brother harboured no enmity."

"But you admit yourself, Miss Coyle, that they were not friends, do you not? If there was no ill-will from your brother, why should you say that?"

"Because, as you know, Mr. Black, Mr Stubbs killed my brother."

There is a gratifying gasp from the public gallery. I go on.

"For that reason, I do not think that they were friends."

He looks at me then, for the first time. Looks right into my eyes with a surprise that seems genuine. I look back, trying not to sneer at him, thinking of the grubby kerchief in his waistcoat pocket. He has a question in his eyes, but he doesn't ask it. Without breaking eye contact, he addresses the judge.

"No further questions, your honour."

Something Bigger

And that is that. My time is done in court, and I am dismissed. I don't get to say anything about what really happened. About Jimmy reading his evening Divine Office in bravery or stupidity or whatever you want to call it, going ahead and sitting outside like the world was at peace. About how he whistled as he walked, and how that meant he was afraid. But still he walked. I get to say nothing about Jimmy, so nothing about him is said. He is hardly present at the trial. The court-room artists don't sketch his face, only Stubbs's, hard and staring. He watches me as I step off the stand and walk back to my seat, as slow as I can manage, holding myself together until they all look away.

* * * * *

I go home every evening now. To the rectory, I mean. Tony is there and avoids me. He doesn't come to the courthouse. Says it wouldn't be seemly, but I think he's frightened. He was a good man always, but never brave. He follows the trial from the newspapers, which is like looking at them through a glass bottle for all the truth you'll find there. He says he knows two of the prosecution lawyers are Klansmen, but he's hope-ful about the judge. He hasn't seen him, as I have. After the first day, I started coming in the back way instead, to spare him from meeting me, and to have supper with Johanna. She cares for me. She is waiting when I get back, no matter how late it is. She made up my old room — I don't know who was sleeping there while I was in Mobile, but Johanna made it look almost like mine again. I don't unpack at all, just lift my things in and out of the carpetbag each day, not even leaving my shoes on the floor at night. I don't want to leave a mark here. I need to be ready to leave.

Chapter Sixteen: 1921

Johanna feeds me all the old comforting foods from when I was young. I was so young when I came first, and she showed such kindness. Almost like a mother. We sit together as I eat, and we talk about the food, or the trial. I don't ask her about Jackson. I'm afraid to hear her answer, her patience or her anger. When I can't stand to eat in silence, we cast about for anything that seems like a safe thing to talk about. One evening, I ask her about the Uncle Remus books that are still in my room. I read them when I came first, though I was fourteen, and too old, really for a childish story like Brer Rabbit.

"Why did you ask Jimmy to buy them for me, Johanna? He told me you did."

"I don't exactly recall, Miss Cella. I guess I thought you'd like them. There weren't no children's things in the house, and it seemed to me you should have something. You did like them, didn't you?"

"I did. I'm trying to remember now. Brer Rabbit, he was so quick and clever, always one step ahead of getting into trouble. And then there was Brer Fox and Brer Wolf, wasn't it? What was the difference between those two, Johanna?"

Johanna smiles. I can tell she likes that I'm talking, even foolish talk like this.

"I guess Brer Fox, he was the sneaky one, and Brer Wolf, he was the strong one."

"But they worked together, didn't they?"

"No child. They was both just looking out for themselves. They didn't care what happened as long as Brer Rabbit didn't end up happy."

"But it took both of them, usually, to outsmart the rabbit."

"It did. Brer Fox was clever, and he could keep a

secret, but bad old Brer Wolf, he was the one to bring trouble."

"He was. You're right, Johanna. He does."

I finish my grits. There's something satisfying about this kind of talk.

I go early to bed, and when I wake I wish I could just stay in my room but instead I get on my best black clothes again, and go to sit at the back of the courthouse with Esther Gavin. I pass her handkerchiefs from my pocketbook when she starts sniffing, which is early in the day most days. I don't know why she never has handkerchiefs of her own. Still, she's with me. That's kind of her. I shouldn't mock her for feeling what it seems I can't feel yet, whatever it is that causes her emotion to well up in her, flooding her eyes. She looks like she's crying for Jimmy, but more likely she's crying for her own old loss; widowed without children, she says, a worse fate than most. She says it like I'd understand. I suppose it's the same grief, in her eyes. The same loss. But Jimmy wasn't my husband. He was my brother. That's blood. That's stronger. Still, she comes and sits with me. And when I have grace enough to be kind, I am grateful to her.

The courtroom is airless, and this morning it's tedious, covering pointless detail about the gun. What is there to discuss? It was a gun, used to kill Jimmy. But still it goes on, like a slow build up, like a movie where you know there's going to be a fight, but it hasn't started yet. From my seat at the back of the crowds, I watch Hugo Black spinning those jurors a story, playing them like his own personal orchestra. He speaks well, using small words in a way that shows he could use bigger ones if he chose to. He holds his education back like a bowstring, almost out of sight but ready if needed.

Chapter Sixteen: 1921

Instead he uses the homely language of the men in the box. He smiles at everyone, even the prosecution lawyers.

"Our friends here, these men who want to lock the Reverend Stubbs away, they're gonna tell you good men that he's a murderer, but you know a lie like that won't fly. It's just like my Daddy used to say, that dog won't hunt!"

He smiles like he's said something clever, and every man on the jury grins at him as if he knew what it was to hunt with a dog. As if they all did. As if it was something they might do together. But he doesn't need a dog to hunt, this man with his well-cut clothes and his well-cut words. I can see that in his eyes, in the way he holds himself, conscious of the figure he cuts as he half swaggers around the open space of the court, performing to his own script. He hunts down their hearts and minds with his words and with silence. He wants them eating out of his hand, not just when he's talking, but when he's done. It's been a long morning and I'm hoping for a recess, but the judge glances at the clock at the end of the court and says he will allow one more witness.

"I call Bess Rivera."

The whole court inhales sharply, and heads turn towards the exit doors to see her come in. Darned if she isn't wearing my blue hat, and a floaty blue dress that seems fit for a social. Her head is thrown back, and she sashays a little as she walks up the courtroom aisle, looking confident and alone, reminding me of her wedding day. As she passes, I see she's wearing too much powder and rouge that I can't tell if she's pale or not. She takes her seat on the stand with a coy smile for the court photographer, and she doesn't meet her father's eye.

Something Bigger

She answers questions well, I'll give her that. The prosecution is running through all the settling-in questions — her age, her home, her schooling. I look away, numbed by the heat, and my attention is called back by a new hesitancy in her voice.

"He was ... a controlling man. I was punished as a child."

"Punished?"

"Yes, sir."

Her voice, so small and so submissive, is strange to me. The court is very quiet, and her voice gets soft and softer. There's a shaft of light that crosses her face, casting a deep shadow under her chin. When she moves her head, as she does when speaking, she looks like an angel one moment, and like a much older woman the next. She talks about times she ran away, and about looking for a safe place. She talks about joining the Catholic Church over in St. Michael's, but the prosecutor doesn't question her about that.

"And your father didn't know of this?"

"No, sir, I had not told him."

"Did you ever hear him express his feelings towards Father Coyle? Or towards Catholics?"

"Yes sir. All my life."

"And what were his feelings?"

"He hates Catholics. My mother hates them too. They wanted St. Paul's gone from our street, and Father Coyle too."

There isn't even a rustle of surprise at this. Abner Stubbs is staring at his daughter like he never saw her before. She is talking about Diego now.

"How long have you known your husband?"

"Three years, sir."

Now that's a shock, to me at least. Could they have met when she was barely fifteen? But yes, it seems that is the case, that he came and stayed with the family for a summer working on the renovation of the barbershop. He would have been in his thirties then, surely? And she a child.

"And where does he come from, your husband?"

"He's a Birmingham man, sir. He's lived here most of his life."

Some laughter from the crowd makes her look up.

"I mean sure, he's Spanish, but he lives here since the war."

"Spanish? Don't you mean Porto Rican?"

"His people were Spanish. And it's Puerto Rican, he says, not Porto."

"And when did you first meet Father Coyle? When did you first visit the rectory?"

She looks back at the crowd now. I wonder if she's looking for my face? She looks right past me."

"I've visited the rectory and the church since I was a little girl. I've always visited the rectory."

I wonder why she said that, and if it will matter? Hugo Black moves on to questions around the wedding. She tells it like a fairy tale — her handsome bridegroom, the flowers, the church. She smiles a lot and looks down, as though she is trying to express the word demure. I wish I felt more kind towards her. I don't like myself when I feel so mean, but I can hardly bear to listen to her. I look away for distraction and see her father leaning forward, staring at her as though she wasn't real, but a vision just out of grasp. Then I understand. It's him she's talking to, really. He's the reason she's looking so cool and blue, so self-possessed and happy. It's all for him. She's performing for him. I'm glad when the recess is finally called, and I can slip outside.

I walk to the ladies' cloakroom, and it's empty, as it has been all week. Courthouses are for men, I've learned. I lean forward, the mirror cool against my forehead. I let my face go, and am shocked when I look up to see how it droops. How it has aged. Oh Jimmy. What you've put us all through. I might have whispered that. I open my eyes again and see her, reflected, still as a nun in the back of the room.

"Bess?"

"Miss Coyle."

Up close I can see that the confidence she showed in court was just for show. I can see the strain on her. Now she looks ready to cry. Her mouth has changed – that full pout is gone and she looks defeated, like her mother used to. I realise I haven't seen her mother. Ethel hasn't been in the courtroom at all. That absence seems odd, like a clock that doesn't tick.

"I been hoping you'd come in here, Miss Coyle. I wanted to talk."

"Why, Bess? What could you possibly say that would make a difference? Did you want to say you're sorry? Is that it? Are you looking for forgiveness for dragging Jimmy into all of this? For choosing St. Paul's for your wedding? Because if that's what you want, it ..."

"No, Miss Coyle. Why would I need forgiveness for that?"

"Then what are you doing here if not to apologise for all the trouble you've caused?"

"I caused no trouble, least not by getting married. But I did want to apologise. I'm sorry for leaving my diary on my bed. It wasn't rightly an accident. I ..."

"What diary?"

"My own diary. You told me when I was young that I should write one, and so I have. Not often, but

Chapter Sixteen: 1921

enough. I should have burned it, or taken it with me, but I didn't."

"I didn't tell you to keep a diary, Bess. I never told you to do anything. You've always done what pleased you, as far as I can see."

A sudden wave of tiredness washes over me. I want to sit down, but there is nowhere. So I lean back against the sink and wait.

"Well, that ain't exactly so, Miss Coyle. The diary was your idea — writing things down so I wouldn't forget things. You said it. I thought you meant it. I thought it might be important. But I should have burned it when I left. It would have burned up real easy."

I think of Jimmy then, suddenly, and he's smiling in my head. Something about the mention of burning is making him straighten up and pay attention. What is it? Why does that matter? Bess is still talking.

"I'm gonna tell the truth, so I won't have to confess a lie. I didn't forget it. I wanted Daddy to know. I wanted him to see what I could do. I just didn't think they'd find it so soon. It was wrong. But I ain't the only one that was wrong."

"Go on."

"Me and Diego, it's not how I thought it would be. Your brother was wrong when he said we would make a good marriage. I thought he was kind and easy to be with, and that was enough. I just needed to marry."

"And why would a slip of a thing like you need to marry?"

She looks at me, honestly, as though I were an imbecile.

"Ma'am. I'm 18."

I'm tired. Too tired for these games.

"So what, Bess? What does it matter what age you are?"

Something Bigger

"This is Alabama, Miss Coyle. That means I gotta do everything my Daddy says til I'm 21. '"Subject to him,"' is what they say. He could stop me leaving home, stop me getting a job. Less I'm married. You can marry when you're 18. So I did."

"So you did all this to get away from Abner, from your Daddy. I know that. You told me he was cruel to you."

Her eyes are half full of tears.

"No Ma'am. I never said that. He's a good man, my Daddy."

"You just said in court he was controlling. And you told me he hurt you, Bess. You said he used his belt and ..."

"No, Miss Coyle. I never said that to you. You might have thought that, cause we're poor, and you made assumptions, but that just ain't the case."

"But that was why I helped you, Bess. I thought you needed help."

She smiled at me still with those aching eyes.

"I'm grateful for your help, Miss. Coyle. But you were wrong about Daddy. And your brother was wrong about me and Diego."

And darned if she doesn't start crying, right there and then. I can hardly look at her. I am shaking with rage. I stand and watch her cry, don't even try to help. Then I hear Jimmy's voice saying 'Ah come on now, Siss. What are you doing getting angry? Sure it's not her fault.' And still she keeps snivelling away, because Jimmy's voice is only in my head now, and she can't hear it. He's saying something I've heard before. Something about hate, and not giving in to it. So I have to fish in my pocket book and get her a handkerchief. And I have to tell her it will all be alright. And then she hugs me, and darned if I don't start crying too, and I'm afraid to talk in case she sees I'm crying for different reasons than her. I'm crying for Jimmy. And for myself. I'm the one who was wrong, too many times. I don't know how long we are there like this. I'm just glad nobody comes and sees us.

And then she straightens herself, and dabs cold water on her face, tries to put her pout back on. But those eyes won't rise to it; those eyes are blank and broken now.

"Well, Miss Coyle, I'd best be getting on. Perhaps I'll see you ..."

Her voice tails off.

"Where would you see me, Bess?"

"Perhaps at Mass, Miss Coyle. Perhaps in St. Paul's.

"Goodbye, Bess. Take care."

I almost mean it. I try to wish her well, at least in my head. I watch her walk out, and I stay, leaning on the cloakroom sink. I'm picturing Stubbs finding out about how she got away, how she found a way to escape him. I'm seeing him differently now, like a father, not a bully. I can almost see it breaking him, the barber in him stronger than the preacher. I suppose it was her mother who found the diary. That seems more likely to me. I can't imagine Old Man Stubbs having the patience to read a journal written by a teenage girl, his daughter or not. I can see her mother though, sitting on the bed, reading it from start to end, and then walking out of that grimy little house to test the truth of it. I suddenly know who it was I thought I saw in the back of the church that day, that dark shape that moved in front of the bank of candles. I can see her. I can suddenly see her doing almost anything.

Something Bigger

I stay in the cloakroom until it's time for them to lock up the building. It's not that I don't want to leave. I just don't want to face the daylight.

* * * * *

It's the last day of the trial. I don't expect much to happen. I've testified, so has Bess. So have a dozen people who saw the shooting. I thought there'd be nothing to write about today, but I should have counted on Hugo Black. This is his big finale, and the young men in the press bench sit forward, excited. One of the photographers from the Birmingham Age Herald starts firing up his flash. Hugo Black steps closer to him, and then turns dramatically to one side, allowing his profile to be captured as he sums up his client. He's talking about old man Stubbs now. Abner Stubbs. I never knew his first name until this trial. Hugo Black points to him and he's calling him a worried father, a minister, a good upstanding American man, faced with the marriage of his only daughter, barely eighteen, not only to a Romanist, but to a ... he pauses, and drops his voice.

"Well, let's see what you think of him. Let's see what you think he is."

He turned to the court bailiff.

"I call Diego Rivera."

He smiles then, just to himself, relishing the drama of his announcement, the scramble on the press benches as they send runners to break this story, the excitement running through the crowd. The judge calls a recess. He says it's to give the witness a chance to prepare, but really, it's for the reporters who all flood out to phone in their stories — hot news this, the calling of the bridegroom, and it's about to get hotter. Esther

Chapter Sixteen: 1921

and I stay where we are, along with all the other hangers-on and watchers, afraid of losing our seats if we leave. Hugo Black talks to the custodian, and has the courthouse blinds half closed. "We gotta keep that sun from dazzling our star witness," he says. On this, the most overcast of Fall days, with hardly a shadow being cast from one end of the city to another. Nobody questions him. He has been the scriptwriter and director of this show, and now he becomes the stage manager. We are only the audience. I wonder why he is bothering to have Diego there. He can't give any evidence that matters. The lovebirds were flown a good fifteen minutes before Jimmy was shot. He's the one person in this whole sorry drama who has nothing to do with the killing. But the killing isn't the part of the story that Hugo Black wants the jury to think about today. He has a different play to stage.

The crowds mill back in and the recess ends. With the windows darkened, the witness box is in shadow. Every seat is packed, and a hush falls, like in the Lyric Theatre before a show.

"Call Diego Rivera."

The back-door swings open, admitting a shaft of light from the corridor, back-lighting Diego and the deputy who escorts him to the witness box. I see it now. In the shadow, he looks dark. Darker than he is. I see what that's doing to the crowd. They're not used to seeing Black folks in the courthouse, and though Diego isn't Black, the light makes him look that way.

Diego is nervous, and I realise I've never heard him speak more than a few words. He avoided all the reporters who interviewed Bess, and he has hardly even had his picture in the paper. He looks like a man who likes to keep his head down in times of trouble.

"Come closer to the jury."

Hugo Black is imperious, and Diego steps up before the jury box.

"Closer. Move closer."

He stands in silence, confused, waiting for questions. The white men in the jury box look at him as though he were an exhibit of the court. They take in his sallow skin, his dark curly hair. Finally, Diego can bear it no longer and turns to the judge.

"What do you want? What do you want of me?"

His accent is strong, and he sounds angry and weak.

Hugo Black steps forward, gestures to the deputy.

"No questions, your honour. I just wanted them to see the man."

Diego spins towards him, seeing the game too late, his eyes wild. The deputy forcibly leads him from the court, which makes him look like a criminal. Hugo Black steps back a little, and lets a silence gather around him before he speaks straight to the jury.

"He says he's Spanish. He says he is of proud Castilian descent."

He turns a little to one side, looks down and smiles, as though he's being casual, as though he's going to say something unguarded.

"Well, I'm sure you'll agree, gentlemen — he's descended a mighty long way."

A ripple of laughter runs around the court. Some tension has escaped the room. Hugo Black takes a step back and opens his arms wide in a gesture that seems to disclaim everything, walking slowly backwards away from the jury. It's familiar, somehow. I remember the fire. The Klansmen in the valley. The ones who had the torches, who lit the cross in the centre did that

Chapter Sixteen: 1921

same thing. Once the wood was lit and burning, they threw their hands wide and walked backwards into the waiting circle of their brothers. The men on the jury look curiously happy, as though something unsaid has been resolved for them. Hugo Black is walking and talking now, spinning this new thread into his main story. Bad enough that Jimmy was a Roman, a priest; worse still that he brainwashed an innocent girl to make her a Catholic and married her at only eighteen years of age against her father's wishes. But look at the man he married her to? Does he look white? Does he look like a real American? Sure, he has a passport, but that's just something he won in the war. You saw him. Well, that's about too much for a father to bear, isn't it? More than a man should have to stand for in this American city, in these progressive times. More than anyone could be expected to take. Wouldn't any man worth his britches lose his mind faced with an assault like that? Wouldn't he want to take a stand against it? Wouldn't you?

Like I said, he plays them like an orchestra. He walks to his desk and lifts up a notebook, clearing his throat before reading out a page from the diary Bess left on her bed for her father to find. He stumbles over the words "married to a Catholic boy," and pauses, taking out his white handkerchief to dab his left eye. He looks down for a moment before going on. I glance up at Abner Stubbs in time to see a flash of faint surprise cross his face at this show of half concealed, contrived emotion. His own face is stiff as stone. I guess he is afraid. The trial is almost over, and soon the jury will decide his fate. Hugo Black carries on reading the diary, and then he asks the open court as well as the jury, if this isn't the very thing that would be your worst nightmare? "This young, innocent girl," he calls Bess. "I guess," he says, looking over at Abner with something that looks for all the world like sorrow, "it would make any man lose control."

The verdict comes in quick. Not guilty. Hugo Black smiles his private smile for the last time, all for himself, as though he was ignoring the applause. Stubbs looks bewildered. He almost buckles, grips the handrail, and doesn't fall. Then he gathers himself and looks at me, right at me, right through me, maybe. Like an old eagle, his mouth twisted down at the corners and his eyes shining. Bess's controlled smile has fallen off her face. She looks like she lost. Her mother is there for the first time, standing beside her, looking triumphant. Outside, crowds start whooping and hollering as the news spreads. Esther is crying again. Men surge in and lift up Hugo Black and Abner Stubbs, carrying them both out the door on their shoulders like some kind of heroes. The court empties behind them, and I am suddenly reminded of a chaotic railway platform, some long ago hot day, and the crowd suddenly ebbing away until I was left alone at the last with a hot smell of dust and coal. It's such a clear and sudden memory but I can't place it at all. I wonder where it comes from.

I walk out the side door of the court and stand in the hot alleyway listening to cheering from the other side of the block. They are cheering the man who killed my brother. Cheering the man who made sure he got away with it. The street must be full of men with dark suits and red faces. All triumphant now. I don't feel angry. Just empty. I am done with this city.

* * * *

Chapter Sixteen: 1921

I make the short walk to the rectory and let myself in the back door. Johanna has already heard the news, and she looks like she's been crying. I hug her properly at last, and we sit together, finally sharing something real. I tell her I'm leaving in the morning, and she talks to me like she hasn't before, like she's been saving it up. She says I'm stronger than I think. She says she knew it from the beginning, from the first time she saw me, and she knows now I'm burst open like a dropped glass of water, but she swears to me I will be strong again.

And I believe her. She should know. She's put herself back together more than once. She says she still can't believe old man Stubbs came for Jimmy, for the Father, as she calls him. She never thought there'd be trouble for him, like there was for Jackson. "White like them," she calls Jimmy. White like the men wearing hoods on their heads. They hate us, I tell her. They hate us too. She nods. Says still, it's a different kind of hate. Hate's all the same as far as I can see.

We don't talk for long, but it's the most real conversation I've ever had with her, with this woman who's cared for me most of my life. She asks me to write to her if I see Jackson, out there, in Mobile or wherever I'm going. I promise to watch for him. I ask if she'll be ok here. She says she'll stay. She doesn't have another place, and she's still hoping Jackson will come back. She says the rectory is a good house. Always was.

And it was for me too, I guess, for a long time, but not anymore.

Chapter Seventeen

1921

Birmingham Age Herald, October, 1921
**JURY'S VERDICT WILL BE
HARD TO EXPLAIN**

**Twelve men sworn to render true
verdict according to the evidence have
found the Rev. A. Stubbs not guilty of
the murder of the Rev. Father James
E. Coyle, and thus ends one of the most
unfortunate tragedies ever enacted in
Jefferson county.**

I don't feel like I slept at all. I feel like I watched
the window all night, the net curtains never moving.
Not a breath of wind. Light from the street hardly
reached my room, but a high riding moon drifted by
in the small hours. Just as it got light, I drifted off, and
then woke still half in a dream that was slow to fade. I

Chapter Seventeen: 1921

was home with Fran, up on the Steps Hill where we'd been picking hazelnuts, but in the dream, it was also summer, and the meadow grass was long and loud with grasshoppers and bees. Fran was wearing a wedding dress, though shorter than she would have worn, and she was younger than me and she walked ahead of me looking beautiful. I followed. I wasn't wearing any shoes, but the grass was warm and soft, and there were no nettles or thorns. She smiled back over her shoulder like a girl on a chocolate box lid and then she looked past me, and her face froze and she began to scream. It looked like screaming but no sound came. She was looking behind me and when I turned it was into darkness, a long corridor with a door at the end with yellow glass panels through which I could see outlines, silhouettes of men with tall hats carrying something, a slumped body, carrying him past the door, out of sight. I turned back but the meadow was dark, and Fran was old again, older, as old as Mother and as small, and her wedding dress turned black before my eyes.

I open my eyes and remember he's dead.

* * * * *

I go back to Mobile by train the day after the trial, sick to my stomach. Everything has changed. Jimmy often spoke about Mobile. Sometimes I thought he'd move there, he seemed so fond of it, calling it a gentle, scholarly place. But he was wrong. There are Klansmen here too, I realise. I can smell it from them, their bright hard eyes on a Sunday morning. The things I loved about the South have become sinister, like a chord in a favourite song changing abruptly to minor, or a shadow falling suddenly across a child's face. I

271

used to love the slow accents and morning heat and evening crickets and the sweet, sweet tea. I can hardly bear to drink it now, too sweet, too cold. Like the ladies who go walking just to watch one another, who dress up for church just to gather gossip like food for the week. I never actually decide to stop going to Mass, but one Sunday I realise it has been weeks, and that I don't seem to be a churchgoer anymore. This as much as anything else marks me off here. It seems part of the same thing to me, all part of what pushes me away. I always thought the South was home, but now it's a foreign land.

Birmingham would be even worse. Imagine if I were still there, walking to and from the rectory, passing the courthouse and seeing him, up there above the street, mooching on the court room steps like a cat, ambushing all the young couples who came to be married with his pockets full of cheap brass rings. I imagine him watching me pass, and the thought of his eyes on my back as I pass is too much to take. If I got work in Loveman's, if they took me on again like Lucille says they would, even then, living on another street, I know I'd be drawn to the place. I would come walking down 3rd, walking slow past the church and the rectory, leaning back into the shadow of Huckston's awning, to watch without being seen. That's what Bess said she did for years before she got her courage together to cross the street and go into the church. I would have turned into a reflection of her, hiding in the shadows to watch her father like she used to watch my brother. I'd be drawn to it like a stray cat to milk. I'd want to see the rectory without being seen, see the space I used to hold. What would I do if I saw anyone, anyone at all sitting on the swing seat on the porch? What if I met

Chapter Seventeen: 1921

Johanna? Would I have anything at all to say to her? What if I met Bess?

I try to be better than I am. I try to get past it, to get past him. If I could get to a place where I could read his name like it just was just a word: Stubbs with a small "s," killer with a small "k." If I could get to a place where 3rd Street was just like any other street to me. Then I could live there. But I can't do it. I can't forgive him.

No. I'll go North, like Bess and Diego. Like Jackson and Mimi. It feels natural, like a swallow migrating in summer. I don't know New York, but Mimi is there, and she has a small place, she and this man she's so mysterious about. They can help me make a home there, in a new place without this dark audience, with no memory of what was before.

* * * * *

There was awkwardness from the beginning. I suppose I should have seen it as soon as I got off the train — Mimi with her too-bright smile, her eyes darting, like she used to when she'd done something awful at school and was hoping Sr. Levinus wouldn't find out. Perhaps I shouldn't have come to her. Well, I suppose I shouldn't have come, but how was I to know how things were?

Anyway, she met me. Grand Central Station, high and curved and beautiful. The centre of the world, it feels like, full of people with places to go. I've never felt so alone or aimless as I feel there. If you stand still in the centre of that big marble space, you can feel life rushing past you in all directions, like wind. Mimi was stylish, bright and brittle. She had a light in her eyes and a gaiety that I should have been glad for. I should try to be glad. She took me to a coffee shop at the corner of 42nd, and we ordered like two city ladies. She was glad to see me, she said. She bubbled, welcomed me to the Big Apple. She said that's what they're calling it now. I tried to raise my smile, but when she mentioned meeting up for a show sometime, I just blurted it out.

"Mimi, I'm not here to see a show. I need to make a new start. I need somewhere to stay while I find a job. You're the person I know best in this whole place, so can you help? Can I stay with you for a while? Just a few weeks."

I would have said more, but something about the concentrated way she was stirring her coffee, the purse in her lips, stopped me. There was a silence. Not a long one, but long enough for me to have my answer.

"You see, Cella ..."

She stopped, and I waited. I wanted to stretch the silence, to make her come up with the words herself, but I hadn't the strength.

"What, Mimi? Is it something I said or did or didn't do ...?"

"No. No of course, not, Cella. It's not that. It's ..."

"Is it where you're living?"

"No, Cella, look. I'm sorry. It's Carlo. He wouldn't have it. He ..."

"Carlo? My ... Carlo Moretti? Are you ..."

She smiled in a way that should have made me kinder. She smiled and looked down like a teenager. She might have even blushed under all that face powder. It should have made me kinder, that smile, but it didn't.

"You and Carlo, Mimi? Really?"

"Yes, Cella. I'm sorry. Carlo and me, we've been

Chapter Seventeen: 1921

together for, oh, it's been a year now. He came north doing some work for that husband of Lucille's, and he's really making it. He's got people working for him now and everything. Not many, not yet, but ..."

She broke off, maybe seeing my face.

"Now Cella. He's a good man. And he's Southern. Do you know how hard it is to meet a good Southern man around here? These Northerners don't know how to treat a lady."

"Mimi, he's Italian! He's no more Southern than I am!"

"Well, yes, Cella. Exactly that. He's as Southern as you or me."

"He's Italian, Mimi. Like I'm Irish."

"Cella, honey, you're not Irish now. You're as Southern as sweet tea. Carlo's the same. He's a fine Southern man, and well, he's my man now. And I'm sorry, but we can't ..."

It took all my strength not to just get up and walk out of the coffee shop. I wanted to, so much, but that's not what a lady does, is it? I said nothing, and I let her babble. Their apartment, so darling, but so tiny. Hardly room for them to turn. No room for a guest. Her job on the Upper East Side, taking care of some Jewish lady's children. Carlo's business, delivering, organising, meeting. Something to do with prohibition; something that didn't sound exactly legal, but that was hardly a surprise. I let her talk, and I said nothing. I was thinking, furiously, who else I might know in New York. And when the coffee was cold, we kissed each other on the cheek, lightly, barely touching, and made false promises to meet up for that show sometime. And as she left, I sincerely hoped I would never see her face again.

* * * * *

275

Something Bigger

St. Paul's Rectory
221 Third Avenue
Birmingham, Alabama
November 15, 1921

Dear Mother,

How are you? This letter comes from Jimmy and me. He asked me to write since he is so busy with the parish these days. Everything is good here, as ever. We are working hard with schools, and James is having a new one founded out on the edge of the city for a new community from Italy. There are many Italians here, and they are good people. And he likes to practice his Italian. He says "Buon Giorno" to you. I hope I spelled that right.

We have a little news, Mother. The parish is going to build a new rectory for us. Soon we will move out of this house, just for a year or so, while they knock down this old wooden place and build a new house on the site. They're building a small orphanage too, and some convent rooms for the sisters who will care for the children. We will be living here and there for the year we are out. I don't know exactly when we will get to come back again. Jimmy says it is better for me to keep writing the letters for now, since he will be travelling a bit, until our new rectory is built. He's just come by as I am writing this and sends you his love. He says he hopes you are not trying too hard to look after everyone, and that you should let everyone look after you for a while instead. He's right, of course. He is wearing his straw hat, as our weather has been wonderful — long hot days and no storms.

How is Fran and all her family? I suppose they are

Chapter Seventeen: 1921

growing up. Jimmy is so proud he has one named for him. I'm sorry I don't have a photograph to send you as you asked. Our camera has broken and is in to be repaired. We'll see. In the meantime, as I have filled this page I must finish here and get this letter to the mail.

Please give our love to all there, especially Fran, and tell her I wrote.

Your loving daughter and son,
Marcella and Jimmy

* * * * *

160 Bleecker St.
New York City
November 15, 1921

Dear Fran,

You see my new address on this letter. I think this will be my home for some time, so you can use this to write to me. Mother can still write to the rectory for now. Tony Brennan still sends on my letters, and any Irish ones for Jimmy. Sometimes he adds a note, saying I'm in his prayers. He never gives news of the parish, and I'm glad of that.

This place where I live is better than a boarding house. It's so tall — thirteen stories of apartments, a clean house, and safe, but it's not home. I share a room with two other women, my narrow bed pushed under the slope of the roof so I can't sit up straight in it. That's fair. I'm the last one in. The women are fine — Tessa is from Mayo. She's young, and has dreams of meeting someone, settling down and having children. She dresses up to go out at the weekends. I like the hope she has. We live carefully around each other, invisible lines in the worn matting that mark which part of the musty room is mine, and which is theirs. The hallways smell of cabbage and mould. The running water is cold, and not always clear. The privy is down three flights of stairs. I hadn't realised the luxury of the rectory, but I care a lot less about those things now.

They let him off, Fran. Stubbs. They acquitted him. Said he couldn't be blamed for killing the man who had married his daughter in a Catholic ceremony to a Puerto Rican man. They made it sound like Jimmy was the one who did bad things, like they had to find him guilty, so they could get Stubbs off. I couldn't stay anywhere near Birmingham after that.

I hope you and Martin and the children are OK. Write and tell me if those RIC men came around again. I always thought Rockfield was the safest place in the world, but maybe no place is safe. I wonder sometimes if it would have been different if you'd come to Alabama with Jimmy instead of me. Well, I don't wonder. Of course it would have been different. It would have been better. You always knew what to do, Fran. I thought I did. But I was wrong.

All my love,
Marcella

* * * * *

Two letters to post, one that tells some of my life, one that tells of the life we might have had, Jimmy and me. Writing is company, and I'm short of company now, even in this crowded place. There are too many people here that I don't care about; too few who care about me. I walk out of this building in the mornings and right away, I'm nobody. I pass those fish-lipped

Chapter Seventeen: 1921

sisters on the seventh floor, one or other of them always standing at the doorway, watching me walk up the steps. Jeering without saying a word. I've long given up smiling at them, or even trying to tell one from another. They blur like bad wallpaper.

Last night made me think it might be possible to make a life here. I shouldn't have gone – Mother would be scandalised. But Tessa kept pleading, and she's right about this much: I'm not getting any younger. The Bowery Ballroom looked so beautiful from outside – white lights curving around the facade, and music drifting out on the street. But that was early in the evening. Later it was so crowded I could hardly keep my eye on Tessa, and those boys have no respect. Tessa took up with a Spaniard, and I couldn't find her after that. I walked around and around the edge of the dance floor, looking for her until I saw that I was being noticed. I think they were laughing, those younger girls in their more fashionable dresses. So I left. It's a short walk home, and it wasn't so late. Still, the unfamiliar street was dark and empty, and scared me a little. I could see the lights on Houston, but I walked the wrong way, and then turned back too quickly so my heel broke. I felt useless hobbling there. I stopped, trying hard not to cry. And that's when the policeman stopped. He walked past me, and before he turned back, I thought for a minute he might be Jackson.

"Excuse me, Miss. You OK? These streets ain't safe, you know. All kinds of strangers out here. No place for a lady like you. Let me walk you up the street here."

It was his voice that made me trust him. A Southern voice – deep, drawling and kind, familiar as a blanket. I remembered what Mimi said about wanting a Southern man that time she talked about Carlo being Southern. It made sense now. He walked me home, talking all the time because he could see I was embarrassed and tearful. He talked about his wife, and his grown-up daughter. He walked me all the way to the building.

It was just a kindness, a comfort to walk with him, and I felt something opening that had been wound tight since I got here. At first, I thought it was his accent that made me relaxed, that it was the South I'd missed and wanted to get back to. Then I thought, if we were in the South, we wouldn't be walking together like this, so easy in the middle of the street. I'd never have spoken to him, not after what happened when I tried to talk to Jackson. And that's when it came to me, maybe this is a better city to live in, to be with people, to know new people. Maybe I could make a life here that won't break. That's what I was thinking, all the way along Bleecker St, weighing this place against that, letting the policeman's talk wash over me hardly listening to his words. I wondered what Jimmy might have said and I could hear him again for a minute. There was a smile in his voice. He said 'yes, Siss. Find yourself a life to call your own.'

It felt so settling, I right away wrote to Fran again, and told her as much of the story as I thought she'd understand.

* * * * *

Chapter Seventeen: 1921

Crancam
Rockfield
Athlone
Ireland
December 3, 1921

Dear Siss,

I got your letter, and Mother got hers. Thank you for that. You are doing the right thing in keeping all this from her. She doesn't go out now and would never be able for the shock.

Siss. I can't believe you went to a ballroom just months after poor Jimmy died. Even if you only went to take care of some stranger, it's not right. I suppose at least you didn't go in.

Thanks for the patterns. These are better than the ones you sent from Alabama. I like them, though I have no time to sew these days, and of course where would I wear such glamorous clothes? Still, I like to see what all the fancy ladies of New York City are wearing. What a life you are living. What places you see, and all on your own now. I can't imagine the city, but the way you describe it, so modern and noisy, I don't know that I'd like it. Are you still set on staying up there, not moving back down South? Are those places in America really so different from each other that you have to go to the trouble of moving?

Don't expect any big news from me. We are all still here, doing the same things. The children get more interesting every day, though. Elizabeth is like you. She has your eyes, I think. And your ways. Jamesie is not like his namesake, being more like his father. In fact, all the others are like their father, so it looks as though all the Coyle looks in my family came from you. You should see Elizabeth, Siss. She should see you. We all should.

Keep writing to Mother. She's gone very quiet in herself, and letters from Jimmy are what she needs. And I don't like to ask, Siss, but with things as they are here, we miss the money too. God love him, Jimmy was great for sending money, and I hadn't realised how much it meant. So if you can spare some, it would help a lot.

Things are quiet here now. Is it odd that I miss Jimmy more, now he's died, though I haven't seen him in years? I miss knowing he is walking the earth. I miss you, but I still hope to see you. I will see you, Siss, won't I?

With love always,

Fran

* * * * *

And part of me would love to go to Ireland. Since he died, I've been missing home. I mean Rockfield. Ireland. I still dream of the schoolroom, my father at the top, almost turning. I want more than anything to see his face properly, and even a dream would do. I call the place home even though, when you think about it, when did I live there, really? I was a child in that place, but now it's more real in my head than it used to be, the one small world that I know every inch of. I sit here in this room that means nothing to me, and call it all up like a film set: the shape of the rain puddle that welled up outside my bedroom window; exactly how big that could get on a pouring wet day; the way the heaviest drops would drive bubbles into the surface, huge half spheres floating for just a

Chapter Seventeen: 1921

few seconds and disappearing, maybe scudding side-ways in a high wind. I was so wise, then. I knew everything. I knew to the minute what time the evening crows would come shawling overhead, high and silent in the bleached-out sky. I knew all the sheep paths in the neighbours' fields; where to find mushrooms, sticky and white, hidden under tufts of bright grass. I knew which blackberry bushes had sweet solid fruit, and which were watery and insipid. I knew the best hazel trees, which branches would shake down the heaviest load. I knew all the comfortable stones tucked away in corners out of sight, where you could read undisturbed for hours in the thin May sunlight. I knew how to get frogspawn in the pond, and leebeens in the stream, and in winter, which ice was safe to slide on. I can still taste the bitter tang of sorrel and the pinprick sweetness of tiny wild strawberries, never enough for a mouthful; up the fields with Tanner running ahead of me on his own nose-led adventure, following invisible trails through the long grass. I knew how far my evening shadow would stretch ahead of me when I made my way home. I knew that place inside out.

I thought I'd have it forever. I thought it was the whole world. And now, since he's gone, it's like a photograph developing in my head, growing clear on a page that was blank or forgotten. Fixing itself, as if it were important. Tiny details won't leave me: the swoop and flash of swallows, the metal taste of early frost. I carry those damp Irish fields in my head. I carry them through this hot and cold city more clearly than I ever carried them through Birmingham, Alabama that was the best home in the world until it became the worst. The memories don't fit at all in New York, so I belong here less, hiding this world inside me, like a disloyalty.

Something Bigger

I tried to let it go, let it all go to hell and live with a smile on my face like Tessa does. I'll paint it on, if I have to, I thought. I'll paint my nails and go dancing, hot and light and free like I imagined Mimi might be, the old Mimi at least. But I couldn't make it work. I am still in mourning. I'm tired of it, the heaviness and history, but it won't let me go. I'm tired of memories spreading like weeds in my head until everything here reminds me of there. Nothing here is like home. Everything should be new, but New York is still haunted. The haunting is in me. I can't leave it behind.

There are young men here still, and they notice me sometimes. Tall Italians, shorter ones from home, older ones with nice laughing eyes. A different species, they might as well be. Some like me, but they don't date me. Maybe they can smell the tragedy. Maybe they can't get through. Maybe I don't want them to. Sometimes I can't bear them, so full of swagger and hope. They think the world is theirs for the figuring out. They talk about the things they like – this music, that food, wood smoke or mountains, an automobile they want to buy, a boat maybe – they talk of these things as if they were real. As if they had bulletproof futures. Like children deciding what to be when they grow up. They don't know what's waiting for us, just when we feel our powers are at their highest. They babble on and I let them. Their sudden clumsy kisses take me by surprise, ending what I had thought was a friendship of sorts. Nothing lasts.

And then there's that dread that rises up like hot water in my chest when I'm alone – a weekend or a day off work. I stay home. I stay in my room, not reading. I sit and look at the wall, or the echoing mirrors that swing from side to side on this shared dresser, just like

Chapter Seventeen: 1921

those in the rectory did, reflecting hundreds of me, smaller and smaller, and I feel full and empty at the same time. Heavy and sad, like bad news is coming, will come within the hour, but it never does. It already has. It's like something is trying to prepare me, trying to tell me the world is hard and random. Telling me not to get comfortable. Like I didn't know that already. Hot water rising in my chest, crowding out song and speech. I can't shake it. So I sit and wait. That's all I do. I let time pass.

When I left the rectory that last time, I gathered things in a chocolate box: a comb with some of his hairs caught in the tines; a bundle of his scribbled poems; his pen a little worn for which no ink can be bought anymore; one small river stone. I gathered as much as I could but now that I've left, it's not enough. When Tessa saw it first, she thought it was candy, that I was hoarding something sweet. She was nearly right.

Fran thinks it's a kindness, my letters to Mother that keep Jimmy alive. Fran thinks I am being good to Mother. It's true that she couldn't bear the loss of Jimmy, her one good son, her hope. But the truth is it's no hardship to me to write about Jimmy as though he still lived in my life. It keeps him close. Writing, I don't have to wonder where he's gone. Sometimes, I believe what I write, and that makes me smile. More, it makes me warm and relaxed to write how smart he thinks Fran's children must be, how his arguments have ended, and the city officials are asking his advice on building schools, what he said in his sermon last Sunday. I read his missal most days. I read his Divine Office, so that I know what the readings are for the season, and I imagine what he might say to it, in this fearless, open life he's living now in my letters, with no threats or enemies, and no bullet in his brain. I write a better life than the one I lead, better than the one he would have had. But it's good for me. It feels natural and easy.

Too easy, I suppose. I suppose there would be words for it, words to call it hysterical, if Fran knew how much it meant to me. It's better to be thought kind.

This is the best of it now. This chocolate box of relics, the letters I write, the full, imagined life I'm not living with him. Maybe that's all home ever is – small things, memories and ideas. People I loved once, love still. People who live in my head. Maybe that's all I'll ever have.

But sometimes it crashes down on me, and I think I've lost laughter forever. On those days I walk through the streets here, watching nothing, letting nothing in, not even the smiling men who sometimes try to catch my eye. I walk past the most beautiful buildings and the brightest lights. I see lovers in the park, and dancers, sometimes, in big upstairs windows on Lexington Avenue. I even go to movies but it's like the stories are not for me, and nothing can wake the part of me that used to feel so happy.

I didn't pay the Klan enough attention. They never seemed as important as they were. They were just men, doing men's things: arguing in the papers and getting themselves known. I could see it getting bitter, even frightening, but I didn't worry until it was too late. I never worried about us. Jimmy moved through it, like a giant in a storm, letting it all blow around him. I never thought it would come to much. I never thought anyone would die, and if they did, I never thought it would be him. But it was. All it took was bullets, in the end.

Chapter Seventeen: 1921

Now, here in this spinning city, it all might as well never have happened. Tony wrote to me only a month after the trial, describing how President Wilson visited Birmingham, and all the crowds and banners and flags made the city a festival. Here too, in this busy city. The streets are teeming, people pushing themselves forward into the future all the time with no looking back. Sometimes I sit at the window and look up, try to catch some meaning in one patch of windless sky between the high buildings. There might be clouds there. Or the swift flight of a bird, leaving no trace behind. Or nothing. Just a piece of emptiness that won't be filled.

Chapter Eighteen

1950

A letter came today from Fran to say Mother has died. Peacefully, she says, at home. Where else would she die? I can't imagine her anywhere else.

I'm to light a candle for her, Fran says.

I feel the sharpness of loss, and selfishly, I can't tell how much is the loss of the letters I won't write now, the life I can't imagine any more for Jimmy and me. I've no reason to pretend any more.

So I try to be good. I plan to light the candle. I walk up fifth avenue to St. Patrick's, but I can't go in. The steps to the door remind me of St. Paul's, and I can imagine candles inside, like on Bess and Diego's wedding day. I saw a shadow that day. I saw the candles flicker as though a door had opened, and a shadow passed in front of the bank of candles at the back of the dark church. And I said nothing. There's no reason to pretend any more.

It was my fault, wasn't it, in the end? Abner Stubbs came with his gun, because Ethel Stubbs told him, and

Chapter Eighteen: 1950

she would have known nothing if it weren't for the diary I encouraged Bess to write. And I was the one who brought Bess round the rectory, though Johanna tried to warn me. I was the one who knocked on her door.

I don't go in the cathedral. I walk home, all the way south through crowded sidewalks, alone.

* * * * *

A parcel from Ireland. I open it on my bed, and letters spill out on this blue airmail paper, thumbed and curled at the corners like Jimmy's were, on the mantlepiece in Rockfield where Mother kept them up behind the tea caddy, over the fire. It takes me a while to recognise them. These letters are from me. These are the letters I've been writing to Mother from Jimmy and me, for more than thirty years now, going right back to the years before he died, when I was hardly making things up at all. They spill over the bright crocheted wool of my bedspread like treasure.

There's a short note from Fran, explaining.

"She said I had to send them to you. She was very insistent on that. To send you all the letters you wrote her. She said you'd want them, to read like a novel. I don't know why you'd be reading your own letters, but she was very strong about it, so here they are.

Of course she knew, Siss. She's known for years. You couldn't keep a secret like that from a place like Rockfield, where everyone knows everyone's thoughts before they think them. But she loved them, your letters, and made me promise not to tell you. I'm not sure when she figured it out, but it got so she only talked about you, never about Jimmy anymore. She'd say things like, 'She makes him sound happy, doesn't she?' She stopped wondering when he'd come home.

Something Bigger

She knew well what you were doing, and she loved it, Siss. She knew it was love."

Now I cry for her, that woman in the dark cottage who lost us both so long ago. I cry for what I never knew of her, what lay behind her shell of grumbling and guilt. I cry for what might have been, had I stayed. Imagine if I'd never left? Imagine what might have been then?

Chapter Nineteen

1962

I woke with a question — what am I doing here, still in New York, and that was still in my head this morning before the mailman came. Friday, mid-morning is my weekly treat. I go to the small café next door to my building, dressed in my best. I have my regular table, a small one in the corner just inside the plate glass window. I sit, just being in a room with others, watching the quiet street.

This morning I ordered a cola. It's not sweet tea. It's better, with bubbles that break, tart on my tongue while the sweetness lingers. A flat-tailed squirrel did that springing thing they do, straight from the sidewalk to halfway up the tree trunk right outside the glass, and he turned his little raisin eyes on me without curiosity. It made me wonder how I looked to him: an old lady in a dark dress, holding a glass in her thin hand, peering through pale-framed glasses at the bright street.

Something Bigger

And it came to me, then, that I should go home. I should go walking with Fran while we can, tell her the truth about why I wrote those letters home to Mother, about Bess Stubbs and why it was my fault she came to the rectory, about what I might have seen down the back of the church, how I should have warned Jimmy, if I'd taken enough time to understand it. I wanted in that moment to be with her, to just tell her for once and for all what I knew.

I think that's when I decided to go. All I can remember for sure is the moment — watching the squirrel watching me, thinking of Fran and how to get to her, to spend some time — some years? Was that in my head? Or even a short visit. A little time to be sisters with her.

The mailman passed, dropping off at my building. I left my soda, half-drunk, on the café table and slipped out to pick up the letter that had come — an Irish stamp that made me smile. Fran's letters mean so much. Back in the café, I took another drink, savouring the moment before reading, loving that she thinks of me as I think of her, all the distance between us disappearing when I hold her words in my hand. But the letter was not from her.

Fran passed, Jamesie wrote, in her sleep. I wondered what that meant? Did she wake at all? Did she know she was dying? Had she time to say goodbye to anyone? Did she think of me at the end? And where is she now? Where is she now, Jimmy Coyle, tell me that?

I counted back the days from when the letter was posted, from her funeral, and remember what I was doing then — shopping for gloves, I think, as they brought her body to the church; still sleeping, as they

Chapter Nineteen: 1962

said her last Mass; having breakfast of juice and eggs, as they buried her in the new graveyard. Jamesie's letter said it's beside the old one. I can't picture either of them.

The letter is short. I suppose they didn't have much to say. They hardly know me, these babies of Fran's, grown up now. After I read it, I stood up, looking out at the street, wondering how everything could look so much the same, and feel so different. The squirrel was still there, not bothering with me anymore, taking little acrobatic runs along the branch like a clockwork toy. And then he jumped and was gone. The leaves shook on the empty branch, but no sound reached me through the plate glass of the window. I sat back again, quiet. I picked up my glass, amazed by the clinking sound it made, amazed that the ice had not melted.

* * * * *

I go to light a candle for her. Years ago, she told me to light one for Mother, and I didn't. I couldn't. But now I must. This is for Fran.

When I got the letter with the news of Mother, I felt grief that wasn't clean. I know now it was because of those letters I wrote, because I thought she believed that Jimmy was alive. Those made-up stories of church dinners and tennis matches and sunny, sunny days in Alabama kept me from ever going back to visit her. I couldn't have kept those lies up in person. She was too sharp for that — she'd catch me out for sure. So my grieving was complicated — I kept myself from her, so she could believe Jimmy was alive. That's what I told myself.

But I grieved, too, for the writing of those letters that I wouldn't need to write any more. I grieved for that pretended life with Jimmy that had seemed more real than this cold New York wind whistling up the stairs of one building or another. I grieved for what my life had become, and I grieved back then for Jimmy — gone at last, now I couldn't write him into life anymore. Fran told me to light a candle for Mother and I wrote back that I had, and that I'd had a Mass said for her in St. Patrick's Cathedral, and she was glad. It wasn't a difficult lie, but it was the last one. Now there's nobody to lie to.

I make my way all the way uptown to St. Patrick's to light the finest candle I can find. It's a long walk. I should have worn better shoes. Fifth Avenue is crowded, full of people who have not just lost the last person they loved. They brush against me, rushing from one unimportant thing to another. I can't bear them, can't bear the ordinariness of their lives, the way they have people to shop for and cook for and write letters to. I step into the cathedral, tired and overwhelmed, and sit down in the back to be quiet and alone for a while.

Through the stained-glass window, I watch the light change as a cloud passes over. I am thinking of a psalm Jimmy liked, but I can't remember the words. Something about the sky declaring the glory of God. From my seat, I can't see the cloud, but the colours change as it passes, darkening and brightening. The sky is different from in here. Light looks different. There is dust on the pew and from habit, my left hand traces a sideways figure of eight. I add a vertical line to make it a cross. I smudge it all out again.

And I hear his voice behind me, like I haven't heard it since his funeral.

'Siss. There you are. Isn't it time you called?'

I don't turn around. The voice is real, but I know,

Chapter Nineteen: 1962

even as my heart skips faster, I know it is inside my head.

'Is this where you are?' I ask without words, bowing my head so nobody can see my face. I might be smiling. I might be glowing.

'Where else would I be? I'm glad to see you, Siss. I'm glad you came.'

I sit for a long time, and we are together. I talk to him, and he answers, and I'm so glad. I tell him about Fran, but he knows already. Over the following days and weeks, I come more often, early in the mornings. It's a fine church. A better place to spend the day than my own small room. Nobody notices one more old lady in a half dark cathedral. Nobody notices him but me. He's always waiting, and when I come in, and put down my bag, I feel lighter. I sit and rest, or maybe light a candle, or talk to someone who looks like they need to talk. I like it here. Jimmy likes it too. He always seems happy. Always content now. I hear his voice in my head often, in grocery stores or subway trains, but here, in the cathedral, this quiet and familiar place, his voice is always clear.

I thought again about going to Ireland. You can fly there now. It only takes a day. But instead I wrote to Jamesie and asked him to send me pictures. He sent snaps of his family, and of the ruins of the house I grew up in. The pictures were in colour, and I thought, oh, it's gone, the place where I lived.

* * * * *

This is how I spend my days now. This is home, this half-dark vaulted space, letting my life grow long, watching for the women who need help — the young ones, the lost ones. I'm here for them as well as for me.

Something Bigger

Sometimes, even still, it's hard to accept the things that remain the same, now that so many people have died. The breeze in the morning when I go outside my front door, it still freshens my face as though it were hope. Candles still in their softness promise something more than light. The laughter of women together still sounds like sisters, sounds like the kind of love that will put up with small things and bear with it. Tea tastes sharp. Sunlight burns.

A memory comes flooding back of my father at the top of the classroom, chalk dust hanging in the damp air, the smell of boys' boots and turf smoke. It's clearer than when I dream it, and I see what he is writing. I hear his voice asking the class — what's the last number? What's the biggest number you can think of? And he's writing them down, the line of numbers getting bigger and bigger and suddenly I have my hand up, and he turns and says "Yes? Marcella?" I remember in my gut how it felt, to be a child and to suddenly understand it, that there is no end to counting, that there is always a bigger number, always another step. I was five, maybe six years old. Properly, now I remember his face when he saw that I understood. His beaming smile. And he turned and lifted his chalky hand and drew on the blackboard that looping symbol of infinity, and said "Good girl."

I hold it, the clear memory, like a baby bird in my open hand, and it doesn't fly away.

I used to draw that sideways eight in the dust on the desk in the accounts room at Loveman's, not knowing where I learned it. Loveman's is gone, long ago torn down. My father's schoolroom is in ruins now. People I worked with, school friends, the ones I loved, the ones I feared, all gone. And still it doesn't end. There's always something else, infinitely present, something bigger than all our lives.

At some point, I must have decided my life could be long, just as Jimmy decided his did not need to be. I wonder when it was that he started looking around for a way to make it count? Was it when he left, really? Was it the war? Was it when he couldn't get to Dublin? Was it Bess after all, that singular girl and me the one who brought her in to our small house?

Or was he always going to find a way to die? Did he think that would make him matter more? Me, I've decided you don't have to die young to be a hero, and there's nothing wrong with growing old. It's all one line in the end, the time we live, the time after we have lived, all our history in one never-ending twisting ribbon.

Sometimes it amazes me that Birmingham still exists, a real place I could go back to. The train still runs from Penn Station every day. I could get a ticket, and climb on board, but it wouldn't take me anywhere I want to go. I remember the place like a hot, hateful movie. It's unlikely that Johanna is there still, but she could be. Once I thought I saw Jackson in a newspaper photograph, three men sitting up at a lunch counter and one half-turned away from the camera. I think it was him. I hope it was him. Back at the rectory, there might, even now, be a cat nosing around the front porch, looking for scraps, with nobody to call him Captain. I play it in my head, preserved like candied orange peel, too sweet, too bitter to be real.

And then there's Bess. She could be there. She could be anywhere.

Something Bigger

'And you, Siss. Aren't you still here?'

Jimmy's voice is teasing, and I almost laugh in this silent space.

I am. For now. Still here.

Acknowledgements

The first person to thank for this book is Marcella, who taught me to read, and so ultimately to write, and gave me the best of all stories to start with. The next is my family, especially John, whose consistent encouragement has kept this train on the rails. Thanks to my Mam and Dad, and the sisters and brothers, in-laws and outlaws who have been a huge source of encouragement and inspiration for this book. Thanks to the cousins I've gotten to know through this last year, who are cheerleaders and historians for Jimmy's story. Thanks to everyone in those bookclubs which are about books, and those which are about wine and friendship. Thanks to friends at the kitchen table, the Wednesday night house group, to old friends and new ones. All my good friends believed in this even (or especially) when I didn't and helped me to keep going. Thank you so much. You know who you are!

In Alabama, I was greatly helped by the good people in Birmingham Public Library and the Alabama State Archives, by the Catholic Diocese of Birmingham, by Jim Pinto, by the late John Wright, by the work of Sharon Davies and by Laura Pratt. Thank you all. I also am grateful to the Tenement Museum in New York, and to Sherron Killingsworth Roberts for that one great anecdote which is adapted herein. And the Tyrone Guthrie Centre, the Big House that makes writing possible – thank you for providing space to create.

Thanks also to the brilliant, generous people in the writing and publishing business who have helped in a million ways, especially the Writepacers of Limerick, and Sherry Boas for really seeing this story from the very start, and for making this book possible. A special thanks to Benedicta Norell, Bob Burke, Brian Langan, Cat Hogan, Ciara Fleming, Claire Maxwell, Crystal Warren, Dan Mooney, Donal Ryan, Eoin Devereux, Geri Maye, Gielty's (for coffee), God (for everything), Gráinne O'Brien, Hilda McHugh, Jesse Dillard, Jim Pinto, Jim Sheridan, Jo Gibney, Karen Ryan McNamara, Karin Schimke, Kerry Neville, Liesl Jobson, Liz Nugent, Mary Watson, Mindy Stanford, Muire Graham, Niamh Boyce, Noel Harrington, Noreen Clifford, Philip and Veronica O'Regan, Rita Buckley, Robert Berold, Roisin Cahalan, Sarah Moore Fitzgerald, Sarah Togher, Sinead Hanley, Sybille Schiffman, and everyone I forgot to name here. There's no end to the list of people whose fingerprints are on this book, in one way or another, most of all, John, Finn, Cian and Aoife. This wouldn't be in the world without you. Go raibh míle maith agaibh go léir.

PRAISE FROM BESTSELLING NOVELISTS

"This is a stunning, intensely engaging novel by a consummate storyteller. It's tense and gripping and beautifully written in restrained, elegant, crystalline prose. This is a book that I would eagerly recommend to any reader, anywhere."

—Donal Ryan

"With a most appealing protagonist and a deft literary talent, Sheila Killian brings us a story to make us cry and make us think. Compelling, intriguing and skillful."

— Liz Nugent

"Beautifully written and full of heart — *Something Bigger* tells us the story of Marcella and her brother Jimmy in a way that brings them vividly to life. We see their bonds to Ireland, and their loyalty to their new home in Alabama, we witness their strength, love and the power of words. This is an honest, lyrical and heart-warming novel that shines a light on what life was like for Marcella in Alabama, and gives us one of the warmest voices I've read in years."

—Niamh Boyce

"One heck of an impressive debut. Sheila Killian's writing voice is confident and brave. Everything rings true: characters, dialogue, location and story. It's a long time since I enjoyed a debut this much."

— Roisín Meaney

"*Something Bigger* is a wonderful novel that takes complex and consequential moments from history and places them in a beautiful, almost intimate context. Drawing together universal themes of emigration, family, racism and social justice in a style that is at once compelling and lyrical, Sheila has written a novel that spans generations and yet feels extremely personal. This book is a stunning reach into the past to explore moments we're living through in the present."

—Dan Mooney

"It's not just the compelling, tenderly-researched story that kept me turning the pages of Sheila Killian's debut novel *Something Bigger*. It's also the gorgeous, lyrical, multisensory writing. Page after page I was dazzled. Marcella is so fully formed and utterly believable that I wouldn't have been surprised if I'd looked up from the book and found her sitting beside me, writing that letter to her mother or quietly playing memories in her head 'preserved like candied orange peel, too sweet, too bitter to be real'. She will take your breath away. What a beautiful book."

— Sarah Moore Fitzgerald

Sheila Killian grew up in the dead centre of Ireland, a childhood enlivened by her grandaunt Marcella, her Southern drawl, tales of Brer Rabbit, and darker, true stories of the South and the unforgettable drama that unfolded there. That singular family story inspired this debut novel. Sheila's fiction, poetry and travel writing have won awards in Ireland and the UK, and her work has been broadcast on RTE. She teaches at the University of Limerick, is a member of Writepace, and spends as much time as she can by the sea.

CPSIA information can be obtained
at www.ICGtesting.com
Printed in the USA
BVHW071113180821
614612BV00010B/712